ILL-FATED FORTUNE

Jennifer J. Chow

St. Martin's Paperbacks

This is a work of fiction. All of the characters, organizations, and events portrayed in this novel are either products of the author's imagination or are used fictitiously.

First published in the United States by St. Martin's Paperbacks, an imprint of St. Martin's Publishing Group.

ILL-FATED FORTUNE

For information, address St. Martin's Publishing Group, 120 Broadway, New York, NY 10271.

www.stmartins.com

ISBN: 978-1-250-32303-3

Our books may be purchased in bulk for promotional, educational, or business use. Please contact your local bookseller or the Macmillan Corporate and Premium Sales Department at 1-800-221-7945, ext. 5442, or by email at MacmillanSpecialMarkets@macmillan.com.

St. Martin's Paperbacks edition / March 2024

Printed in the United States of America

10 9 8 7 6 5 4 3 2 1

For Bella, who brings me magic and joy

"Charming isn't adequate to describe Jennifer J. Chow's series debut, *Ill-Fated Fortune.* There is real magic in this story—and not just from the baking skills of Felicity and her mom. . . . A new series is about to be born."
—Carolyn Haines, *USA Today* bestselling author of the Sara Booth Delaney series

Praise for Jennifer J. Chow

"Yale and Celine's growing loyalty to each other, coupled with the warmth of Chow's prose, adds extra depth, just like the tapioca balls nestled in a glass of bubble tea."
—*The New York Times Book Review* on *Death by Bubble Tea*

"[A] delightful treat for lovers of culinary cozies. With its intrepid sleuth and vividly drawn setting, this clever whodunit will have you greedily turning the pages for more."
—Leslie Karst, author of the Lefty Award–nominated Sally Solari series, on *Death by Bubble Tea*

"The second installment of Chow's cozy mystery series set at a California market, *Hot Pot Murder* is as charming and delightful as the first. . . . Spending time with these characters is a treat, but—full warning—this book will make you hungry."
—*Parade*

"A frothy read for any pet lover who enjoys a little mystery and romance."
—*Criminal Element* on *Mimi Lee Gets a Clue*

Praise for *Ill-Fated Fortune*

"Nobody writes cozy mysteries quite like Jennifer J. Chow. No matter what is going wrong in my life, I know that all I need to do for some comfort is turn to one of Chow's books. Chow has done it again with *Ill-Fated Fortune.* I did not want to leave Felicity's side even for a moment, and you won't want to either."

—Jesse Q. Sutanto, author of *Vera Wong's Unsolicited Advice for Murderers*

"Who doesn't love a magical bakery? Readers will enjoy following Felicity Jin, her friends, and her mother in *Ill-Fated Fortune.* Check your fortune: I believe it will tell you to read this book."

—Emmeline Duncan, author of the Ground Rules mystery series

"*Ill-Fated Fortune* expertly combines magic and murder. This story is an absolute treat that you'll want to binge read."

—Olivia Matthews, author of the Spice Isle Bakery mysteries

"A magical new culinary cozy mystery series filled with family, friendship, and heart—and a pinch of real magic."

—Gigi Pandian, *USA Today* bestselling author of the Secret Staircase mysteries

"A deliciously magical culinary cozy that will leave you hungry for the next delectable installment in this new series by Jennifer J. Chow."

—Valerie Burns, Agatha, Anthony, Edgar, and Next Generation Award finalist

ACKNOWLEDGMENTS

To you, dear readers: Thanks for letting me fiddle with police jurisdiction (duties of sheriff's department versus city police) to streamline the novel and for allowing me to change up specific police station locations. And thank you for embracing Felicity and her family. It's pure magic every time I interact with someone who enjoys my books.

I'm grateful to my literary agent, Jessica Faust, for encouraging me to expand my fledgling fortune-cookie idea. You were right—magic and mystery pair well together! Special thanks to the entire BookEnds team, especially Jenissa Graham and Eva Dooley, for making my authorly life easier.

Sweet appreciation goes out to the Minotaur crew. Lily Cronig—you are an amazing editor. Thank you for your keen eye, and you deserve all the cookies. I'm also indebted to the Saras (Sara Eslami-Black and Sara LaCotti) for their marketing and publicity magic. Many thanks to Janna Dokos, Olya Kirilyuk, Kelley Ragland, John Simko, Tania Bissell, Ryan Jenkins, and Nathan Weaver for truly making my book sparkle.

I couldn't write without community, so special thank-yous to my Chicks on the Case blogging buddies, Crime

Writers of Color friends, and Sisters in Crime siblings (with an extra nod to Bao, Stephanie Gayle's adorable bunny).

The generous blurbs from great authors, including Valerie Burns, Emmeline Duncan, Carolyn Haines, Olivia Matthews, Gigi Pandian, and Jesse Q. Sutano, made me blush. Thank you all for being wonderful and extremely kind.

I'm delighted to be in conversation with incredible fellow authors like Iris Yamashita and Gigi Pandian and participate in fun activities like Murderous March. Discover more bookish events and learn about my *Cozy Connection* newsletter at jenniferjchow.com.

And, finally, never-ending pineapple buns and egg tarts to my entire extended family. I'm particularly blessed by my nearest and dearest: Steve, Bella, and Ellie: You are the real J-O-Y in my life.

CHAPTER 1

It only took twenty-eight years and one bad take-out meal to unlock my superpower. Okay, "power" might be stretching the definition. I don't fly or shoot beams out of my eyes or have absurd strength. I may be able to bring supreme joy, though . . . by baking. Like my mom and all the other women in the Jin family line before her.

Legend has it that once upon a dynasty, my ancestors lived in a tiny village that had been punished with drought. For two long years they suffered, until every villager had reached the last of their wheat reserves. Using her final grains, our Jin ancestor poured all her hope for the future into the batter and baked a tiny cake—but not for herself. She fed every last bite of pastry to her sickly mother; on her deathbed, the matriarch smiled and blessed her daughter and all future daughters down the line. The matriarch's soul rose to the upper realms, and whether it was because of her pleas to heaven or the celestial notice of a daughter's devotion, a miracle happened. The skies opened, filling the earth with cleansing, nourishing rain. The villagers rejoiced, and every Jin pastry from then on has spread joy.

With a last name like ours, of course the family shop is called Gold Bakery because Jin literally means "gold" in Mandarin. Not that I'm good with the language. I'm a third-generation Chinese American, so I'm surprised *any* vocab has stuck with me. That, plus being raised in the small town of Pixie, California, where most people don't look anything like me—which meant getting bullied as a child and feeling out of place as an adult. White faces all around me. Except in a certain beloved cul-de-sac in our quaint downtown. The three shops nestled close together there might offer the most diverse demographics around Pixie.

Besides Gold Bakery, my bestie Kelvin owns a store next to ours called Love Blooms. His floral arrangements are gorgeous, and I'm not just saying that because I'm biased. We've been pals ever since our diaper days.

Paz Illuminations is on the other side of us, and the owner is my godmother, Alma Paz. She's in her sixties or her seventies (I've never quite pinned down her age) and gives out enigmatic bits of wisdom while providing the latest on-trend candles through her physical store and Etsy offerings.

Meanwhile, Mom and I are traditional and focused on our small, curated selection of treats. We offer our customers what we call our *specialized* supply of two types of baked goods. Mom has perfected Grandma's pineapple buns and also created her own magical spin on egg tarts. Per tradition, recipes are only passed by Jin word of mouth and a carefully monitored apprenticeship. I'm not sure what happened, because none of the other Jin secret recipes made it to America when Grandma, my Po Po, immigrated over.

Po Po was going to continue the Jin tradition here since her magical baking also worked in the United States. Mom dutifully followed in her footsteps; she adored being a magical Jin and described how she felt wrapped in sunshine when crafting pastries, as though the ancestors had bestowed on her a mighty glow of approval. The baking skills had come easy to Mom, her fingers moving in a quick, confident rhythm whenever she mixed and kneaded.

Then I was born, and I broke the trend. Instead of crafting magical treats, I ended up staffing the cash register. Admittedly, it's gotten tedious over the years—but everything changed last night when I unleashed my own superpower.

Because when I say magic, I really mean it. There's true magic in Mom's baking, just as there was in Grandma's, that creates feelings of temporary bliss in our customers. Every daughter in our family, across the ages, has discovered her own baking recipe that provides pure joy to others. I thought the magical talent had skipped me—until now.

So today, I rushed out the door with a renewed sense of optimism. After sprinting past the other stores in the cul-de-sac, I arrived at Gold Bakery just before opening time. I should've taken Mom up on her offer to wake me in the wee hours of the morning, but I didn't want to get up *that* early. Thank goodness our small apartment is a short distance away, just around the corner from the shop.

"Sorry," I said to my mom when I showed up, huffing and puffing. (While I looked wild from my run, Mom appeared as put together as ever, from her side-swept bob to her unwrinkled white linen apron.) "I'm used to cashier duties. I should have come in a lot earlier to prep."

"That's okay," she said. "Your body's not yet trained to getting up so early." Mom placed a calming hand on my shoulder. "Are you ready for this, Felicity?"

I swallowed hard. "I sure hope so."

Mom checked her pocket watch. She doesn't wear

anything on her wrists—it'd interfere with the baking. "You still have time before the first customer arrives to try out the recipe."

"Do you think it might not work? That it was a fluke?" I asked as I surveyed the glass display case in the front of the shop. Mom had already set out trays of her scrumptious pineapple buns. No real pineapple in them, but the crisscross marks on top of the buns made them appear like the eponymous treat. The pastries were golden in color and perfectly round. Her signature egg tarts must be somewhere close by, too. Maybe she was letting their smooth custard centers cool down before she slid the tarts alongside the pineapple buns.

I took in the smell of sugar and happiness floating in the air.

"Felicity, I believe in you," Mom said.

"But my track record isn't that great, remember?" I gave her a lopsided smile. As if she could forget. We'd tried for years in the kitchen to shape me into a worthy Jin baker.

She batted away my doubts. "Those were growing pains, Felicity."

Twenty-some years is a lot of growing pains. Ever since I could mix batter, I'd tried to bake—and failed. Forget about making pastries that brought happiness, I couldn't even create edible treats. I would burn the cookies and flatten the cupcakes. My mom had continued to encourage me all throughout that time, but after I turned twenty, I'd avoided baking. Too much heartache.

And yet, I said now, "Let's go for round two." Hopefully, my night magic also worked during the day. I went to the kitchen in the back.

The beautiful space brought forth mixed emotions. The baking equipment all gleamed a sparkling silver, polished daily by my mom. A massive triple-deck industrial oven stood sentry at the rear wall, overlooking two long silver tables in the center, at the ready for pastry-making. Off to the sides, we had a drop-in stainless steel sink and our refrigeration units. The modern married with the whimsical in the kitchen, what with the bright tangerine-colored tile floor, the pastel glass bottles of ingredients, and the teal pendant lamps dangling from the ceiling.

I loved the cozy warmth and heady fragrance found in the kitchen, but I'd also experienced many culinary fails in this very same baking arena. What would happen today? I gathered my needed ingredients, starting with the eggs. After cracking them, I was grateful not to have flung yolk everywhere, though I found myself scooping out bits of shell from the bowl. My nerves must be getting to me.

Mom perched at a nearby counter, watching my every move. She was like a mama bird waiting for me to spread my wings and soar in triumph . . . I only hoped I wouldn't fall flat on my face.

"Sorry, but could you give me a little space?" I said. "Maybe you can put some egg tarts out on display?" I thought I could do this, but having an audience distracted me from the peace I needed to replicate the recipe.

My mom nodded understandingly and carried off a tray of the mini pastries out through the arched doorway. I whipped the eggs and some sugar together while she busied herself in the front.

Suddenly, she straightened and darted to the glass door at the entrance. We weren't even open yet. Who could she be hurrying to see?

"Kelvin!" my mom said, a delighted squeal to her voice. "Felicity's in the back. Why don't you go see her?"

Maybe she thought he could provide moral support.

Or perhaps because he'd been on the scene last night, she thought he'd bring me good luck. Well, I might need it.

I could hear the clomping of his size-twelve feet even before he strode through the kitchen archway. He sure loved those sturdy Doc Martens.

"Hey, Lissa," he said, the only person I let get away with a nickname.

"Hi," I said, showing him the mixing bowl. "Does this look like the same amount of batter as I made last night?"

Kelvin shrugged. "Beats me. Anything I can do to lend a hand?"

I glanced at his white Henley shirt, a sharp contrast to his dark skin. "Ha. You better roll up those shirtsleeves if you don't want them to get messy."

He chuckled. "I trust you, and you did great yesterday."

True, but I'd created the fortune cookies on a whim after I tried the horrible ones we'd gotten with our Chinese takeout. After years of avoiding baking anything at all, I'd been struck by a sudden inspiration. In my mind's eye, I could envision the fully formed fortune cookies. Then the recipe had materialized in my imagination, and my fingers had happily danced along to each step I'd pictured. Last night, I'd successfully baked fortune cookies. Only two of them, but they'd been edible and had smelled of enchanting possibility.

Could I do it again? I mentally went through every part of the new recipe to calm my nerves. Okay, I think I've got this.

I turned to Kelvin and asked, "Can you get the butter for me?"

He took out a stick from the fridge and handed it over.

I removed the wrapper, placing the butter in a dish and into the microwave.

Mom returned as I added the melted butter and the other needed ingredients to the bowl. She cupped a hand behind her ear and leaned in toward me.

"I can't hear you." My mom nudged Kelvin. "Can you check her lips? Anything happening there?"

I stopped mixing. "Mom," I said, "come on."

"It helps me when *I* bake," she said. "The joy comes out of the cheerful sounds we make."

"Does it really?" That was Mom's theory. She figured that the humming she did while baking infused her egg tarts with love. Mom claimed that my grandmother, Po Po, had also sung while she made her exquisite pineapple buns; I couldn't reach that far back in my memory to know for sure since she'd died when I was a toddler.

I gave Kelvin the side eye now. "Please don't stare at my lips."

"Can't help it, they're gigantic," he quipped. Whatever.

Kelvin and I were purely platonic. He'd gone for a romantic promposal our senior year, but I told him we should go as pals. He'd been in the friend zone for so long, I never allowed my mind to contemplate an alternative. Now, I debated whether to dump the bowl of batter on him and his pristine shirt. It would serve him right.

I swear the man could read my mind because he gave me a subtle head shake.

Time to concentrate, Felicity. I focused on the bowl before me, my senses centered on the soothing vanilla essence drifting in the air.

My mind visualized the completed fortune cookies, and my hands, on automatic pilot, completed the meditative motion of whisking in slow, concentric circles. After a couple of minutes, I scooped out tiny portions of the golden batter onto a baking mat and carefully placed the tray in the preheated oven.

"Here's hoping." I crossed my fingers and set the timer for six minutes.

The fortune cookies I'd made last night—the pair of them—had been yummy. For once. Kelvin and I had munched on the cookies with glee. Or maybe that was because we'd wanted to get rid of the taste of the mediocre takeout. We'd (unfortunately) ordered from Foo Fusion, the new restaurant that had sprung up right outside of Pixie's town limits.

The timer dinged, and I pulled the small batch of three cookies from the oven. They smelled like vanilla spice and everything nice. I couldn't detect the same sweet scent of magic that usually wafted from my mom's creations, but then again the stress might be blocking my senses.

With fumbling hands, I managed to shape the newly baked discs over the rim of a mug to get the distinctive fortune cookie fold. I set them aside to cool, but my mom snatched one up right away.

"Time to find out," Mom said, popping the cookie into her mouth. She closed her eyes and chewed.

I bit the side of my cheek as I waited for her verdict.

"Delicious." A smile bloomed across her face. "Only a hint of happiness in it, but that should increase over time."

Kelvin soft-punched me in the arm. "You did it, Lissa. Congrats." He was the only one I'd ever shared my family's magical history with—recklessly so in a childhood game of Truth or Dare, but I'd pinkie-sworn him to secrecy. I doubted he even believed me . . . until his mother fell ill. The treatments stopped working in the end, and only our pastries brought her comfort. At her funeral, Kelvin had pulled my mom and me to the side, thanking us for the "precious, truly magical" moments. My mom got flustered I'd shared the Jin secret, but Kelvin's earnest gratitude softened her heart. She eventually forgave me and accepted Kelvin into our inner circle of trust.

And now, my mom wasn't the only one with magic at her baking fingertips. After all these years, I had finally claimed my birthright. It felt so good. Redemptive almost, especially after all of my previous fails.

My best friend smirked at me. "Even though fortune cookies aren't really Chinese."

"Well," I said, "they're made in the USA like me." Authentically American.

"So I guess now is not the time to tell you about their Japanese roots?" Kelvin said.

I goggled at him. *Wait, what?* "Uh, can you save the history lesson for later? I'm trying to stake my baking claim here."

"Whatever their origins, you did it, Felicity. Made these beautiful fortune cookies." Mom rubbed her hands together. "Guess we'll be unveiling a new line of pastries at Gold Bakery today."

I glanced at the remaining two cookies left on the baking sheet. Since I had to fold the treats by hand before they cooled, I could only make tiny batches of three at a time. It'd take a while before I'd be able to fill an entire tray.

"Looks like you've got a lot of work ahead of you," Kelvin said as he grabbed a cookie. "I'll leave you to it."

I sputtered. "Hey, I thought you were going to help me."

He jingled the keys in his hand. "Fetched the butter for you, didn't I? Besides, I've got a floral shop to open."

"Jerk," I said with love.

"Aw, have a fortune cookie." He winked at me. "It'll make you feel better."

If only. I needed to save that last one. Especially since we'd just opened up shop. Time was not my friend today.

The first customer who walked into the bakery fawned over the pineapple buns. "Angela, you outdid yourself again," she told my mom, buying three dozen of them.

Quite a stash. As a reward, Mom handed her my last fortune cookie. "On the house," my mom said. "Felicity made it. If—I mean, when—you like it, tell all your friends."

I felt my cheeks heat up.

"Why, thank you." The lady cracked open the cookie and stared at it for a moment, perplexed. "Odd. Where's the fortune?"

I slapped a palm against my forehead. Thankfully, she didn't pay attention to the smacking noise.

Of course people would be expecting a morsel of written wisdom with their treats. I'd have to throw something together for the next batch.

The lady chomped on the fortune cookie. Her features softened, as though she was reliving a good memory in her mind.

She gave me a smile. "Very tasty," she said, finishing the cookie. "I'm sure these will be a huge hit."

I decided to handwrite some generic fortunes and slip those papers into the cookies. Unfortunately, there was only a small window of opportunity to sneak the lucky messages into the baked goods. I had to time it just right, inserting them after the fortune cookies had been baked but before I folded them.

Writing had never been my preferred medium of creative expression. But at least I had neat penmanship. Maybe that would make up for the generic messages I'd thought to give to customers. Variations of "You will have a nice day" repeated themselves.

I hit a snag with the after-lunch crowd. Folks didn't want to buy only a single fortune cookie but multiples of them, so I was running out of cookies. And written messages.

I'd finished with an onslaught of people and inserted another mini batch in the oven when one more customer, a guy in his mid-twenties, showed up.

"I just heard about these new fortune cookies," the man wearing a Fresno State Bulldogs jersey said. "My buddy can't get enough but won't share his with me. Do you have any more in stock?"

"Yep, they're in the oven." I gestured through the archway. "You okay waiting?"

"Sure, I've got some time."

"Thanks," I said.

He tapped his sneaker-clad foot against the ground. "You know what I like best about fortune cookies?"

I shrugged at him.

"The cool messages inside."

I suppressed a groan. *Please don't judge me by my sayings.*

He spoke again. "I keep all my fortunes, you know."

A fortune message collector. What were the chances? I didn't want to disappoint him with my lackluster writings.

He pulled his wallet out. "How much are they?"

I named a price, and he slapped some cash into my hand. "Just one, and keep the change. I hope I get the perfect fortune." No pressure, huh?

The timer dinged and saved me from having to

respond. I sprinted to the kitchen. My palm still tingled with warmth from where he'd thrust the money at me.

Even as I washed my hands, the cool water didn't lower their temperature. I pulled out the tray and worked on writing the ideal fortune for the expectant cookie collector.

Only before I could make something up, my hand automatically twirled across the slip of paper. I didn't even know what I wrote—rainbow colors swam across my vision, and a buzzing sounded in my ears. Strange. It must be because I hadn't bothered to take a lunch break on this super busy day.

I wobbled back to the Bulldogs fan and gave him his cookie.

"Excellent," he said, slipping out the front door. I saw him break open the cookie and take a bite. Then he read the piece of paper, and a wide grin appeared on his face.

I wondered what I'd written. Hopefully not some sort of pickup line by accident. I had half a mind to go out there and correct the message. But then the man stumbled on the sidewalk and fell down hard.

CHAPTER 2

I rushed out the door just as the man in the Bulldogs jersey sprang up from the sidewalk.

"Are you okay?" I asked.

"Better than that." He brushed off his knees and waved some cash in the air. "Your fortune was right. I did find money on the ground."

"What are you talking about?"

He showed me a fifty-dollar bill. After he plucked out his wallet and placed the cash tenderly inside, he flashed me a familiar-looking slip of paper.

The fortune cookie message I'd written. I hovered near him and read my own words. "You will find lucky money on the sidewalk."

He beamed. "And that's exactly what happened. Right outside the bakery, I saw a hint of green. Fell spectacularly while picking up the cash, but I'm no worse for the wear."

Huh. My fortune for him had literally come true. What were the chances?

"Thanks again," he said with a wave. "I'll be sure to come back and spread the word about your bakery."

Still in shock, I managed to make a garbled noise in

the back of my throat—which I hoped he took as thanks. The customer sauntered off.

A merry bell tinkled nearby, and I turned toward the sound. My godmother, Alma, had exited her shop.

"What was that all about?" She crossed her arms over her ample bosom and watched while the customer turned the corner.

"Um, that guy fell down." I scratched the tip of my nose. "But he didn't mind since he ended up finding fifty dollars on the ground."

"A very *fortunate* tumble." Alma narrowed her eyes at me, as though she saw straight inside my soul.

I took a step backward. As far as I understood, Alma didn't know about our magic. Mom certainly never shared it with anyone in Pixie. She said she'd been burned before and that Jin secrets should stay in the family (except she'd eventually relented with Kelvin).

Anyway, Alma's weathered face held a constant inscrutable expression, so I never knew what she was thinking.

"Want a word of advice?" she said now.

I nodded. My godmother loved to drop indecipherable pearls of wisdom on me. Even though they were confusing, I loved trying to figure them (and her) out.

"All things will be known in the end," she said.

"Thanks, I guess." Was Alma referring to knowing my talent? Or to the reason for the guy falling down? Or something else entirely?

The shrill ringing of a phone drew my godmother's attention back to her store with its dimly lit interior. Her shop's windows and door were covered in swaths of black velvet curtains that she kept mostly closed. Customers had been known to wander away during business hours, thinking she'd already shut down for the day.

Alma bustled off, and I watched as she disappeared inside Paz Illuminations. Her braided bun of silver hair wobbled with her quick motions, and I hoped I would be as spry as her when I turned sixty . . . or seventy . . . or whatever her real age was.

I reentered Gold Bakery, where I could hear my mom humming up a storm in the back. She needed to restock her supply of pineapple buns.

Right after I gobbled down a much-delayed lunch, more customers arrived. It was like they could smell the happiness baking in the air.

Over the next few hours, we sold a lot of our inventory, including the rest of my fortune cookies. I didn't bother to make another batch when evening rolled around. We closed at five, and I figured nobody would stroll in at the last minute.

Unluckily, someone did. I didn't recognize the thirty-something Asian man. Maybe he was a tourist. Pixie was a small place, so I usually knew a lot of people by name or at least by sight, especially those in the Asian community.

He did a thorough study of our place, making sure to walk and inspect every corner of the shop. The man checked out our decorations and even sniffed the air. In the end, he muttered, "So this is Gold Bakery."

Innocuous enough, except I didn't like how he said our name with a hint of disgust.

"Can I help you?" I said. "We have a dozen egg tarts left and two pineapple buns."

He shook his head, and I noticed his long bangs, distrusting them at once. They were styled in a specific way to hide his receding hairline. "I heard you make fortune cookies here."

My mom popped her head through the archway of

the kitchen. "That's right. My daughter, Felicity, added the new item just this morning. They're fabulous."

Embarrassed by her glowing remarks, I focused on my sneakers.

The man snorted. "We'll see about that. I'd like to try one of your 'fabulous' fortune cookies."

"Okay, but I'll need to go bake a fresh one," I said.

"Sure, just don't take too long." He looked at the huge gold watch on his wrist. "I've got places to be."

I nodded, letting his snooty manner and words pass, and swapped places with my mom as she rang him up and tried to engage in polite conversation.

While I created another batch of fortune cookies, I heard snippets of their chat. He didn't live in Pixie but in Fresno. He'd come by when someone had shared about the fortune cookies offered at Gold Bakery.

The man gave out short, sharp answers to my mom. He didn't seem to enjoy making small talk, so I rushed to shape his fortune cookie and almost burned my fingers in the process.

By the time I brought the treat out, Mom and he had finished their conversation, and he was focused on his phone. Mom stood behind the counter.

I whispered to her, "Oh no. I was in such a rush, I forgot to put in the fortune. Maybe he won't notice?"

She bit her bottom lip.

In a louder voice, I told the customer, "Here you go."

"Finally," he said, putting away his cell.

To temper his grumpiness, I said, "It's handcrafted. I made sure to pay special attention to each step." Except for the message.

I placed the fortune cookie in a little to-go container. He grabbed at the box, and the tips of his fingers and accompanying sharp nails scraped my wrist.

I winced but covered it with a smile. Then I felt an overwhelming urge. Like a strange force pushing me forward. What was happening?

I lurched toward the paper and pen on the counter, compelled to write something down. Buzzing filled my ears, and dizzying, colorful lines appeared before my eyes.

Once I finished writing, my mom snatched the piece of paper out of my hand and gave it to the man. "Oops, your fortune. It must have fallen out of the cookie."

He raised his eyebrows. "What kind of poor quality control do you have at this shop?"

Then he glanced at the slip of paper and made a sour face.

What had I written for him?

He crumpled the paper up and stuffed it in his pocket. "Ha. Even if we're short-staffed, I don't think you'll be a problem," he murmured as he strode out the door.

"What was that all about?" my mom asked after he'd left.

"Beats me," I said, "but I hope he doesn't darken our door again anytime soon."

My mom nodded and turned our bakery sign to CLOSED. I busied myself wiping down the counters in the kitchen. Mom would take care of everything in the front, including reconciling receipts and packing away the leftover pastries.

It took me an hour to clean everything in the back. While wiping up the messes, I couldn't help but grin. Splashes of vanilla. Sprinkles of flour. The messiness didn't faze me. It all reminded me of my new accomplishment. I'd actually baked for others after a lifetime of trying . . . I got lost in daydreams of accolades and praise.

Mom had to call my name twice to get my attention to

remind me to take out the trash. Oh, right. The garbage truck was scheduled to come by early the next morning.

When I walked into the alley, though, I noticed that the communal dumpster was already overflowing. Fast-food bags and torn condiment packets littered the ground. Guess the bakery trash would have to wait. I placed the tied sack next to our back door. I'd heave it into the dumpster after it got emptied tomorrow.

In the morning, my mom and I got up early and walked over to Gold Bakery together. But something had happened on our sleepy street of stores.

Several police cars were crookedly parked in the cul-de-sac. One vehicle still had its lights flashing, as though the cop had been in too much of a rush to turn them off.

I gaped at the strange scene while my mom's brow furrowed, causing a deep crease to appear on her forehead. What was going on? Did one of the stores get broken into? A quick inspection showed me that Love Blooms, Paz Illuminations, and our own bakery were seemingly untouched.

Besides, Pixie was known for its low crime rate. We had a very tiny police station for minor complaints. If there was any real trouble, services had to be contracted and authorities had to be sent in from the surrounding area. I'd rarely spotted officers out and about, unless they were visiting from nearby Fresno and wanted to relax in our little town on a day trip.

Then I noticed the EMT vehicle. It half blocked the entrance to the area behind our shops, the alleyway. The ambulance's back doors were thrown open. There must be some kind of medical emergency.

"Do you think it's someone we know?" I asked Mom.

It wouldn't be Alma, right? She wasn't *that* old and anyway, she didn't usually come in this early.

Mom shivered. "I hope not."

We hurried over to the ambulance. "Is everything okay?" I called out, hoping for an answer. No response. I checked, and the vehicle was empty.

Then, from the alley, a few medical technicians pushed a gurney toward us and the vehicle.

"Who's injured?" Mom asked one of the paramedics. He cast his eyes down, shook his head, and mumbled, "Coroner assist."

I studied the stretcher again. It didn't have someone lying underneath a blanket. Instead, it held a human-shaped, closed bag. "Mom, that person on there . . . I don't think they're just hurt—"

She followed my line of sight and gripped my arm. "Someone died?" We were now both trembling.

After exchanging mutual looks of horror, we rushed to the alley. A garbage truck sat there, parked. The nervous-looking driver puffed on his inhaler before he spoke to a tall Asian woman in a camel-colored suit.

As though feeling my gaze on her, she turned around and spied us. The flash of a shiny badge at her waistband let me know that she was working the investigation.

She approached Mom and me with confident strides. "No civilians allowed in this area."

My mom appeared flustered, gesticulating with her hands as she spoke. "We work here. I mean, not *exactly* here in the alley . . ."

I pointed to the back door of our store. "Mom and I work at Gold Bakery. It's our family shop."

The woman's dark eyes focused on me. "And is there a particular reason you didn't put your trash in the dumpster?"

I glanced at the garbage bag from last night, which lay sagging on the ground near our bakery's back door. "The dumpster was too full yesterday. I figured I'd wait until the truck came and collected things."

"It certainly was full, given the dead body."

If the woman had meant to shock us, it worked. I gasped, and Mom swayed against me. I steadied her. "What are you saying? Who is it?"

The woman dodged my questions but showed me her badge. "I'm Detective Rylan Sun. With Fresno's homicide department."

Someone had definitely died then. And the homicide department. Could the death have been suspicious? I reminded myself the body had been found in a dumpster: It didn't get much more suspicious than that.

Mom spoke in a tiny voice. "How did this happen?"

The detective turned her attention to my mom. "Ma'am, I'll have to record you and your daughter's statements about last night separately."

Maybe she noticed Mom's pallor because her demeanor shifted and softened. She added in a more polite tone, "Is there someplace you can sit down where we can chat?"

"In the bakery," I said. Behind the register. The only option. We didn't have any tables or stools for our customers, and the kitchen wasn't made for sitting around in. "Let me guide her there."

"She can't go by herself?" the detective asked.

I hated talking about my mom as if she wasn't right next to me, but I said, "Not in this state."

The detective nodded, as though giving me permission, but followed close behind us into the bakery. Did she think we were going to collude or something?

I sat Mom down on the chair behind the register and gave her a glass of water.

Detective Sun motioned me over. "Let's give her some time to recover from the shock. I'll take your statement first, outside. Your name?"

"Felicity Jin."

We returned to the alley, the detective asking me to shut the rear door to the bakery. Guess she didn't want Mom overhearing anything from our conversation.

Detective Sun pulled out her phone and informed me she'd be recording our conversation. I took her through the timeline of yesterday's events. She seemed especially interested in the evening hours after we closed up shop.

When the detective ended the formal recording session, she asked in a forced light manner, "What kind of goodies do you make in your bakery?"

"Pineapple buns and egg tarts are our signature treats."

She cocked her head. "Nothing else?"

"Um, I just started making fortune cookies."

"Fascinating."

"How so?"

The detective seemed to have an internal debate before she took out a clear evidence bag. I recognized the small slip of paper inside it.

"That's mine!" I blurted out.

She startled at my words, and her ponytailed black hair shifted with the movement.

Maybe I shouldn't have admitted to anything. Could it be used against me? I didn't know how.

"The fortune is handwritten," she said. "Do you remember what it said?"

"Not a clue."

"Interesting, because it was found in the vic's pocket. And it was spot-on about his manner of death."

I shuddered. "Really?"

She watched my reaction carefully as she spilled her next words: "It said 'Too much concrete knowledge will surely suffocate you.'"

"He suffocated? I don't remember writing that." I spoke the truth. At the time, I'd felt too dizzy to pay any attention to what I was scribbling. What had that nausea been all about anyway?

The detective continued to give me a hard stare, but I couldn't add anything enlightening to my statement.

"I hope your memory clears up soon," she said before striding into the bakery to interrogate my mom.

CHAPTER 3

When Detective Sun left the bakery after questioning Mom, she walked by me without a word. She wasn't smiling. That didn't bode well. I hurried inside and found Mom sitting behind the cash register, frozen, staring straight ahead of her.

I touched my mom on her shoulder, and she blinked. Turning to me, she said, "That detective asked a lot of questions . . . about you."

"What did she want to know?"

"Everything you did last night. I told her you were with me the whole time. We served that last customer together and then cleaned up like usual." She paused. "Maybe the detective can track down that man who came near closing time. He could vouch for us."

I shook my head. "I don't think so."

"You're right. He paid with cash. He'd be hard to find."

That wasn't the only problem. Detective Sun had shown me a written fortune customized by me. I'd only personalized two fortunes yesterday, and I was pretty sure the man they'd fished out of the dumpster *was* our last customer.

My mom brushed her hands like she was getting rid

of excess flour. "I'm sure Detective Sun is very competent at her job."

Mom had always believed in authority figures—and staying on the right side of them. Not making waves.

I made a noncommittal murmur.

She got out of the chair and said, "Well, the egg tarts aren't going to bake themselves. Best to keep busy." Mom turned practical when confronted with any mess in life. She always talked about moving upward and onward. Plus, she couldn't stay sad when she got into her sweet baking groove, an apron tied firmly around her waist.

On the flip side, I liked taking a moment to think, to pause. The unexpected always bothered me. Still feeling shaken by the events of the morning, I asked her, "Do you mind if I hop over next door? Kelvin should be there by now, and I promise I'll come back soon."

"Yes, of course." She touched my shoulder. "Take your time. We've both had a huge shock this morning."

Practically getting accused of murder will do that to you, I thought, but didn't say aloud to my mom. The detective had definitely seemed suspicious of me. She'd started off by telling me about the dead body in the dumpster and ended with sharing the fortune cookie message. Both times she'd been intent on my reaction, and I thought I'd heard somewhere that the police analyzed potential suspects' reactions for tells.

"Thanks for understanding, Mom," I said, putting on a stoic smile before I walked next door.

Love Blooms was the shop I went to when I needed solace. Not only could I find Kelvin there most of the time, but its whole environment put me at ease.

I walked through the door, and the fresh, jungle-like interior of the shop greeted me. Kelvin had covered almost every open space with greenery. Somehow, though, the pathways remained clear, and nobody had ever knocked a vase over.

Kelvin, as usual, didn't even look up from where he stood at a long table at the back of the shop. Whenever he got lost in flower arranging, he stayed concentrated on the task. While I could be dreamy and disconnected with the world around me at times, Kelvin stayed grounded and focused so hard on the thing right in front of him that he blocked out everything else. Maybe our opposite approaches complemented one another and made us well-suited as best friends.

I watched as his hands flew over the greenery. Kelvin's fingers danced among the branches and leaves. Flower arranging seemed like the perfect combination of his parents' skills. He got the surgical dexterity from his dad and the plant-growing talent from his mom, who'd been an amateur gardener and ikebana artist. Kelvin still used blossoms from the garden of his childhood home to create special arrangements for people.

He wrapped the bouquet in brown kraft paper, tied a sky blue ribbon around it all, and then looked up. "Oh, Lissa, I didn't hear you come in."

"You never do," I teased. "Not when you're hard at work."

Had he gotten distracted by flower arranging earlier and tuned out the drama this morning? Kelvin didn't seem disturbed at all. Or maybe he'd managed to miss the cops. All the other shops on the street opened later than Gold Bakery.

"Can't help it. Flowers are like a portal into another world." He gave an embarrassed grin before coming closer to study me. "What's wrong?"

Of course, he would know something was up. Kelvin had always been sensitive to his surroundings and people's moods. He joked that he'd been trained to do so because he'd had to navigate growing up with an African American dad and an Asian mom.

I stood there, silent. Strong emotions swirled around my heart, but I couldn't voice them. Could Kelvin read the tumult inside me just by my tense posture?

He turned to a side table, extracted a sprig of lavender, and gave it to me. "Here's what you need."

I sniffed the flower. It gave off a sharp, clean scent. It did make me feel better, and I focused on the present moment instead of my misgivings. "Thanks. What's it symbolize?"

Kelvin enjoyed investigating the meanings behind flowers. He really should write a guidebook on floral symbolism one day. "Peace," he said. "Plus, lavender helps you sleep better."

"Guess it'd be asking too much for it to ward off trouble," I said. "Or get someone out of jail."

He sucked in a deep breath. "Whoa. What happened?"

"I take it you didn't see the police activity?"

He glanced out the door at the serene street. "When was this?"

"Early in the morning. The cops were swarming around the cul-de-sac when Mom and I came to prep."

He rubbed the back of his neck. "I was running a little late today."

"It was like a crime show over here." I gulped. "They ended up pulling a dead body out of the dumpster in the back alley."

Kelvin stared at me, maybe waiting for the punch line.

When I didn't tell him it was a joke, he said, "Gee, Lissa. That's horrible. Are you okay?"

"Yeah. I mean I'll be fine eventually. But there's more."

He raised his eyebrows.

I proceeded to share with Kelvin my interactions with Detective Sun and how it seemed like I was her primary suspect at this point.

When I finished, he tugged at his earlobe. "I don't know, Lissa. Your mom is vouching for you, and you've got no motive, so there shouldn't be any trouble. Maybe this detective will get off your case soon."

Kelvin was right. Perhaps I was overthinking things. It did feel good to get everything out in the open, though, and I felt reassured by what he'd said.

I pretend-punched him in the arm. "Thanks for the pep talk, Coach."

"Sure, anyt—"

The door to Love Blooms swished open. A woman came in, gabbing on her phone. "I'm at the flower shop right now picking up the bouquet." She motioned for Kelvin to ring her up.

The customer continued her conversation as she tapped her credit card against the reader. "Rumor has it that he died with a fortune cookie in his hand."

I flinched. Could it be? Was she talking about the man who'd been found in the dumpster?

The woman accepted the bouquet from Kelvin and left the shop without acknowledging either of us. As she exited, I heard her say, "I'll be at the gathering soon. Foo Fusion, right? See you there."

How many men died with fortune cookies on them? I brought the sprig of lavender up to my nose and inhaled deeply. It didn't work this time around. My nerves seemed to tense up even more.

I had a bad feeling about everything that was happening, and I thought Foo Fusion might hold the answer to a few of my questions.

Kelvin nodded at the flower in my hand. "Not working? I think you may need something else to ease your mind."

"Or someplace else," I murmured.

"Foo Fusion," he said. "I heard her, too. And, being the stellar guy that I am, I'm willing to go with you on my lunch break."

"Thanks. You're the best." I didn't want to do this on my own, but I also wanted answers.

When I asked Mom, she assured me I could go out for lunch and get a breather. "Go for as long as you need to," she said, giving me a brief pat on the back.

When we'd had Chinese takeout a few nights before, it had been from Foo Fusion but Kelvin had picked it up, so I didn't know what the restaurant looked like or even where it was located exactly. He drove us across the boundary line between the towns and into the City of Fresno proper, soon pulling into a wide parking lot.

There was no doubt that the owner had had a grand vision for their establishment. The standalone building was stylized with imposing columns, a peaked roof, and a pair of Foo lions guarding the entrance. The fierce statues seemed to stare at me with challenge and fury.

I hurried past them but was blocked from entering the actual restaurant because of a small crowd. *Wow, the place was packed for lunchtime.* Or wait, that wasn't quite right. Nobody was walking into Foo Fusion. Instead, they lingered under the overhang.

Kelvin, who stood half a foot taller than me, craned his neck. "I see an impromptu memorial," he whispered, pointing to the side.

I shuffled around until I found a gap in the crowd.

Peeking through the tiny space, I glimpsed the tip of the flower bouquet Kelvin had made earlier. It was positioned on top of a mix of eclectic gifts, including plushies and candles, all piled on the ground.

"This was his favorite new restaurant," a lady said, then started sobbing. "Truly, the Fortune Cookie King has crumbled."

Someone in the crowd snorted. "Ha, that's a good pun."

Fortune Cookie King? Who had this guy been? I tapped the crying woman on the shoulder, but before I could ask her any questions, the front door to Foo Fusion flew open.

A middle-aged Asian man with a balding head glared at us. "You can't block the entrance to my restaurant like this. Come inside to eat, or get off my property."

A few people disentangled themselves from the crowd and snuck off. The rest of them entered Foo Fusion.

I glanced over at Kelvin, and he seemed to understand my intentions. The least we could do was financially help out the owner at a time like this. Besides, my stomach had started grumbling, and I'd give the place a second chance. Especially since it'd led (in a zigzagging way) to regaining my magical birthright.

The spacious interior of the restaurant boasted three distinct eating stations. It wasn't a lie that the place served fusion food, because each area boasted a separate specialty: Chinese cuisine, doughnuts, and hamburgers. The owner had really tried to cater to different tastes.

When Kelvin and I got to the front of the line, I insisted on paying for our take-out meal. I wanted to keep things platonic, and alternating who paid kept our budgets and relationship on surer footing. Kelvin, really giving the restaurant another chance, ordered the beef chow fun. I decided on a cheeseburger.

Once the owner disappeared inside the kitchen, I swiped a business card from the holder on the counter, auspiciously placed next to a potted money tree. I studied the card. The man who owned the place was named Michael Fu.

Soon, Michael came back and plopped a bag in front of us. Kelvin peeked inside and asked, "Can we get some fortune cookies, too?"

Remembering their rancid taste, I wrinkled my nose at him, but my best friend mouthed, "Trust me."

"Too bad. We don't have any more," Michael said. "Out of stock."

Kelvin pointed to a large, opened cardboard box behind the owner. "There's an overflowing pile of them right there."

"Are you absolutely certain you want to eat them? Of your own choice?"

Kelvin nodded.

"Okay, if you're sure," Michael said. He reached into the box and dropped two wrapped fortune cookies in the to-go bag.

Strange, I thought, as I followed Kelvin out the door. *Why had Michael seemed so hesitant about giving us the cookies?*

Lost in my own world, I didn't pay attention to where I was going and knocked into a woman coming through the door.

"Whoops, sorry," I said.

The woman didn't respond and planted herself in front of me to block my exit. What was going on? After all, I'd apologized.

I looked up. Detective Sun's eyes bored into mine.

"What are you doing here?" she asked, a hard edge to her voice.

CHAPTER 4

I backed away from the detective and stammered out nonsensical garbage. Kelvin saved me by popping back through the door. "Lissa, you coming or what?"

I gave an apologetic shrug to the cop. "I'm just here for lunch, Detective Sun. Takeout," I said, pointing at the brown bag.

She gave a grunt but let me pass.

Once outside, Kelvin turned to me and whistled. "So that was the detective, huh?"

"Yeah, no love lost between us."

Under the awning of the restaurant, I took a moment to study the makeshift memorial. While we'd been ordering our food, everything had gotten knocked over. Stuffed animals lay prone, and petals from wayward flowers were scattered on the ground. Who'd done this?

I noticed a message in vivid red on lined notebook paper—could it have been written in blood? Creepy. On closer inspection, I realized the liquid was glossier. The texture and vibrant hue of sweet-and-sour sauce. It read "The Cookie Prince Had It Coming."

Kelvin and I glanced around for any obvious onlookers, but the crowd had dispersed. They had all left quickly after Michael had railed at the loiterers. Would he know who had left the mean message? Not that the owner had been too friendly with us. I checked the peaked roof above me, but couldn't find a camera lodged in a hollowed space up there. *Unfortunate.*

"Okay, let's go," I said.

Back in our familiar cul-de-sac of shops, Kelvin and I sat on the curb eating from the take-out containers. Admittedly, I wasn't too hungry, and Foo Fusion really did have subpar food. Even the cheeseburger tasted like cardboard. I'd given it another chance, but maybe I shouldn't have.

I closed up the food container and handed it over to Kelvin. "Stock up your fridge."

My best friend was not a food snob like me. As long as something was edible, Kelvin scarfed it down. In fact, he'd already eaten his entire box of chow fun without any complaints.

"Thanks," he said. "Now on to dessert."

I took the wrapped fortune cookie he offered me. "But why did Michael hesitate to give them to us?"

"Who knows?" Kelvin unwrapped his cookie and munched on it.

I stared at the cellophane wrapper labeled "Smiley Fortunes" with a yellow happy face design. Flipping it to the back, I located the address of the fortune cookie distributor in tiny print. A local place. They made their cookies in Fresno.

"How is it?" I asked.

"About the same as before." Kelvin worked hard at crunching down on the cookie. "Don't feel like smiling much after eating it. And it definitely isn't as fresh as yours."

That was an understatement. On my first bite, I

couldn't break through the rock-hard surface. I brought a paper napkin to my mouth and spit out the cookie. "Ugh, talk about a choking hazard."

"You know," Kelvin said, "Foo Fusion should stock your more *fortunate* cookies instead."

I chuckled at his weird but endearing sense of humor.

The door to the bakery opened, and my mom bustled out. There was a smattering of flour in her hair. "Felicity," she said, "I need your help right away."

"Time for me to go." I stuffed the cellophane wrapper and rock-hard cookie in my pocket before I hurried to assist Mom.

Kelvin gave me a brief wave as I ducked inside the shop.

"What's going on, Mom?"

"Someone just called and ordered two dozen fortune cookies. They'll be here in twenty minutes."

I was glad that whoever had phoned hadn't heard about the ill-fated fortune cookie episode in the alley, but yikes. I'd need to rush to get the order done to keep the customer satisfied.

As I prepared the oven and mixed the batter, I wished I had more assistance. Wouldn't it be nice to have other workers helping do some of the more tedious tasks? Then again, my mom's guarantee to our customers was her focused personal dedication to each sweet treat we served. How many times had she called it the Jin way of baking? Besides, she insisted that a true baker did every single step herself. Or maybe that was because I'd made such a lousy helper in the kitchen even from an early age.

While I waited for the cookies to bake, I stuffed my hands in my pockets and rammed my fingers against something hard. The fortune cookie from Foo Fusion. I tossed out the inedible treat, but I kept the wrapper with the location of the business. An entire fortune cookie factory? What would that even look like?

Maybe I could do some research at Smiley Fortunes. At least I might be able to make my cookies more efficiently—but without sacrificing quality. I tucked the wrapper back into my pocket.

The oven timer dinged, and I turned my attention to baking. For these next couple of batches, at least, I'd have to do it the old-fashioned way.

After fulfilling the order (for a birthday party, I discovered), I stretched out my fingers from their cramped positions. Thank goodness I got a chance to rest. No other callers had phoned in, requesting dozens of cookies.

As the afternoon progressed, I began to hope I could get off from the bakery early because we'd hit an unusual lull. When I asked Mom if I could leave before closing, she didn't mind and said, "It takes a lot of strength to be a professional baker. You need to build up to it."

I knew she was trying to encourage me even if, at the same time, I felt a little put down by her remark. Either way, I decided to complete another dozen cookies before leaving for the day. I left the treats cooling on a metal tray for her.

After I finished, I popped back over to Love Blooms. As luck would have it, Kelvin didn't have anybody in line. Flower buyers tended to come in on special occasions, and we'd passed Valentine's Day and hadn't hit Mother's Day yet.

"Want to give me a ride?" I asked, hoping he'd say yes. Otherwise, I'd have to borrow my mom's clunker of a car. Sometimes it started, and other times it stayed icily silent on us.

"Can't you just walk back home?" Kelvin asked.

"I can, but I want to go on a field trip."

"With what class?"

"Ha-ha," I said.

"Seriously, where to?"

"A very specific fortune cookie factory," I said as I showed him the wrapper of Smiley Fortunes and pointed at the address in tiny print.

Much of Fresno is now developed, as opposed to its agrarian roots. It's a true urban city but without the towering skyscrapers crowding the view. It's kept some of the original San Joaquin Valley roots—for example, acting as a base for tons of fresh produce—and the outskirts of the city still feel peaceful.

The factory's location clung to the edges of Fresno on the Blossom Trail. We passed by many fruit orchards known for their plentiful petals, but I was more in awe of the hearty wildflowers that bloomed on the roadside, showing off their floral glory.

Kelvin started identifying each specimen as though he was on an episode of gardening-themed *Jeopardy!* (he even used the question format), but I tried to tune him out. Flower geek. The man had even named his car after a plant: Dahlia.

When we arrived at the factory, I did a double take. The building looked rundown. And the concrete sidewalk near it was torn up. A bulldozer lay parked across the street.

"You sure you took us to the right place?" I asked after we'd parked on the side of the dirt road.

Kelvin tapped at his noggin. "Please, I'm Mr. GPS."

True. He had an unerring sense of direction. For which I was grateful because I was directionally challenged. His navigational skills had saved me on multiple past occasions.

"Besides," Kelvin said, "I see a fruit—I mean a fortune cookie—stand."

I squinted at the table display through the windshield. A row of pint-size green open-weave baskets stood at the ready. Instead of holding berries, though, they contained stacks of fortune cookies. "We must be at the right place."

Nobody was behind the table selling the treats, so Kelvin and I headed to the structure in the back. Once we walked inside the dim warehouse, an unnerving smell assaulted my nose: a wretched combination of sugar, vanilla, and despondency. No happy scents here.

I glanced around the dilapidated building. A string of bulbs snaking around the rafters gave off some meager illumination. There was a small office with a glass window to one side, but the rest of the space was devoted to housing some massive machinery.

I'd expected a crowded factory of workers but found only three employees walking around. And one of them didn't even appear to be doing anything besides staring at her clipboard and marking things off a list. She had to be the one in charge, what with her glossy hair pinned back by two delicate pearl barrettes and her dangly beige clay earrings, while the other two wore hairnets and moved around with exhausted expressions.

After clearing her throat, the manager said to the workers, "Hurry up. We're behind on production. Remember: Satisfied customers mean orders mean continued jobs."

The employees scrambled to their work stations. One of them concentrated on making batter, pouring out a large bag of flour into an orange construction bucket. The other, after emitting a loud groan, sat on a stool before a large machine with a running conveyor belt.

Kelvin and I walked closer to the woman with the

clipboard, and she turned around. Once she noticed us, she pasted a fake smile on her face. "Oh, I didn't see you come in. Are you here to buy fortune cookies? Let me grab the cashbox."

"Thanks," Kelvin said, "there wasn't anyone outside."

"Sadly, we're short-staffed." The woman frowned. "We have an employee out on leave."

I would have thought they'd need more than a single additional worker to keep this operation running.

The woman continued speaking to Kelvin. "Do you want to pick out the *multiple* bags you'd like to purchase? If you buy three or more, you get a special deal."

He nodded, but I gestured to the space around us. "Is there any way I can check out the factory?"

"Certainly." This time the woman put on a genuine smile. "Costs ten bucks for a self-guided tour."

"Do you have headphones for the tour?"

"No," she said as she held out her palm for payment.

I gave her the money. Wow, the place must be desperate for cold hard cash. "Go ahead and pick the cookies without me," I said to Kelvin, hoping he'd take the hint.

If the manager wasn't hovering over me and busy helping Kelvin, I'd get a better chance to examine the equipment and get into honest conversations with the employees.

"Of course," he said.

"Ten minutes tops," the woman said to me. "Otherwise we charge twenty dollars for every additional fifteen minutes after that."

Desperate was right. "I'm sure I'll be done soon," I said.

Once they turned their backs to me, I started investigating.

CHAPTER 5

I moved toward the employee hovering over a heavy-duty industrial bucket. She used a stirring stick, and if I hadn't known better, I'd have thought she was mixing a vat of paint. The woman paused, opened a large opaque bottle, and dumped some of its contents in.

Vanilla floated in the air, and I peeked into the bucket. The swirl of dark brown against the cream of the batter almost looked like edible art.

"How do you like working here?" I asked the woman.

Even before she spoke, I could predict her answer because she exuded a heavy amount of despondency. "It's a paying job," she said.

Not the best of endorsements.

"Don't know for how much longer," she muttered.

"Why's that?" I leaned in closer, inviting further conversation.

The woman glanced over her shoulder toward the exit. Through the open doorway, I could spy the silhouettes of the manager and Kelvin. The worker's lips twisted. "Excuse me," she said, hauling away the finished batter.

I watched as she moved to another machine and poured it in there.

"What happens next in the process?" I asked.

She jerked her thumb to the left.

I followed the movement to an assembly line. Tubes were pumping the batter onto individual hot plates. An automated process ensured a trip through a hot gas oven—flames licked its metal underbelly—and the baking of fortune cookie rounds, looking very much like mini pancakes.

The second worker sat on a stool as the golden discs came out of the oven, speeding his way on a conveyor belt. A long metal rod was positioned before him. He grabbed a disc, stuffed in a fortune, and used the rod to bend the disc into a fortune cookie shape. Despite his heavy-duty gloves, his fingers worked quickly. He had to, given the rapid rate of the cookies being spat out by the machine.

"Nice gloves," I told him. They were made of a thick material but still seemed slim-fitting.

"Thanks," he said. "I'm Dakota, and I've been using these babies ever since the *incident*."

"What incident?"

He shook his head, but his fingers kept up with the work. "Let me tell ya, I'm so glad management has changed. Before, we weren't allowed to wear gloves in the factory."

I gaped at Dakota. "But the temperatures are so hot straight out of the oven." The workers didn't have my luxury of the extra minutes of cooling down I incorporated into making my fortune cookies.

"Don't I know it? That's how my buddy burned his hand. The incident I mentioned."

A shuffling of footsteps sounded from behind us.

"Time's up," the manager said.

I didn't know if she'd heard the tail end of our conversation, but she didn't offer to extend my factory tour.

Back in the car, I vented to Kelvin. "Something is going on with Smiley Fortunes. That manager didn't want me hanging around the factory one moment longer."

Kelvin kept his eyes on the road but said, "Her name's Cayla, spelled with a *C*. Cayla Jung."

I clicked my tongue. "On a first-name basis with her, huh? What'd you learn?"

He groaned. "That she sure can upsell. Check out the back seat."

I turned my head and counted three bags of fortune cookies in the rear of the car. "What are you going to do with all those? If you recall, they're barely edible."

"I don't know."

"You could do some beautifying of your landscaping," I said. "They *are* as hard as rocks."

"Don't even joke about it. My yard is perfect as is."

That was true. He had an oasis of lush plants and flowers. I held my hands up. "Sorry, I know that's your sacred space."

He grumbled, but I knew he'd already forgiven me. Kelvin didn't hold grudges.

"One of the workers told me the management's different," I said. "Looks like Cayla is running the operation now."

"Makes sense. She's the most senior employee there."

"I hear she's been making changes for the better," I said. "After another worker burned his hand there."

Kelvin hazarded a glance at my hands. "Have you gotten hurt while baking, Lissa?"

"Nah. It's been fine. I let my cookies cool down before

folding them." Except when I'd hurried to appease the impatient Fortune Cookie King himself.

"Good." He turned his attention to the road, and before long, we arrived back in Pixie.

Kelvin said he'd drop me off at home, which wasn't an inconvenience since he lived down the street from us. My mom and his mother used to coordinate playdates together all the time, from when we were toddlers (when nobody else wanted to play with "a foreigner") until our sophomore year. That's when Mrs. Love got sick and hid away from the rest of the world; her family had focused on her care during those rough home hospice months before she eventually passed on.

"Why the big frown?" Kelvin asked, pulling to a smooth stop in front of the apartment.

"Nothing." I wasn't about to go down memory lane with him. Even though years had passed since then, he could still plunge into intense bouts of grief. "Just worried about my new baking venture. I really want to live up to the family name."

"I believe in you, Lissa," he said. "Besides, you haven't burned down the bakery yet. That's a big step."

"You gotta bring that up? It was only ever the once." I let out a dramatic sigh. I'd been multitasking in the kitchen when I learned that parchment paper, to my complete astonishment, could actually catch on fire.

I left Kelvin snickering in the car and entered our apartment. Mom and I shared the space, but I didn't mind the cozy quarters. It was a one-bedroom, and while Mom got the actual room, I had my own partitioned-off section in the living room. A heavy curtain did a great job of giving me privacy and muffling outside noises.

Mom was stationed at the kitchen and peeling a mandarin orange, a common sight in our family. She'd packed one in my lunch box every school day for years. Oranges were considered lucky, particularly during the Lunar New Year, but Mom liked to give them to me all year round to bring me good fortune.

She turned her head toward me. "There you are. Where'd you go with Kelvin?"

"To a fortune cookie factory."

She finished with the orange and handed half of it to me. "Why?"

"For inspiration." Baking tips, I hoped she assumed, and not, say, insight about a murder.

Mom made a face at me, and it wasn't because of the fruit. I'd popped an orange section in my mouth, and its sweet citrus juice ran down my throat.

"Factory schmactory," she said. "We Jins believe in small batches of handmade baked goods."

"Yes, I know." I'd heard this lecture many times over in my youth. "Every item baked with delicious magic."

"That's right. Remember, there's no magic without love, care, and joy in the baking process." She gave a slight head shake. "And that can't be done when you try to mass-produce something."

"Except that's how you get to be Fortune Cookie King," I said. A cheesy title, sure, but I wondered what it would be like to have customers streaming into Gold Bakery, and not just the locals and regulars. Mom didn't talk about expenses much, but I figured there was a solid reason we'd never moved to a bigger apartment and why we clipped coupons and scrimped on things.

Mom ate the final pieces of her orange with a faraway look on her face. "Why does that nickname sound familiar?" She glanced around the apartment before her gaze landed on our small dining table. "Aha. It was mentioned in the paper."

The household budget did include a requisite subscription to the *Pixie Courier,* the local newspaper. Mom preferred the actual newsprint and pages over the online version. I think it had something to do with family lore; it was said that my grandmother chose her English name based on an article from a newspaper.

I went over to the dining table to peruse the *Courier.* While I chewed the remainder of the orange, I spotted the article my mom had mentioned. Though it focused mostly on the disturbing circumstances of his death, I gleaned several facts about the Fortune Cookie King.

His real name was Charlie Gong, and he'd cornered the market on the fortune cookie business in Fresno over the past decade. His name had been tied to quite a few restaurants, but they'd all gone belly up for a variety of reasons.

I choked a little when I encountered a surprising quote from an anonymous source. They'd indicated that Smiley Fortunes' finances were in rough shape and that Gong had recently experienced a falling out with the owner of Foo Fusion, even though they'd had a one-year contract.

Michael's reluctance in giving Kelvin and me fortune cookies came to my mind. Had he known something sinister about the treats?

CHAPTER 6

My alarm blared, and I grumbled at the clock. I felt like a walking zombie getting up so early for the bakery. Even the sun had continued to sleep.

"Do we really have to go before sunrise?" I asked my mom.

"No complaining," Mom said. "It messes with your magical energy."

Unfortunately, so did caffeine, according to my mom. I made do with a cup of ice-cold water to wake me up before I stumbled out the door.

As we strolled down the sidewalk together, Mom said, "Another word of advice? I find that the sooner I feel happier in the morning, the easier it is to harness that joy for my baking."

I stuffed down another complaint. It was no wonder that Mom had detected only a hint of happiness in my fortune cookie the other day. I didn't consider myself a morning person.

The early pre-sunrise hours passed in a blur of yawning and tired baking, but I was proud that I'd managed to make several trays of fortune cookies before we opened the doors. In fact, I was in the kitchen slipping another tray into the cooling rack on our wheeled cart when the first customer arrived.

Mom and he were chatting in the front about our fortune cookies. The guy even mentioned someone telling him about luckily finding money on the ground right after eating my treat—must've been that Bulldogs fan from the other day.

The customer mentioned something about a business proposition to my mom. Now that I thought about it, his voice sounded vaguely familiar.

She replied, "You'll have to speak with my daughter, Felicity, about that. She's the one in charge of the fortune cookies."

I figured it was time to stock our glass display case with a dozen cookies anyway. As I walked to the front of the store, I almost slipped on the floor. I recognized the newest customer with a single glance at his balding head. Michael Fu.

His eyes narrowed in recognition, and his calculating gaze took in the cookies I was carrying. He nodded at them. "Are they edible?"

What kind of question was that? "Of course they are."

"The cookies are delicious," Mom said, snatching one up and offering it to Michael. "Go ahead and taste one. It's on the house."

He nibbled at the end of the cookie, and a flicker of a smile emerged. "Yes, very nice. This will do."

Mom turned my way, maternal pride shining in her eyes.

"And where are the fortunes?" Michael asked, peering at the cookie in his hand.

Ack, I'd forgotten about them again. "That's a sample batch," I said, "to, um, get the flavoring figured out."

I wondered if I could sneak some messages into the gaps before other customers arrived.

I grabbed at some paper behind the register and furtively scribbled. "One fortune coming up."

Michael took the slip of paper I offered him.

I'd written "You will enter into a lucrative business deal."

He gave a longer, luxurious smile this time around, full of greed. "Just the kind of fortune that speaks to my heart."

I bet.

"How fast can you make the cookies?" he asked.

"Depends on how many you need," I said.

"Let's do an initial run. Three hundred pieces," he said, "by tomorrow morning."

I gulped, and my mom inserted herself into the conversation. "We don't rush our baking," she said. "Every treat needs to be made with care and joy."

Michael shrugged. "Tomorrow by ten," he said. "Unless you can't handle it."

I stood up straighter. Did he think I couldn't do it? I'd finally crafted my own signature magical treat after years—no, over two decades—of struggling. There was no baking obstacle that I couldn't tackle. "Don't worry, I'll bring them by tomorrow."

After he left, I turned to my mom, who stared at me with widened eyes. "Three hundred fortune cookies by tomorrow, Felicity? Are you sure you'll be able to make them with love?"

Doubt crept in, and I wrung my hands. "What have I done? Should I back out?" I'd never made that high of a quantity before. Moreover, I wondered if I was selling out by baking in bulk.

I'd always stuck with my mom's advice in the past.

She'd never led me astray, always taking the time to give counsel, though she must've been tired raising me by herself. My dad had left not long after I'd been born. She'd never complained about it—much. In fact, she tried to ignore the topic of him whenever possible.

Mom's lips tightened now. "Maybe you should go and talk to Alma about it."

I wasn't sure if she was dismissing me out of frustration or truly thought my godmother had better insight into running a lucrative business. I didn't want to upset my mom, but a standing order with Foo Fusion would work its own kind of magic on our bottom line.

My mom waved me out the door.

Entering Paz Illuminations was like being transported to a new universe. The drawn curtains and the dim atmosphere made me feel adrift, like I'd gone outside of normal reality into a mystical realm.

I blinked to adjust my eyes to the gloom, and by the time I got reoriented, my godmother had already appeared by my side.

"Felicity," she said, "everything all right?"

"Yes, no. Oh, I don't know." I explained the business proposition with Foo Fusion. "Do you think I'm tarnishing the Jin name somehow? Shouldn't I be content with the traditional way of doing things, turning out small, handcrafted batches in our family bakery?"

Alma tilted my chin up with her finger to gaze into my eyes. "You've always wanted more, child."

"What do you mean?"

She answered me by asking a question of her own. "Why did you keep trying different recipes while you were growing up?"

I thought about my past baking attempts. I'd aimed for magical cupcakes, pies, even croissants one year. As I went over the list in my head, I realized that they weren't random recipes I'd attempted. I'd been influenced by the culture around me, and the food all had something in common—my avoidance of inserting any hint of Asian flavor into them. Of course things had finally clicked when I'd tried fortune cookies, even if they were possibly Japanese in origin.

As though Alma had read my mind, she said, "Don't be afraid to be yourself."

If only I knew what that meant. Why wasn't giving happiness to one customer at a time enough for me? I mean, my mom certainly was content in her cozy corner of Pixie. She'd never once thought of expanding and bringing more attention to the shop or herself.

My head began to throb, and I swiped at my forehead.

"Your thinking is sieved," Alma said. Or maybe she'd said, "Your thinking is grieved." She'd be right in both cases. Troubled thoughts were tumbling through my mind and escaping.

I started asking for more clarification from her when Alma sprang forward and rubbed the top of my head. She said, "Sana, sana, colita de rana."

When I was small, that's how she'd fix my boo-boos. I once asked her what the chant was about, and she mentioned something about frog tails. I didn't ask for more details after that. Too bad my current distorted thinking wasn't like a scraped knee from my childhood and so readily fixed.

Alma's computer chimed with a notification, and she stepped back to check it. "Another Etsy order. How wonderful."

My godmother managed to balance old-school candle making with high-tech sales. I admired her for it. Maybe her example also made me want more for our family business.

Alma echoed my inner thoughts. "It's okay to want more, Felicity, or to be different than the rest of your family."

I didn't know about that. I'd only barely found my way into the Jin Legacy (yes, with a capital *L*). It'd be foolish of me to stray from the traditional path now.

"Wait right here." My godmother moseyed to the back of the shop and returned with a candle. "A new creation of mine," she said. "I call it Wishes. Light it tonight."

"But it'll be a full moon," I said. "I won't need a candle."

"I think you will," she said. "Promise me that you'll light it tonight."

I always found it easier to go along with my godmother, so I nodded and thanked her for the gift. When I exited her shop, the candle she'd given me seemed to glimmer and glow. I knew it was a trick of the light; the candle was a beautiful golden color with sparkles that caught the brilliant sun, but it still reminded me of fairy dust as I stared at it.

CHAPTER 7

Why on earth had I agreed to create three hundred fortune cookies for Michael Fu? It proved to be no small feat. Beyond the stifling heat of the kitchen and the clumsy dropping of ingredients, it took me longer than I'd anticipated just to produce the first fifty.

After that meager triumph, Gold Bakery welcomed a steady stream of customers who, unfortunately, all wanted to talk to me. Pixie is a small town, and word travels fast. The interruptions came from people wishing me good luck on my new business venture. Each arriving customer came with more extensive congratulations because the rumor grew more elaborate over time. First, people wanted to wish me well on landing a dream delivery to a famed local restaurant. Then, they cheered me on about adding stock to the shelves of various branches of a regional supermarket chain. Next, they wished me success on supplying an international warehouse and sending my fortune cookies overseas. I hated to squelch that last glamorous vision, but I told every customer who came in the truth; I was only doing an initial batch for a Fresno eatery. After I cleared up all the confusion, I holed myself up in the kitchen.

"I don't know, Mom," I said as she took a break to

check on my progress. “I’ve only made half of the order so far, and it’s already late afternoon.”

“Let’s do some quality control,” she said, biting into my latest creation with its generic fortune about good health. I’d written the same message for the last hundred cookies to save on time.

She shook her head in dismay but not because of the slip of paper. “Tastes wrong. The cookie’s too bland.” Her frustration peppered the air, making me want to sneeze.

“Are you saying that I should redo all of them?” I said.

“Only if you want to bring real happiness to your eaters.” And, clearly, keep up with the Jin tradition. My mom could be very passive-aggressive when she wanted to be.

“What will we do with the extras?” I said.

She glanced at the clock on the wall. “You might be baking for a while yet. The not-so-good ones will be great to snack on.”

I’d be lucky if the rest of my fortune cookies didn’t turn out bitter, given my increasing irritation. If only I had an automated machine like the one at the Smiley Fortunes factory. I swallowed a rising sigh and went to work.

Mom was right that it’d take us into the evening by the time I finished with my required order of three hundred cookies—at least to her level of quality assurance. She’d sampled the last treats and deemed them passable, but barely—with “only a sprinkle of happiness” in their flavoring. We trudged back home, my fingers feeling stiff after folding cookie after cookie.

At the apartment, I forced myself to eat a quick dinner of stir-fried veggies and noodles, but I didn’t taste anything. Mom and I even skipped our usual light-hearted banter; a few months ago, we’d even had a laughing game, where we'd tried to copy each other's laughs, which had left us in stitches. But tonight, my thoughts weighed me down and left me speechless.

What was happening to me? Was I losing my new-found talent already? How could I be putting forth even less happiness than when I had first started baking fortune cookies? My magical ability should be leveling up, not decreasing.

I finished eating and glanced out the window near our dining table. The full moon hung low in the sky, and I could see the outline of the beautiful goddess who lived there. Next to her, the Moon Rabbit was busy making an elixir of immortality. Many myths declared the bunny to be a companion of the moon goddess, a woman who had either selfishly taken the immortal potion for herself—or drank the elixir to keep it away from someone greedy.

I'd always been more partial to the Moon Rabbit legend, who also had a noble story. When a deity, disguised as a beggar, came to earth and asked for food from the animals, the rabbit quickly jumped into the fire. The sacrificial offer of itself led to the honored place in the moon. If only I'd had my own celestial companion to help me through life.

Seeing the night sky reminded me of Alma's candle. I'd promised my godmother to light it. What was the least amount of effort I could put in while still adhering to my promise? Maybe if I let it burn for only a few seconds, that would fulfill my pledge.

I pulled out the golden candle and balanced it on the windowsill. "Wishes," Alma had called her new creation. Striking a match, I lit the wick and watched it burn for a few moments.

The golden flame seemed to dance before me. I recalled my godmother's words, about it being okay to want more and to be different. A sense of extreme peace filled my soul. And then the flame flickered out.

What? I hadn't opened a window. Where had the draft come from?

My mom tutted. "This was Alma's advice to you? Lighting a candle to make things better?" They were close friends despite their age gap of a decade or more, but that didn't mean they understood each other's ways sometimes.

"I'm sure she meant well," I said.

"I don't doubt that but, really, a candle?"

I was about to defend my godmother some more when I heard a quick thumping from beyond our front door. It almost sounded like a bouncing ball out there.

"What's that?" my mom asked.

We went over to the front door and opened it. There on our stoop, a bunny hopped up and down. It was a gorgeous white rabbit with long pink ears and eyes like sweet chocolate chips. The bunny stopped moving when I focused my attention on it.

It twitched its whiskers at me and, without any warning, bounced itself into our apartment. As though already familiar with the layout, the rabbit went straight to an unoccupied corner of the kitchen. It settled there and paused, staring at my mom with expectation.

At first, Mom and I just looked at each other in shock. Then we burst out laughing—the entrance of this adorable and determined rabbit had broken the tension between us, at least for the moment.

After our laughter subsided, I said, "It must be someone's pet. It's so cute, and clearly very comfortable with humans."

The rabbit swiveled its head back and forth between us.

"Would you like something to eat?" Mom asked the bunny.

The rabbit responded by going on its hind legs, like a begging puppy.

"I take that as a yes." Mom foraged in the refrigerator and provided the bunny with fresh crisp lettuce.

While it nibbled on the greens, Mom inspected the rabbit. "No collar or tags of any kind."

"Why would the owner let their pet roam around at night?" I asked.

Mom shook her head. "How did you get here?" she asked in a soft voice while petting the bunny's back.

"It *is* strange," I said.

"Well, I'll make a few calls. Check if anybody's missing a rabbit." Pixie was small enough that anyone living here for long enough didn't need to open the phone directory.

Mom left the room, and I went back to the candle. Should I try lighting it again? How had it gone out so quickly?

I stared through the window at the dark sky as I mused. Something had shifted in the night scene. I easily found the goddess in the moon . . . but not the rabbit.

No. It couldn't be.

Glancing back at the bunny, I noticed it lying content in a sleeping position. Kind of like a fuzzy loaf of bread. The rabbit winked at me.

"Wait. Did you just—" I stepped closer to the rabbit and looked once more.

No, I must have been mistaken. It lay there, innocent and fast asleep.

CHAPTER 8

Mom had used her Pixie connections and called around last night, but nobody had reported a missing rabbit. So we officially got a new house bunny. I dubbed her Whiskers. She seemed quite docile and hadn't attempted to chew on a single cord or slipper in sight.

"Stay good," I said to Whiskers, stroking her silky ears. "We'll be back later today to check on you."

Whiskers bobbed her head as though she agreed with the plan.

I grabbed Mom's car keys from the hook near the entryway. I'd need to use her old, unreliable Corolla to make my delivery to Foo Fusion this morning. While Mom had already left to start the usual baking day, I'd be driving to Fresno and dropping off my batch of fortune cookies.

Thank goodness the car worked when I put the key in and I was able to get right on the road. I'd timed my arrival at the restaurant to an hour before their official opening. Surely Michael would be on the premises by then.

After parking next to a shiny black Lexus in the parking lot once I arrived, I tugged on the door to the restaurant. Still locked, but I figured I could go around the back to find the kitchen entrance.

I scuttled around the building and located the rear door, propped open at this hour. Someone was around. Two people, actually. I could hear their loud arguing even from outside.

A woman whined, saying, "You had a contract with Charlie, and we worked hard for you."

"'Hard' is the key word." I recognized Michael's voice. "Smiley Fortunes' products are killer on my customers. Did you know someone cracked their tooth on one of your cookies last week? I had to pay for their dental visit."

"Maybe the kid had a wiggly tooth."

"It was an adult," he said. "Besides, I did more research on your company. I know about the recent lawsuit. Does the name Moana Clark ring any bells?"

The other person huffed. "I'm the manager now, and I promise I'll make things better. In fact, I already have."

It must be Cayla Jung. She continued. "I bet you'll be back for the new versions of our fortune cookies in no time."

"Since I never had a formal written agreement with Smiley Fortunes," Michael said, "I can do whatever I want, and I've certainly made up my mind about your cookies." Michael asked Cayla to leave in a polite but firm manner.

A few moments later, I heard clomping footsteps coming toward me. I scrambled to hide and crouched behind a rusted Schwinn bike.

Sure enough, Cayla soon came into view. "If only I knew who he's using now . . ."

I held my breath and hoped I stayed hidden. She seemed angry, and I didn't want to bear the brunt of her wrath.

Avoiding confrontation was my specialty. I wanted

people to be happy around me; isn't that what Jins were born to do?

Cayla didn't appear to see me in my dubious hiding spot, so I relaxed. At least I wouldn't have to deal with her.

I waited for a full ten minutes before I returned to the front entrance. The door was now unlocked. I grabbed the fortune cookies from the car and marched right through the kitchen of Foo Fusion to present my baked goods.

Michael's expression changed from sour to sweet the moment he saw me. "You made it. And so early in the day, too."

I beamed at his compliment. I'd gotten a verbal gold star. "I worked hard on them. Practically baking all night."

"Time for a taste test then."

I offered him a cookie, but he shook his head.

"There's a better man for this job." He strolled over to the walk-in fridge and banged against the metal door.

To my surprise, a broad-shouldered man wearing a work apron stepped out of it. How long had he been inside? Though maybe he'd come to work through the front entrance while I'd been busy hiding from Cayla or carrying the fortune cookies from my car.

Michael pointed to the man. "This is Foo Fusion's award-winning chef, Grant Allard."

I tried to hide my disdain. He'd won awards for his food?

"I know you're busy," Michael said to Grant, "but give me your honest opinion of this fortune cookie."

I offered the cookie to Grant, and he chewed on it with deliberation. He even closed his eyes to focus on the flavor. When his eyes popped open, he wore a slight smile on his face. "I like it. There's pure vanilla extract in it, a touch of almond, and . . . something else I can't put my finger on."

Magic maybe? Not that I'd tell him our family's secret ingredient.

Instead I said, "You've got a superb sense of taste."

He patted his stomach. "Honed from years of crafting artisanal doughnuts. But I'm still working on my other offerings." Maybe that's why I hadn't liked Foo Fusion's entrees so far. I'd been a guinea pig for this chef's experimental cooking.

Michael clapped his hands, drawing the attention back to himself. "Excellent work, Miss Jin. I'll need regular shipments on a monthly, if not weekly, basis."

I remembered the private conversation with Cayla I'd overheard. Michael hadn't put together a formal contract for Smiley Fortunes. "Can I get the deal with Gold Bakery in writing?"

"Smart woman," he said. "Be back in a few."

After Michael left, Grant returned to the fridge. He pulled out several soggy cardboard boxes of produce. Their outsides were stained with weird marks, and a slight stench permeated the air. "How am I supposed to work without fresh ingredients?" he grumbled, half to himself.

I decided to add my thoughts. "Where'd you get those?"

"They're imported. Flown in from overseas."

I clucked my tongue. "If you're looking for quality ingredients, you should try local sources. Central California grows a lot of its own fruit and veggies."

"Good idea," he said. "If Mikey will agree to it."

I gave Grant info on the farmers markets close by as Michael stepped back inside the kitchen.

"What's all this chattering?" the owner asked.

"Your fortune cooking gal is sharing tips about great local produce," Grant said.

"You stick to your specialty, fortune cookies," Michael said, handing me our new contract. "I'll run the restaurant my way."

I read it over while Michael and Grant held a whispered conversation about produce suppliers. Everything on the document looked accurate and complete, including his signature. "Thanks," I told the restaurant owner.

"Keep it for your records," Michael said and handed me a check. Maybe I should raise the prices for my cookies.

Nevertheless, I pocketed the papers and did a happy strut out the door. On the way back to Pixie, I stopped at a pet store and splurged on supplies for Whiskers. I still wasn't sure if she really was the Moon Rabbit or if some other family would eventually reclaim her, but at least while she was staying with us, we'd make sure to spoil her.

When I arrived at Gold Bakery, there was a long line of customers at the counter. Mom grinned at each person as she served them. Strangely, one ponytailed woman stood off to the side. As I got closer and noticed her taupe suit—she must have a thing for variations of brown—I had a sinking feeling.

"Detective Sun," I said. "Did you happen to feel like getting a pastry?"

She turned to me with her sharp gaze. "I hear congratulations are in order."

"We *are* buzzing with customers." I gestured to the cluster of people salivating over our baked goods.

The detective tilted her head. "The buzz seems to be about your fortune cookies. And your huge delivery to

Foo Fusion. Your mom told me about it. How'd the meeting go this morning?"

I shuffled my feet and tried to avoid answering.

Detective Sun pointed to the check sticking out of my back pocket. "Must have gone well."

A wave of shame hit me. Was she insinuating that I was money hungry? "My cookies are baked with quality and care."

The detective nodded. "Of course they are. But sometimes you need to push things to the next level."

"What do you mean?" I said the words slowly.

"It's funny how Charlie Gong, your competitor, died recently. And now you're networking and making deals with his old contacts."

I held my hands up. "You've got it all wrong, Detective. Michael Fu came to me, not the other way around. And he never had a written contract with Smiley Fortunes, even before I came on the scene." All's fair in business, right?

"How'd you get that insider info?"

I faltered for an answer. It probably didn't look good that I'd known the intimate details of Charlie's deal with Foo Fusion, and admitting to eavesdropping wouldn't help my cause. I crossed my fingers behind my back. "Oh, you know how it is with small towns. Pixie gossip gets around."

"Both the fortune cookie factory and the restaurant are in Fresno City limits."

Fine. I'd have to clear my name another way. I motioned to the detective to follow me and led her to a quiet corner of the bakery. The line had dwindled at the register, but I didn't want any local residents to overhear the detective's potential accusations.

I looked her in the eyes. "Everything has been pure

coincidence, Detective Sun. Michael Fu coming to me. My fortune cookie message found you-know-where."

"Your very specific message, I'll remind you. And I don't believe in coincidences, I believe in evidence."

"I didn't even know what I wrote," I said, trying for complete honesty.

She raised her eyebrow. "It was your handwriting, your thoughts, so I don't buy that. Maybe you just figured he'd throw away the written trail incriminating you. Who keeps their fortune cookie messages anyway?"

The thought of fortune cookie collecting niggled at me, but I had a more important question to ask the detective first. "Are you investigating other people?" Didn't I deserve a fair justice process?

She shrugged. "Yes, but the vic didn't have much interaction with people beyond his fortune cookie making circle. Not too many prime leads."

Except me. Not that the detective said that. She only left the bakery with a flippant "I'll see you around" dismissal. By that, I hoped she didn't mean seeing me in the county jail.

CHAPTER 9

What Detective Sun had said about not believing in coincidences struck a resounding chord with me. I stood in the corner of the bakery, staring out the glass door at her receding figure. The fortune I'd jotted down for Charlie had been too specific. As had the one I'd customized for the Bulldogs fan, the fortune cookie message collector I'd remembered about after chatting with Detective Sun. And both my predictions had come true.

It'd only been two people, but didn't more than one mean a pattern? I furrowed my brow as I concentrated on my memories of writing those messages. I'd experienced a buzzing noise and dizzying rainbow colors swimming across my vision both times. In each case, I couldn't remember what I'd written down, but the fortunes had turned out to be prophetic.

My mom shuffled up beside me, placing a hand on my shoulder. "Are you okay, Felicity?"

I glanced around the bakery. All the customers had been helped, and the place was empty. No better time than the present to have this conversation.

"Mom," I said. "Is baking happiness our only magical skill?"

She squeezed my shoulder. "Well, we also give out joy, peace . . . any pleasant emotion, really."

"We don't have any other gifts?"

She looked confused and backed up a step. "Like what?"

"Maybe prediction." I chewed on my bottom lip.

"Of course not, don't be sil—" Mom's eyes seemed to cloud for a moment.

"What is it?"

"Could it be?" she whispered to herself. "Can you explain to me where this is coming from, Felicity?"

I told her about the two customers and their unerringly accurate fortunes.

"We can do a test," she said. "Make a fortune for me."

"Okay." I hurried into the kitchen and did some speed baking. By the time the oven dinged, I was ready with pen and paper for a prophecy. Nothing came to me.

I handed the fresh cookie to my mom. Maybe she needed to take physical hold of it for the magic to work. Still nothing happened.

Distracting thoughts and emotions floated around in my head. Fear about getting hauled off by Detective Sun for a crime I didn't commit. Anxiety about this deal I'd signed with Michael Fu. Confusion about this maybe gift I had involving fortune-telling.

Finally, I sighed. "Guess it doesn't work all the time. Maybe the message writing comes and goes. Or perhaps it really was random. Coincidental."

My mom tapped her index finger against her chin. "Another alternative is that I could be immune to you. Magic blocks magic sometimes."

"Oh," I said. "Like how you can taste happiness in my baking? But you're not actually swayed by the emotion?"

"Uh-huh. We can't influence family. Or at least my mother wasn't able to bake my troubled feelings away."

"How will I find out if I have extra magic then?"

"You need to test your skill on someone else," she said.

Well, what are best friends for? I decided to bring a fortune cookie over to Love Blooms to see what would happen.

Kelvin didn't look alarmed when I rushed into his store waving a fortune cookie in the air. "Eat this," I said, shoving it into his face.

"All right, I will." I could've brought him a poisoned apple, and he wouldn't have flinched.

Kelvin put a finished floral arrangement to the side and reached for the cookie.

I reared back. "No, wait. Pretend you're a customer and order the cookie from me."

"Sure thing." He deepened his voice. "I'd like to get one of your supercalifragilisticexpialidocious fortune cookies, please."

Usually, his hamming it up would make me giggle, but this was serious business. I wanted the fortune-telling to work. After dropping the cookie into his hand, I waited for the dizziness to hit me. Maybe I should help the process? I started swaying on my feet.

Kelvin eyed me with concern.

I uncapped my pen. No words came to me. I motioned for him to start eating the fortune cookie.

Kelvin obliged. Throughout his crunching, I still didn't get a message. Instead, I got distracted by the many childhood memories I had of us goofing around together.

"It's gone," I said. "My talent has disappeared."

"I disagree. This is one good cookie," he said. "And I'm pretty content right now."

"Not *that* talent."

"How many do you have?" he asked, his voice semi-muffled with chewing.

"Apparently I make fortune-coming-true cookies as well."

He swallowed. "I don't think that's a real dictionary word. And the wrong description for your family's talent. Aren't the Jins all about baking joy into every bite?"

I jabbed my chest with my thumb. "Not this Jin. I've got a second gift. I'm even more special."

His mouth dropped open. Thankfully, no cookie crumbs in sight.

"Let me explain," I said. "Charlie Gong wasn't the only person to fulfill one of my fortunes."

"He wasn't?"

I'd forgotten that Kelvin hadn't been around when the Bulldogs fan had tripped. Only my godmother had rushed out of her shop that day. I proceeded to tell him about the guy who had literally stumbled onto money, after reading my fortune about doing just that.

"Interesting," Kelvin said. "Amazing, actually."

"And my mom didn't deny it could be true." She'd acted cagey but had wanted to test out my double-magic theory.

Kelvin rubbed his chin. "Maybe you just need to replicate it somehow. Like you do with a recipe."

"That's why I'm here. I thought it'd work if I used you as a guinea pig."

"I'm honored, I think?" he said with a comical waggle of his eyebrows. "Am I the first person you asked?"

"No, I started with my mom. Nothing happened then, either."

"Maybe your magic only works with a stranger. A real one. Not someone you've known pre-preschool."

"I can't go up to a random person and hawk a fortune cookie on them."

"Free food? Who could refuse?" He genuinely looked stunned.

"A lot of people, freeloader."

He snapped his fingers. "I know some fortune cookie aficionados."

"You do?"

"Our friends at the Smiley Fortunes factory."

I grimaced. "You think they want to try eating their competitor's cookies?"

"The workers didn't seem too happy at their current job. And your mom told me you got a deal with Foo Fusion, so maybe you'll need extra help soon."

He sure dreamt big. "But how did you know about—never mind, everyone does. It's Pixie. Even Detective Sun confronted me about it."

"The detective visited you again?"

"Yes, and she let me know that I'm her number one suspect. Not only did Charlie have my fortune cookie message on him, but I'm basically moving in on his operations, now that he's dead."

"When you put it that way, it does sound suss," Kelvin said.

"Are you on my side or not?"

"I'm Team Lissa, clearly," he said, acting offended. "We just need Detective Sun to join the cheering squad."

"How do you suggest doing that?"

"By finding more suspects to focus on." He pointed toward the bakery. "And bribing them with your fortune cookies. It's a two-for-one deal."

"Why's that?"

"Either you learn more about your mysterious fortune predictions or you learn more about the homicide. Either way, we're winners."

Kelvin had a point, but I didn't really want to run into Cayla so soon after Michael Fu and I had inked our deal. I shared my concern with Kelvin.

"No worries," he said. "You just need an excellent distraction. Me."

With that last word, he swiped a fancy orchid bouquet off a nearby table, packaged it in wrapping, and set out the door. I scrambled to follow after him.

CHAPTER 10

Kelvin drove us to the Smiley Fortunes factory. He checked his hair in the rearview mirror once we'd parked, but his curls looked fine.

"You don't need to impress Cayla for real," I said. "And isn't she kinda old for you anyway?"

"What, are you jealous?"

I flicked my fingers at him. "You wish."

"I'll go through the front to distract her and give a signal when she's out, and you try to sneak in the back."

"Yes, sir." I even gave him a salute for fun.

Kelvin left the bouquet of stunning orchids in the car, his excuse for her to leave the building and follow him outside. I wandered to the back, hoping for an open door.

I found a closed one. Locked or not? I tapped my pockets filled with wrapped fortune cookies for luck. It must have worked because when I twisted the knob, it turned in my hand. But I waited until I got the signal from Kelvin to enter. He soon emitted a short whistle, a passable rendition of a cardinal. During my childhood, we'd spent a lot of time in his backyard, unearthing worms and scouting for birds. Kelvin could imitate a lot of bird calls, even making his voice sound like it came from the sky or a nearby tree.

Trusting that Kelvin had distracted Cayla for the moment, I crept through the back door. Before I entered the factory proper, I noticed a punch card system attached to the wall. The time clock was digital, but a bunch of paper cards were lined up in a rack next to the machine.

I studied the data. The info spanned over the past two weeks—including the day of the murder. Since I was here already . . . I pulled out each card and examined the timestamps.

I'd placed the last paper record back when someone from behind me cleared their throat. I swiveled around in alarm. Had Cayla snuck up on me?

I muffled a sigh of relief. It was Dakota. The guy I'd talk to before, who'd been shaping cookies with his protected hands. In fact, he was wearing the same heavy-duty gloves I'd admired the last time around.

Dakota's lips quirked. "Back for another tour?"

I told him the cover story I'd rehearsed. "Okay, you got me. I'm scoping out the competition."

"You also own a fortune cookie factory?"

I stood up straighter. "What, I don't look like a businesswoman?" I knew I looked younger than my age. New customers sometimes even mistook me for a teen.

His eyes shifted to the punch cards. "So why were you checking those out?"

"Calculating the hours they require you to work here." I congratulated myself. I'd come up with a clever excuse pretty fast.

He shrugged. "Yeah, they're pretty long, but I don't mind it for the short haul. I'm saving up to move out of Fresno, maybe head over to Bakersfield."

"What about the other employees? Do they like working here? One of them didn't punch in at all last week."

Could the same someone who hated working at Smiley Fortunes have killed the boss?

"Oh, that must have been Logan." The man rubbed his gloved hands together. "On account of his injury."

I recalled the name from the card: Logan Miller. If the guy had gotten hurt on the job, maybe he'd been riled enough to kill Charlie Gong. "Did your friend get workers' comp or anything?"

"What's it to you?" Dakota narrowed his eyes at me. "Are you really involved in the fortune cookie business?"

"I am," I said, pulling out a fortune cookie from my pocket to show him my earnestness. "Would you like one?"

"Yeah, actually. I didn't bring a snack with me." He grabbed the fortune cookie with his gloved hand and cracked it open.

I willed the magic to work. A prediction could be helpful right about now, but nothing happened.

"This is good," he said. "It's made in a factory?"

I looked down at the cold, impersonal concrete floor beneath me. "No, it was handcrafted in a bakery."

"No wonder you need more workers. A fortune cookie this good must take a lot of time to craft."

"What about your friend? Do you think he'd be interested in a new job? I'd be up for a chat." Maybe I could also weasel some intel out of Logan. He'd been the only one who hadn't punched in that day. Could he have gone to confront the Fortune Cookie King instead?

"Logan might be exploring job options, and he should've healed by now. Let me text him." After peeling off his gloves, Dakota typed on his phone. "Done. Can you meet him tomorrow at nine in the morning?"

I nodded. Mom gave me every Saturday off for my

"social life." Usually I spent it sleeping in and loafing around.

He texted some more and then flashed me his phone screen. "Here are the deets." I memorized the info.

"I'm giving you fair warning," he added. "Logan's kind of a talker."

Perfect. Even if he turned out to be innocent, Logan could give me the lowdown on Charlie Gong and any enemies he might have had.

I started to offer my thanks to Dakota when I heard yelling coming from the front of the factory.

Cayla's voice echoed in the air. "Hey, I'm not paying people to take breaks. Where's—"

"Coming!" Dakota scurried around the corner to appease his boss.

I took advantage of the commotion to hurry out the back door and meet up with Kelvin. "What happened with Cayla?" I asked. "She just stormed into the warehouse."

"Sorry." He pushed the toe of one of his Docs against the ground. "She ran in before I could do the whistle thing and warn you."

"You're forgiven—as long as you give me the scoop." I speed-walked back to his car, where I noticed the bouquet of flowers still lying on the passenger's seat. "Huh?"

"The good news," he said, pointing to the orchids, "is that I can reuse those. The bad news is that she basically rejected me."

"Whoa, she's no Princess Charming herself."

Kelvin crossed his arms over his chest. "I'm not sure if you insulted me just then or not. It wasn't that she's not into me. She ended a bad relationship recently."

"At least it saves you from needing to ghost her later on."

"I don't know." He glanced toward the factory's front door. "Maybe it would've lasted. She's kinda cute."

"Please." I waved away his comment. "Anyway, wait 'til you hear what I found out."

"Okay, I'll bite."

I leaned against the frame of the car. "I saw the station where they clock in for work. Not all the employees were in the factory the day Charlie died."

"So who wasn't working that day?" Kelvin asked.

"Logan's was the only one that didn't have a timestamp on it."

"Who's Logan?"

"The guy who burned his hand while making fortune cookies at the factory."

"A truly hot lead," Kelvin said, with a wiggle of his eyebrows.

I groaned at his dad joke but told him about the details for meeting up tomorrow morning at Fresno's iconic water tower.

"I'm coming with," he said.

"We're meeting in a public place. I'll be fine," I said.

"Still . . ."

"Aww, it's cute how you're so protective."

He rolled his eyes and then asked, "And what about your fortune-telling superpower? Did you make any progress on that front?"

I yanked open the door to his car. "Absolutely nothing happened even though I tried really hard."

Kelvin didn't reprimand me as I shoved the orchids to the side and sat down. For the rest of the car ride, I fumed while my best friend left me alone, knowing not to pry for the moment.

CHAPTER 11

Still bitter about my dwindling magical powers, I huffed around the apartment, even as I set out the bunny supplies. I'd gotten stacks of Timothy hay for Whiskers and even a litter box. Who knew rabbits could be so well-trained? Plus, Whiskers hadn't destroyed a single item in the time I'd been gone.

"You're a great bunny," I said as I created a cozy corner for my new pet.

Whiskers perked up her ears at my compliment.

"Oh, ready to listen, are you?" I said. "Do you mind if I talk some more? I've had a tough day."

The bunny hopped closer to me.

"You know, it really calms me down to chat with you."

She tilted her head at me for a moment, a sweet expression on her face.

I crouched to meet her gaze straight on. "It's like you can actually understand what I'm saying."

Whiskers stared at me.

"So I was trying to figure out my latest magical power today. The one that helps me predict futures." I listed and counted the people off on my hand. "My mom was the first volunteer, but my skill didn't work on her, probably because she's too magical."

I could have sworn the bunny gave an earnest nod.

"Then I asked Kelvin, my best friend, to help me. He's not magical at all. But maybe too close to me? I couldn't concentrate on making a prediction."

Whiskers offered me another serious nod.

"But then I tested out my fortune-telling with a real stranger, a factory worker, and nothing happened." I tugged at the ends of my hair. "Why not?"

Reflecting on the two customers I'd served when my talent *had* shown up, I wondered what the difference had been. "Could it have been because they paid me for the cookies?"

Whiskers shook her head, hard. I was stunned.

"Gosh, it's almost like you know what's truly happening with me." I couldn't be sure I wasn't just letting my imagination run away with me. Then again, I already knew some kinds of magic were real.

I glanced out the window. Mom wasn't home yet, and the moon wasn't in the sky, but I thought about the rabbit myth. "Do you *actually* know the answer?"

Whiskers did an acrobatic twist in the air.

"Is that a yes? Then what really triggered my fortune-telling?"

The bunny dashed toward me and nudged my open palm. Immediately, I felt a tingle. The memories of the two customers flashed back at me. With the Bulldogs fan, he'd slapped his money into my palm. The Fortune Cookie King had scraped my wrist with his sharp fingers. Both had somehow touched me before I'd written my fortunes.

Skin-to-skin contact. I think that was the difference. Dakota from the factory had been wearing gloves, after all.

Whiskers backed away from me, and the memories

dissolved. I blinked at her. She'd given me a vision. Wait—*she'd given me a vision?* No, I must have played back the memories on my own. "Or did you—"

She hopped back to her corner and twitched her whiskers.

The tingling. Had I imagined it? And accessed the memories on my own? I turned away from the bunny. But then I pivoted back. "Do you have magic, too?"

Whiskers started grooming herself, contentedly.

The next morning, I caught my mom before she left for work to tell her the news about our bunny.

"She's magical," I said. "I got a vision from Whiskers last night." It sounded so weird saying it out loud.

Mom didn't seem fazed. Maybe when you grew up magical, nothing charmed seemed bizarre. I mean, it hadn't taken me too long to accept that I was having an actual conversation with Whiskers yesterday evening either.

"Makes sense," Mom said. "I was wondering, when the candle blew out, what would happen." She fed the rabbit a banana chunk as a treat. "Welcome to the Jin family. You'll fit right into our magical world."

Whiskers circled Mom's feet in apparent happiness.

My mom turned to me, pecking me on the cheek. "Now, enjoy your day off."

"Thanks." I hadn't told her I'd be off investigating this morning. Not that she'd asked. Even though I still technically lived with my mom, she gave me the freedom to adult in my own way.

I'd have to share about the bunny (in a more limited way) with Kelvin. Despite being my best friend, even *he* might feel stretched thinking about a bunny with powers.

When he showed up at my door, I introduced Whiskers to him. Kelvin seemed taken aback that I hadn't told him about our new furry addition earlier, but he forgave me as soon as he got to cuddle Whiskers. They seemed to take to each other well.

"Is your bunny purring at me?" Kelvin asked.

Whiskers did seem content in Kelvin's nap. "Meh. She's just soft grinding her teeth."

"I don't think so." He spoke in a confident tone. "Whiskers is apparently a great judge of character."

"Too bad we can't take her to meet Logan. Give an honest bunny assessment."

"Yeah." Kelvin set Whiskers down on the floor with care. "Speaking of which, it's time to get going. I need to scout out a good place where I can eavesdrop."

We got to the Old Fresno Water Tower well before the appointed hour. Kelvin lay half-hidden in the shade of a nearby tree, lounging on a striped picnic blanket.

I stood in front of the tall building and looked up . . . and up. The structure was quite impressive, at over a hundred feet tall, even though it no longer held any water. I especially loved the iconic red domed roof.

"What's really amazing is that it's been around since 1894," a voice said from behind me.

I turned to take in the huge figure who'd approached. The man had broad shoulders and a strong build that reminded me of California's official state animal, the grizzly bear. "Are you Logan?"

"Yes, pleased to meet you." He held his right hand out to me, a business card at the ready in his fingers; his left hand was sheathed in a wrist splint.

I pocketed the card and shook his unharmed hand. "How's the burn?"

"Too bad it's my dominant hand, but almost done healing. I'm still on medical leave, actually."

"You thinking about going back after?"

He shook his buzz-cut head. "No way. That place is always trying to cut corners. It's not worth it, having a boss like that."

Dakota had mentioned that Logan was a natural talker. "Honestly, I don't know much about the Fortune Cookie King. What was it like to work for him?"

Logan snorted. "'Fortune Cookie King.' Charlie made up that nickname for himself, to sound better than others."

I motioned down the street, where the futuristic-looking City Hall, made of glass and metal, stood. "I thought it was well-deserved since he'd cornered the Fresno market."

"Hardly. He had some business contacts in the beginning, but they dwindled away. Then after the lawsuit, all he had left was the account with Foo Fusion."

I tried to tamp down the enthusiasm in my voice. "You know, I heard about the lawsuit. With Moana Clark, was it?"

"A bout of food poisoning. Guess she wasn't expecting that to happen on her hen night in the Tower District."

The sickness. Had it been a one-off? Or was there something really wrong with Smiley's cookies? Could fortune cookies even give people food poisoning? "I hear the factory is under new management. Cayla Jung. Maybe it's better now?"

"Cayla has always wanted to make changes, so kudos to her. But I still wouldn't want to go back." He gave me a wide grin. "Besides, don't I have a new job prospect with you?"

I hedged. "Possibly. Maybe you should try a fortune cookie of mine before you agree to applying."

"I'd love to get hired somewhere. I do have a top choice, but I'll need any job soon. And yes to the cookie—it's got to be better than what Charlie sold."

When I offered him the treat, I made sure to place the fortune cookie in the palm of his uninjured hand. I angled my fingers so that my pinkie made physical contact.

At once, I felt the dizziness swoop in. White noise rumbled around me, and rainbow lines covered my vision. I reached for the pen and slip of paper in my pocket and scribbled his fortune down.

Logan placed a steadying hand on my back. "Are you feeling okay? We could go inside the tower's gift shop, but I'm not sure they're open quite yet."

I took a deep breath in and out, keeping my grip on the paper. "I'm fine. Just give me a moment."

"It does get hot in Fresno," he said before popping the fortune cookie in his mouth. "Mm, this is delicious."

I smiled. It still floored me that people would enjoy eating something I had baked.

"And what's that you're holding?" he asked.

I glanced down at the paper in my hand and fumbled for an explanation. "Your fortune. Sometimes I like to make personalized messages for special customers." What had I predicted this time? I hoped it wasn't death.

CHAPTER 12

Luckily, I'd foreseen happy news for Logan. He grabbed at the fortune cookie message, read it, gave a whoop of joy, and punched his splinted hand in the air.

My fortune had read "You will receive a generous job offer from your most ideal company." It felt wonderful to give out good news. Wasn't this another way of bringing joy, beyond the baking? In the moment, it made me feel even more of a Jin, and I smiled.

Logan seemed in a better mood and whistled as he walked away. Before he'd even taken ten steps, his phone rang.

He answered it with anticipation. After a moment of listening, he said, "Thanks for getting back to me about my application."

Meanwhile, I noticed subtle movement from the corner of my eye. Kelvin stretched his long arms above his head, folded his blanket, and came over.

"You got a lot of info out of loquacious Logan," he said.

"And here I thought you'd stopped studying for the SATs a long time ago."

He pointed at his head. "What can I say? My brain retains a lot of facts."

"Showoff." I lowered my voice. "But I wonder . . . can your brain make magic?"

"You did it, then?" Kelvin whispered. "Predicted his fortune?"

"Maybe. Or it could just be well wishes on paper affecting his overall mood." I bit my bottom lip. "Let's wait a few minutes for confirmation."

Logan had already walked farther on for privacy, but even from here, I could tell it was a positive call. The man was doing an excited dance while speaking.

"I think he landed his ideal job," I said, "and my prediction let him know early."

"Wow, so how does your new power work?" Kelvin asked.

I explained about needing to physically make contact with the predictee for the magic to happen. (I did not let Kelvin know I discovered that particular requirement through my magic bunny.)

"Cool. Only I wish it didn't make you feel dizzy. I saw you sway a little back there . . ." Kelvin gritted his teeth. "Logan had to steady you."

I waved away his concern (and maybe a touch of jealousy?). "I'm sure I'll learn to control my talent better soon enough. I mean, you don't see my mom fainting in the kitchen or anything."

"She has a different type of magical skill," he said.

I put some force into my next words. "I can handle it."

"Okay, don't get hissy at me. I believe you," he said and (smartly) decided to switch topics. "So what do you think about suspect number one now that you've talked to him?"

I shook my head. "Logan didn't log in to work that day, but he's been out on medical leave. I figure he's too injured to be our guy."

"Maybe, but I still don't trust him."

"Aww, don't feel threatened, Kelvin." I reached up to pat him on the shoulder.

He stiffened. "I'm not. But if he's off your suspects list, then we're at a dead end."

"Except for that lawsuit he mentioned. It's come up several times already."

"The one about Moana Clark."

I nodded. "Aren't lawsuits supposed to be public record? And we know it happened here in Fresno. Logan even mentioned the Tower District."

The Tower District was a fun neighborhood in Fresno that came alive in the evenings. It offered concert venues, a theatre, and unique shops, all in one walkable stretch.

While I'd been thinking, Kelvin had been searching on his phone. "Got it," he said. "The local news has an article about a lawsuit from Fresno native Moana Clark. She sued everyone associated with her possible food poisoning."

"Wow, that's extreme."

"Yeah." Kelvin checked the article. "She's quoted as saying that the sickness '*ruined* my bachelorette party and all my wedding plans!'"

Maybe Moana had lashed out in a rash, angry reaction. "Who's she suing?" I asked.

"Charlie Gong, the fortune cookie factory, even the establishment where she started feeling sick."

"Where was that again?"

"An artsy place in the Tower District known as Sip and Sketch." His fingers moved over his phone. "It's actually open right now."

"And close to here, I hope?"

"Yep."

"Then I guess we know where we're headed next!" I

said brightly. My successful—and happy—fortune-telling had me feeling unstoppable.

It took us less than ten minutes to arrive in the Tower District. I even got to admire the striking Art Deco–styled Tower Theatre as we passed by it. At night, it glowed with vivid neon colors, the attached tall spire with starry orb, a brilliant gem in the dark. Even though it was a historic landmark, concerts and films were still being played there. Mom and I had gone a few times.

The place we ended up at was more modern, with an open-space layout and large glass windows. Sip and Sketch was extremely organized in terms of supplies, with a special spot for every art tool. Paint brushes, pastels, canvases were all tidied up on their own labeled shelf or inside a clear, marked cabinet.

The art studio had high tables with tall stools scattered around the large area. They were all empty of patrons, but the smell of freshly brewed coffee permeated the air. I swear I heard Kelvin's stomach rumble from beside me.

A woman with blond hair tied in a high ponytail came out from a side room to greet us. She had on a paint-splattered smock. "Hello," she said. "I'm Adora. Are you here for Coffee and Creativity time?"

Kelvin nodded. She'd had him at "coffee."

"We have a special deal going on. Two for the price of one."

"Yes," Kelvin said, rubbing his hands together. "Now about that coffee . . ."

I shook my head. "Wait a moment. I want to check out the studio, but I'm a little concerned about that lawsuit I read on the news."

Adora turned a bright red. "That was a misunderstanding. Rest assured. We've been cleared of any charges."

"The lawsuit involved food poisoning, didn't it?" I

said, staring at a nearby cart holding a stack of clean white mugs.

"Nothing that we served," she said. "It was what they'd brought with them. I didn't even know fortune cookies could *give* you food poisoning."

Funny, I'd thought the exact same thing. Sickness from baked goods was much more common with raw dough. And they were so small in size. *Had Smiley's cookies been improperly baked?* Returning my attention to Adora, I asked, "You can bring in your own food?"

"Sure, we only serve drinks here, so BYO snacks are welcome. And people do get a bit hungry, especially in the evening." She glanced around the empty studio and explained, "Nights are our most popular hours."

Kelvin gave a pointed look at the coffee mugs. "Well, I trust you. We're staying, so bring on that coffee." He grabbed a seat at a high table facing a window.

"Sure thing," Adora said and turned to me. "Coffee for you, too?"

"Decaf for me. With plenty of sugar and creamer."

I perched on a high stool next to Kelvin, and it didn't take long before our coffees arrived. We were given steaming mugs of rich roast, complete with a tray of sugar and creamer selections.

Now that we'd gotten on her good side with our patronage, I asked, "Just curious, but what did the tainted fortune cookies look like?"

"They were actually really pretty," Adora said. "Individual cookies coated in pastel colors of icing. Wonderful for a bachelorette party, only . . ."

"What?" I leaned toward her. "You can tell us."

"At first everything seemed fine, and the girls were scarfing them down. But when they slowed down a bit, I noticed them starting to make these weird faces. Moana had it the worst, though. She started choking on hers." Adora shuddered. "Her friend did the Heimlich, and the fortune cookie shot out of her mouth and hit the table with a loud *ping*."

What had gone into those unfortunate cookies? I couldn't imagine anyone having such a hard time swallowing my treats.

"Anyway," Adora continued, "I don't want to waste your paid art time by blathering on. What would you like to do here? Sketch, paint, sculpt?"

"Sketching, please," I said. Even though I only drew stick figures, at least I could make actual marks on paper. I wasn't so sure how I'd fare using a canvas or clay.

"Coming right up," she said.

Adora returned with our art supplies: various sizes of paper, pencils with different lead thicknesses, and even a few fine-tipped brush markers. "I'm giving you a reference image in case you want to sketch that, with a directions sheet and a QR code for the video tutorial. But you can also free draw," she said. "Enjoy your time, but don't forget, you pay by the hour."

Once she'd gone, I whispered to Kelvin that we'd better only stay for an hour. After all, we hadn't even asked her about the actual fee for indulging our creativity.

Kelvin and I took the hour to sip and sketch as promoted by the studio's name. Well, actually, I gulped my beverage down instead of savoring it so I could spend more time drawing. Not stick figures or the suggested image, though.

By the time the hour had finished, Kelvin had a wonderful sign for his floral shop advertising FLOWER SPECIAL OF THE DAY. I, however, had populated my paper with a chart of potential suspects. Because I knew someone close to Charlie Gong had wanted to murder him.

CHAPTER 13

Kelvin skimmed my list of suspects. I'd narrowed my choices to the Fortune Cookie King's close circle: Michael Fu, Cayla Jung, Logan Miller, and Moana Clark.

My best friend tapped his square-cut fingernail on Moana's name. "If only we could talk to her directly instead of relying on secondhand information about the lawsuit."

I agreed, but what could we do about it? Adora bustled over to us.

"Is everything okay?" she asked. "You both look . . . unhappy."

I covered my "drawing" with my arms.

"Things are great," Kelvin said, his voice growing louder, probably to direct attention to him and away from suspicious me. "We were just sad about Moana Clark. It seems unfair that this happened to her right before her wedding."

Adora clucked her tongue. "Moana actually had to delay the event, poor thing."

Making sure I still covered my suspects chart, I asked, "How do you know that?"

She shrugged. "After the charges were cleared, Moana sent me an elaborate apology, along with a link to her GoFundMe."

Bold. Moana must have really wanted money. "Why did she need extra funding?" I asked.

"Last-minute cancellations and all that," Adora said. "Moana was too sick to go on with the wedding and had to postpone everything. They lost their deposits along with a few vendors and need more money for a new ceremony."

"Do you still have her link?" Kelvin asked.

"I'm not sure the fundraiser is still going on, but I think so. If I recall correctly, the wedding got rescheduled to early summer."

"It'd be great if you could give me any info so I can contribute," Kelvin said.

"You're a good man. We need more of your kindness in this world." She picked up our dirty coffee cups. "Maybe I'll take ten percent off today's session."

"How will she make any money, giving us all these discounts?" I said after she left.

"You're one to talk. It's not like you're raking in the profits with your cheaply priced cookies," Kelvin said. "You really should charge more. They're artisanal."

"Don't I know it." I folded up my paper before Adora returned—which she did, a few minutes later.

She spoke directly to Kelvin. "I've got the link and can text it to you."

They exchanged numbers, and I heard a beep from his phone that he'd received a new message.

"Thanks for that," Kelvin said, "and I think our hour's up."

We settled the bill at the register, and I teased Kelvin about the text as we left the building.

"Are you sure there's an actual GoFundMe? She didn't just want an excuse for your number?"

"Nah." He pointed to the link on the message. "Besides I'm sure she wasn't interested in me."

"She gave you a compliment and an extra discount," I pointed out.

"People are generous." Kelvin believed in the goodness of humanity. "Anyway"—he clicked on his phone—"I found how to get in touch with Moana."

"Really?"

He flashed me the screen, and I noted the large "Contact" button on the page.

"But will she respond to a total stranger?"

"I think I might have a way in," he said as he skimmed the fundraiser notes.

"How?"

"Moana was looking for a florist earlier. She might still need one."

"And you're the best in the business," I said.

He beamed. "Can't argue with that."

When we reached the car, I said, "Hope Moana returns your message soon."

"Yeah." Kelvin settled his hands on the steering wheel. "Until then, where do you want to go?"

I buckled my seat belt. It'd be nice to stay longer, and we were already in Fresno. The appropriate thing to do would've been to pick some sort of fun site around town, like the Storyland amusement park. Instead, I wanted answers to something besides the case that had been bothering me. "Can we go back to downtown Pixie? You only take half days on Saturday anyway."

He couldn't disagree with my logic. "Plus," I added, "I want to visit Alma."

"To buy a candle?"

"No. She always gives out good advice."

"*Cryptic* advice."

"Doesn't make it less meaningful." I didn't mention the Wishes candle and my new charmed pet bunny to

Kelvin. Maybe Alma was more in tune with magic than I'd previously thought. "I think she could give me insight into this new fortune-telling ability of mine."

"Back to the cul-de-sac it is then." Kelvin started the car.

As we got on the road, I angled toward him, watching his side profile for his reaction as I spoke. My best friend could help me sort through my jumbled thoughts. "I don't understand, though. How can I foresee some really good events, like job openings, but also horrible ones, like dying by suffocation?"

His hands tightened against the wheel. "I don't know, Lissa. I'm not familiar with the magic stuff."

"If only I could be like Mom and the rest of my Jin ancestors—simply bring pure joy."

"I mean you could try," he said. "Doesn't your mom hum while baking?"

"Uh-huh. She says her happiness transfers over to the pastries that way."

"What if you did something similar?"

I guess I could. Humming hadn't worked in the past when I was still trying to find my baking magic, but there was always a chance it would help with the fortunes. Or maybe I needed to gather more positive vibes to pass on before I wrote a message. Of course I'd need to control the power first and not get all dizzy.

Kelvin threw me a sympathetic glance. "Don't worry, you'll get there soon enough."

Not without help, I thought. Which was why I was glad when we reached our familiar street. I offered Kelvin a brusque goodbye as I hurried into my godmother's candle shop.

Inside Paz Illuminations, the world around me hushed. Maybe it was the darkness, which lent an air of reverence.

It seemed to have the same effect on everyone. Even if there were multiple customers milling around, nobody dared disturb the peace. Instead, they flitted like moths around the different candles until they found the one just right for them.

However, no customers were currently in the shop, and my godmother soon approached me. She had her hair up in her signature silver bun and walked toward me with steady steps. “Back so soon, Felicity?”

“I’ve got a problem—”

“I gave you the Wishes candle.”

I hoped I hadn’t affronted her by coming back. “You did,” I said, “and the candle helped. Kind of. I was wondering . . . Does it, er, summon animals?”

It sounded like a strange question, even to *my* ears. To my godmother’s credit, she didn’t appear rattled. She looked steadily at me, not blinking. I couldn’t tell if she believed me or not.

“Do you think it summoned an animal?” Alma asked.

I chuckled. “Well, somehow we got a new pet.”

“Animals are good for the soul.”

Whiskers did help me, but she couldn’t compare to a wise human, like the one before me now. I took a deep breath. “You know about Mom and her talent, right?” *Did* Alma know?

My godmother’s voice remained matter-of-fact. “At baking. She’s very good at what she does.”

I straightened my shoulders. “I want to be just like her, to make people feel happy after eating my baked goods.”

Alma came closer, peering deep into my eyes. “Is that what you really want?”

“Yes, of course.” At least I *should*. I shook my head to clear it. “Anyway, my mom never gets dizzy when she bakes, so why do I?”

"Are you your mother?" Alma asked.

"No." My godmother's opaque answers were beginning to annoy me. Did she always have to respond back with a question? Why was she so ambiguous? I wanted answers and a clear direction.

I let out a sharp exhale. "How can I make joyful fortune cookie messages when some of them predict pain?"

If she understood the allusion to my magical talent, Alma didn't say so. Instead she offered me one of her indecipherable wise sayings: "Your genuine talent will find its way to success."

Now that sounded like a bona fide fortune cookie message. But what did she mean by it?

My godmother continued. "Fate comes knocking for everyone."

When a sharp rap on the door emphasized her statement, I jumped.

A face appeared outside the shop and tried to peer into the thick darkness. Kelvin.

I yanked open the door. "What is it?"

"Come quickly. Moana. She's over in my shop right now."

CHAPTER 14

Inside the flower shop, I noticed that Moana had that talked-of bridal glow. Her shiny brown locks—straight out of a shampoo ad—were kept neatly back from her rosy and dewy face with a silky headband that matched the color of her aquamarine sundress.

"Sorry, I had to leave you for a bit." Kelvin apologized to Moana and motioned at me. "Needed to tell Lissa you were here."

Moana turned her radiant dark brown eyes on me. "Oh, is that your assistant?"

"Partner," I said, hands on my hips. Kelvin and I were equals, even when in an imaginary role.

"Well, good. Because I know exactly what I want for my bouquet." She tilted her phone screen toward us, and Kelvin loped forward to peer at it.

He nodded. "White stephanotis and peach roses. A classic combination."

Moana turned to me. "Can you put together a sample bouquet?"

Uh . . . I'd been in Love Blooms plenty of times, but I'd never really noticed where the flowers were kept. Plus, should the roses be buds or fully open blooms? And what even was stephanotis?

Kelvin noticed my frozen state. "I'll get the flowers, Lissa. Why don't you grab some greenery? On the table in the back."

That I could do. I made my way to the rear of the store and found myself staring down at baby's breath, fern fronds, and other filler material. Which one would go well with the bouquet she'd requested?

Maybe this was why Mom stuck to two treats in the bakery. It saved her the headache of choosing. My hands hovered over everything, indecisive.

Moana's voice boomed across to me. "Ivy leaves, if you have them."

At least I could identify those. I gathered a bunch of ivy and returned to the pair. Kelvin was already showing off his fresh flowers and letting Moana sniff them. She touched one of the stephanotis petals. So that's what the plant looked like. They were delicate white flowers, reminiscent of jasmine.

"The flower samples are beautiful," Moana said. "But how's your styling ability?"

"Let me show you my online portfolio." Kelvin pulled out his phone and accessed his cloud storage to share his arrangements with her.

The two of them debated back and forth about whether the flowers should be hand-tied or placed in a holder while being carried. I tuned them out as they discussed round, crescent, and hoop bouquets for the bridal party. While they chatted, I wondered how to get this conversation back on track to answer my non-floral, murder-related questions.

Moana had been contacted through the fundraiser page, so maybe that was the best way in. "Moana," I said. "We're so sorry to hear about your wedding delay. Thank goodness for GoFundMe!"

She rubbed her stomach. "Ugh, I wouldn't want to relive that night again. It was like a mild reenactment of that scene from *Bridesmaids*."

I knew the reference and shuddered. "It was something you ate, right?"

"Yeah, these awful fortune cookies I bought."

I snapped my fingers as if I'd suddenly remembered something. "Oh, wasn't there an article about it in the paper? Something related to the Fortune Cookie King—"

"More like Fortune Cookie Clown. Sure, the cookies looked fab. Glazed with pastel colors and everything, and at first the icing was all we could taste. We were feeling pretty snacky and gobbled the first few down. After that, we could tell there was something off about the cookies."

"In what way?" I asked.

Her eyes gazed at the ceiling as if concentrating on an old memory. "Like, weird. An almost chalky aftertaste, and he'd tried to cover the yuck factor with an extra thick sugary coating. Plus, the cookie was way overbaked."

What had Smiley Fortunes put in their cookies? Apparently a toxic ingredient that left their customers *unsmiling*. I gave Moana a sympathetic look. "I'm glad you recovered from your stomach issues. The article also mentioned a lawsuit. How's that going?"

"That man—the alleged Fortune Cookie King—died, so I bet I don't get a single cent." She angled her body away from me. "Kelvin, speaking of money, what are your prices if I throw in some posy bouquets and boutonnieres for the wedding party?"

They busied themselves with shop talk for a while. When Moana finally left, she offered her many thanks to Kelvin and gave me a short nod.

"Moana definitely knows what she wants." Kelvin held up a list of detailed instructions written in his hand.

"As always, I'm sure you'll do a great job. And hey, at least you've gotten a new customer out of our investigation."

Kelvin made a noncommittal noise. "Customers can be hard to please, especially when they come in with lots of expectations and high standards."

"Speaking of standards," I said, "I'm wondering what was in those fortune cookies she ate that made them so awful."

He rubbed his chin. "I don't know, but I do have a few of those unglazed ones from the factory around here."

"You keep them in your shop?"

He shrugged. "I've been using them as decorative pieces." Kelvin rummaged around and brought me back a potted bamboo plant.

Instead of the typical small pebbles as decor, the long green stalks and narrow leaves were surrounded by fortune cookies. "Won't they decompose?"

"They haven't yet."

I picked one up, sniffed at it. No strange scent, only a faint whiff of vanilla. Oddly, it did seem just as crunchy as if it'd been unwrapped moments ago. "Hmm, do you have some wrapped versions?"

"A few." Kelvin left and came back with a handful.

I inspected the clear wrapper all over, and disappointment rose within me. "Of course it wouldn't be so easy for me to find."

"What were you hoping for?"

"A full list of ingredients."

Kelvin squinted at me. "You're a baker. Can't you replicate their taste in the kitchen?"

"A few batches of fortune cookies doesn't make me a bona fide baker," I said.

"Don't sell yourself short. You have the Jin talent."

Did I? But I nodded at his compliment and said, "I can at least try to figure out the recipe." If I could solve this one tiny culinary mystery, it would build up my sleuthing skills and possibly help me tackle the larger case.

I timed my arrival at Gold Bakery for the hour before it closed, hoping there wouldn't be many customers around. I got lucky when there wasn't a soul in sight, and I found my mom in the back.

She gave me a surprised look as I dropped a bag of groceries on the counter in the kitchen.

"What are you doing here on your day off?" she asked. "And what did you bring?"

"Ingredients for a different batch of fortune cookies I'm trying out." I kept it vague; she wouldn't be happy if she learned I'd stuck my nose into an open police investigation, even if I was only trying to clear my name.

What had Moana meant when she said that her cookie had tasted chalky? I opened a bag of barley flour. I'd bought several kinds of flour and different versions of sugar—even rock sugar to try to recreate the texture of a harder cookie. Once I got into the focused zone of baking, maybe the mysterious recipe as well as the entire murder case would make more sense. After all, baking always helped me to process and think through things.

While I prepped an experimental batch of barley-flavored fortune cookies, Mom asked, "Why are you trying something new? What's wrong with your current recipe?"

"Nothing." I paused. "But I *am* curious. How come my fortune cookies don't taste happier? You know, more like your pastries?"

She stilled my hands from mixing. "Jin magic doesn't work like that. It's not about the external ingredients you use but the internal ones."

Mom pointed at her tray of exquisite pineapple buns, with just the right amount of puff and sugar-crusted goodness. "It's about having a clear emotion. When I bake, I pour all my joy into it. Don't you?"

Um . . . Well, I could start now. I tried thinking happy thoughts, memories of my mom and me together while growing up. Then I put the fortune cookie batter into the oven to bake.

When the timer dinged, I shaped the round discs into the more familiar folded form. Then I handed a completed fortune cookie to my mom.

She took a tiny bite and assessed the flavor. "The barley's a little overpowering. Beyond that . . ." Mom closed her eyes. "I taste a bit of happiness but a lot of doubt."

I let out a soft groan. "Maybe the talent didn't pass down correctly through my genes. Something to do with my biological dad perhaps . . . ?"

My mom opened her eyes and dumped the cookie into the nearby trash can. "Let's not talk about things that don't matter." As usual, any mention of my father, and she shut down. I'd googled him before, with no luck. His name was just too common.

She patted my hand. "You're a Jin through and through, Felicity. You just need to trust yourself more."

Maybe, but . . . I took a deep breath before I confessed. "I have these dizzy spells, Mom. Do you ever get them while baking?"

My mom's face grew worried, and she touched my forehead. "Are you feeling sick? When was this? Did you catch something?"

"No, it's not that. I'm not ill. The dizziness passes quickly."

"Hmm, it must be dehydration." She hurried to get me a glass of water. "Drink this, Felicity. All of it."

I knew in my heart that the dizzy spells didn't have anything to do with thirst or liquid intake, but I swallowed down the water she offered me. "Feeling much better now," I lied.

Over my mom's protests, I took the next half hour to craft new versions of fortune cookies. Nothing could compare to my original recipe. And I wasn't ever able to replicate the texture or taste of the Smiley Fortunes cookie. Or use the meditative baking process to unlock any clues in the case.

In the end, I quit my efforts with a loud sigh. My mom gave me a gentle pat on the arm and offered me a clean towel to wipe off my flour-covered clothes.

Reminded of my early baking attempts, I took my failed creations and headed straight for the dumpster. A shiver traveled down my spine when I yanked open the heavy lid. Charlie Gong's body had been found in that dark abyss. Among the stench and the filth. Like he'd been worth nothing. Who could have done such a thing?

After dumping my garbage, I peeked inside the bin. I didn't know what I was looking for. Maybe a leftover clue, however irrational that seemed. I didn't get anything but an eyeful of general garbage—bits and pieces from the other shops.

Rubbish. But as I closed the lid, an idea sparked.

CHAPTER 15

Kelvin stood in the middle of my room and looked at me funny. "You want to go dumpster diving? Did I hear that right?"

"Yep. There's nothing wrong with your ears."

"And you want to go in the dark?"

I tossed him a flashlight. "Nobody will be around then."

"But if they are, wouldn't it seem suspicious?"

"Technically, it's not illegal," I said. "Trash is public property."

"Maybe the lightheaded episodes *are* affecting you."

"Ha," I said. "The best way to figure out what ingredients are being used in the fortune cookies is to go to the physical source, the factory."

He scratched the back of his head. "For what it's worth, I think this idea literally stinks."

"No worries. I have some nose plugs lying around. Take those, along with the disposable gloves."

"Thick ones, I hope."

I nodded. "Heavy-duty, the vinyl kind."

Great. If he'd moved on to commenting on the gear, he was in on the idea. I knew I could always talk Kelvin into anything.

I'd timed our exit for right when Mom was in the middle of her favorite sitcom. I hoped she didn't notice our creeping past her as she petted Whiskers in her lap. It had been a while since I'd had a curfew, but I really didn't want to explain our current mission.

Kelvin and I left the apartment while Mom was in mid-laugh and hurried to the car. Without traffic, it took us almost no time to get to the factory.

We parked a little distance away from the building, not wanting to draw any suspicion to ourselves in case there were late-night workers or people out and about in the street. We needn't have worried. Nobody seemed to be walking anywhere near the deserted stretch of block, and the lights were off in the factory.

After circling around the building on foot, I realized that Smiley Fortunes didn't have a back alley. "That's strange. There's no dumpster here. Shouldn't they have one?"

"It can't be too far away," Kelvin said, so we went on searching for a dumpster. I tripped over the broken-up sidewalk in my haste to find an industrial garbage bin.

"Ow." I hoped they finished repaving soon.

"Be careful," Kelvin said. "Are you sure this is a good idea?"

"I'm fine," I assured him, even though my big toe throbbed.

"There it is," Kelvin said, pointing to something in the distance.

Once I squinted, I could see the rectangular outline of the dumpster. Kelvin and I moved faster.

He made it there first and heaved open the lid. I turned on my flashlight, and we both peered over the top.

It definitely held the contents of Smiley Fortunes' junk. I didn't know what I'd expected, but I found the usual suspects inside. Giant bags of flour and sugar. Along with some broken tools and chunks of concrete from the construction effort. Maybe I'd expected a vat of poison with a skull and crossbones etched on it? Too obvious, right?

Kelvin seemed to agree with the lack of findings. "I think we've hit a dead end."

"Ugh, don't remind me of death. That's why we're here in the dark looking through the trash."

He apologized but couldn't help adding, "And whose great idea was this again?"

I flicked off my flashlight. "Well, you're right. Happy now? It's all been a dead end. I should let the detective do her work. I'm not guilty, and surely she'll figure that out on her own soon enough."

"Of course she will," Kelvin said, placing an arm around my shoulder.

And though his kind comment and warmth comforted me, I still felt a wave of doubt.

Although I'd been out late the night before, I still woke up right on time. Maybe my body was finally getting used to the early morning bakery hours.

But I still yawned as Mom and I arrived at the shop. Thankfully, the baking perked me right up. We got into a steady routine, and the rhythm felt soothing.

"Those fortune cookies are looking marvelous," my mom said, glancing at my laden tray.

Some were a little lopsided, but I took the compliment with grace. "Thanks. I feel like I'm getting the hang of it."

She raised an eyebrow. "Did you make any with your new ingredients?"

The baking to figure out how to replicate sick-inducing fortune cookies had been a fail, yielding no answers about the murder. "Nah," I said, "they didn't taste quite right."

She nodded, probably biting back the I-told-you-so from her tongue.

I took a few moments to breathe in the sweet, alluring scent of freshly baked goods. This second home at Gold Bakery meant everything to me. Despite all the ups and downs of the recent days, I knew I belonged here, in the kitchen, baking alongside my mom and carrying on our family tradition.

"Ready?" Mom asked. I turned my attention to her. She held a filled tray in each hand. "It's almost time to greet our first customers."

"Wonderful," I said.

Mom and I organized the glass display case, and it felt exciting to have my fortune cookies resting next to her concoctions. She squeezed my shoulder. "You're doing great. I'm so proud of you."

I still had on a wide smile when the door swung open. My grin flickered. It was Detective Sun. Maybe she was here to buy some treats? But she was scowling as she headed straight my way, and dove right in to the point of her visit, skipping the pleasantries completely.

"What exactly were you doing last night? Tell me the truth."

I was glad a counter separated her from me. In my peripheral vision, I noticed Mom giving me a puzzled look.

I managed to stammer out, "I'm not sure what you're referring to, Detective." How had she known? I started wringing my hands and hid them behind my back.

"Smiley Fortunes has cameras on site."

"They do?"

"Infrared security cameras," she added.

I felt the heat creeping up my neck but didn't want to say anything else incriminating.

She sighed and tugged on her ponytail. "I don't know what you were doing walking around the factory late at night. Innocent people don't do that."

Mom jumped in, offering her an egg tart as a distraction. "Did you have breakfast yet, Detective Sun? I'm sure you need to keep up your energy with this *ongoing* investigation."

"I didn't, and thank you." The detective took the peace offering but said, "I'm trying to be unbiased, Mrs. Jin, but your daughter isn't making it easy for me. I want to wrap up this case quickly. Traveling back and forth from Fresno is a pain."

Geez. It wasn't *that* far. Kelvin and I had done it several times already—not that I'd offer up those details to Detective Sun.

"Please, eat," my mom urged the detective. "Everything will seem better after you have one of my egg tarts."

I leaned over the counter. "If you really want to wrap up the case, Detective, have you looked into Moana Clark? She had a lawsuit against Charlie Gong. It was in the papers and everything."

"I'm well aware of the pending lawsuit." Detective Sun put down her egg tart. "Miss Jin, are you trying to tell me how to do my job?"

Yikes. Had I made the situation worse? I'd only wanted to offer a more viable suspect than, say, me.

My mom moved close by my side and gave me a quick nudge with her elbow. She looked meaningfully at the glass case. It wouldn't hurt to give the detective my own edible peace offering, I guess.

I plucked out the most symmetrical-looking fortune

cookie with a pair of tongs and held it out to her. "Sorry for speaking out of turn. I'm sure you're excellent at your job."

As she reached for the fortune cookie, a devious thought cropped up in my mind. *Could I? Would it potentially help?*

Before I could change my mind, I touched her arm. "Also, let me get you a to-go box for a few more pastries. Free, for your service to the community."

"Oh, okay. Thanks." She took the fortune cookie.

I managed to put two extra pineapple buns into a container and pass it over before the dizziness started. This time, I was ready for it. I trembled slightly, but I hoped the detective wouldn't notice.

The buzzing in my ears happened first. Then the colored lines appeared before my eyes. They swam in bright hues and seemed to almost solidify in the space before me. I touched the floating blue line in wonder.

My mind went blank, my fingers curled and tingled. I itched for paper and pen. Mom must have noticed something happening because she distracted the detective by placing another free egg tart in the box and offering up more pastries.

I grabbed some paper and scribbled down the fortune.

Detective Sun's gaze focused on me. "What have you got there?"

"Nothing."

I hadn't managed to read the piece of paper before she snatched it up.

Detective Sun read the fortune out loud. "'You will travel to the Fresno police station and tackle a mountain of paperwork.' Very funny." She crumpled the note and put it on the counter.

Probably too true, though. The detective must lead

a really boring life. Thank goodness I hadn't predicted anything terrible for her. I should've thought through the potential implications of my impulsive action.

Once Detective Sun left, my mom addressed me. "What was that all about, Felicity?"

I sighed. "I thought I could use my fortune-telling power to find a break in the case somehow."

She tsked at me. "Are you trying to manipulate your gift? Jin magic is meant to be a blessing, an unselfish aid for others."

I shuffled my feet. That wasn't exactly what I'd been trying to do, but maybe my mom was right. "I just wanted to get off her target list."

"Do you? Not from what the detective was saying. What were you up to last night with Kelvin?"

Mom knew I hadn't gone solo even though the detective had only mentioned me being at the factory. "You saw us go?"

"Yes. I knew you two were leaving the house. But, of course, you're free to go hang out with your friends."

Friends? Plural? Kelvin was my only real friend. My peers had tolerated me. I'd always felt like an oddball around town, sticking out in an unwanted way in the sea of white faces.

"I want the truth about last night," Mom said to me with a piercing look.

I gave in. "We wanted to help with the investigation."

"And how exactly have you done that? Tell me everything. And remember: I'm your mom. I'll know if you're lying or leaving anything out."

I squirmed under her intent gaze but, of course, I caved and told her everything. How Kelvin and I had visited different places, including Foo Fusion, Smiley Fortunes, and Sip and Sketch, to figure out the facts behind the murder.

Mom frowned and rubbed her forehead. "I think I'm actually getting a migraine from hearing this."

She walked away and left me alone with my guilt. Normally my mom and I would turn to each other for support. I didn't try to hide things from her. I'd not offered up certain details to the detective for obvious reasons, but keeping Mom in the dark about my activities felt uncalled for, and I still wasn't sure exactly why I'd done it. Was all my investigating creating a wedge between us?

CHAPTER 16

Mom took an ibuprofen for her headache, but her general mood had shifted. When she spoke to customers, she offered a dimmer version of her typical full-wattage smile. She made unusual mistakes: bumping into things, knocking over trays, and spilling sugar everywhere. I couldn't put a finger on it, but the air in the bakery even smelled less happy.

During a lull in the late afternoon, I took her aside. "Want to talk about it, Mom? Because you're worrying me."

She placed one hand on her hip. "It's *you* I'm concerned about."

I gulped. "I'm really sorry about sneaking off last night."

"It's not just the one time. I've always taught you to follow the rules. It's as simple as a recipe. You only need to follow the right steps to create a beautiful life."

It was true: My mom had always encouraged me to do things by the book—not to take shortcuts, and certainly not to break the rules. But in the past few days something had changed for me.

Maybe it wasn't so simple. I felt like I'd lived in our joyous bakery bubble for too long, full of sweet sugar and cozy comfort. It turned out that real life was messy . . . and sometimes murderous. I couldn't figure out how to say this to my mom without taking down her entire philosophy on life, so I stayed quiet.

She continued. "You've changed, Felicity."

My mom didn't say it in a positive tone of voice, either. I bit back an automatic retort that I wasn't her little girl anymore, even though we still shared the same roof over our heads. It might be true, but saying it out loud would only make me seem like a bratty teenager. Instead, I said, "Mom, I just want to find out what really happened that night."

She shook her head. "Detective Sun will figure it out in due time."

Would she? And could she? According to my fortune, the detective had a huge pile of paperwork to handle. I asked, "Don't you think understanding the truth is important?"

"Is it worth your health?" Mom brushed the glass display case. "I noticed you trembling before the detective."

"That's what I was telling you about before. The shakiness seems tied to my gift."

"Impossible," she said. "No Jin has ever experienced any issues with their talent. It flows naturally. I think it's the stress of this recent murder getting to you."

"No, Mom." On this one point at least, I could defend myself. I stood up straighter. "It was happening even from the very beginning. When I first started writing custom fortunes. Before Charlie Gong died."

Her eyes widened, and she went right into mama bear mode. "Then it's your underlying health. You need a checkup. We can go to urgent care right now."

"Actually, I feel like the magic worked better this time around." Sure, I'd trembled, but I hadn't completely blanked, remembering nothing. Maybe expecting it had helped me prepare for the dizziness.

My mom studied my face. "I think you need to rest. Maybe no more baking for a while."

I stepped back from her. "Uh-uh. I want to bake. I *need* to bake. I've waited so long for this moment."

"You've been under too much stress lately," she insisted.

My hands balled into fists. "I'm a Jin, too. I belong here in the kitchen."

Mom softened her voice. "Not if it hurts you, Felicity."

"Please, Mom."

She must have heard the raw yearning in my voice because she sighed. "Fine." Then she walked over to the sign on the door and flipped it to CLOSED. "But we'll compromise, operate the bakery at reduced hours."

"Don't we need more customers, not less?" I asked. "We're not raking in the dough. At least not the money kind."

"I've made up my mind. It's not worth endangering your health." Mom brushed by me to get to the phone at the end of the counter. She dialed up Alma and asked my godmother, our tech guru, to update Gold Bakery's shortened hours on our website and on Yelp.

After she hung up, I asked, "How long are we resting for? A day or two?"

"However long it takes to get some resolution for this case and to bring back your inner peace."

How much time would that take? Once again, I imagined the detective buried under an enormous pile of paperwork. Well, if Mom wanted resolution and someone to crack the case, why couldn't that be me?

* * *

Later that evening, I went over to Kelvin's home. I'd kept secrets from my mom, the person I was closest to in my life, and didn't want to be accused of the same from my bestie.

Kelvin stayed with his widowed dad in a picturesque ranch house down the street from our apartment. I said a fast hello to Mr. Love (his preferred name to the more formal Dr. Love), who was a blur as he ran out the door. Off to another medical emergency no doubt.

Then I slipped into the backyard with Kelvin by my side. It was a good spot for thinking and musing.

Even in the dim twilight, I could make out the riot of colors around me. The garden was filled with all sorts of plants and flowers. In the back corner, there was even a greenhouse, where Kelvin kept a watchful eye over his prized orchids.

"Talk while I make my usual rounds," Kelvin said as he checked on his flowers.

I settled myself in the porch swing and shared about the detective's visit and my mom's growing concern. "She even reduced the hours at the bakery."

"Really?" Kelvin pulled off a few yellowed leaves on a rose bush before turning to me.

"We're pretty much working half days now—until the case is solved." I crossed my arms over my chest. "And I think Detective Sun might need our help to do so."

"I don't know, Lissa. Isn't that what got you into more trouble with the detective—and your mom? The night prowling?"

"In for a penny . . ."

He yanked out a few weeds. "Could we at least do the sleuthing during the daylight?"

I kicked at the ground, causing the bench to swing harder. "Yeah, guess so. Because I've suddenly got spare time. But we'll have to work around your shop hours."

"Unless the suspects come to us," he joked.

Ignoring his attempt at humor, I returned to my mini-rant about the detective. "I even told Detective Sun about a perfectly good suspect besides me, but she didn't bite."

"Who was it?" he asked.

"Moana Clark."

Kelvin stopped moving around the garden and focused on me. "What did the detective say when you brought up Moana?"

"She got all defensive, and accused me of telling her how to do her job."

He pointed at me. "Which, honestly, you were."

"Whatever. I was giving her my informed opinion."

"I'm sure she thought your baking expertise was *invaluable* to her police work."

Before I could offer a sharp retort, Kelvin moved around to the side of the house. Smart guy. Getting away from my verbal wrath. Besides, he kept his green waste bin around the corner, so I bet he was dropping off the weeds he'd collected.

Meanwhile, I swung in the bench and thought about the conversation we'd just finished. When he came back into view, I said, "Kelvin, did you know you're brilliant?"

He took a bow. "Thanks. What amazing thing did I do this time around?"

"You said the suspects can come to us. Couldn't you talk Moana into visiting Love Blooms again?"

He shrugged. "Easy enough, I suppose. She's harping on me to get the wedding party flowers just right. But didn't you try to broach the topic about her lawsuit before, and it didn't lead anywhere?"

"Moana was mopey about the lawsuit because she figured it wouldn't continue after Charlie's death. But I learned something new from the detective's unnerving visit today."

"Which is?"

"The lawsuit is still on," I said. "Maybe if Moana knows that, she'll be willing to share more about it."

"Interesting. Well, I'm sure I can pencil Moana into tomorrow's schedule."

"You're the best, Kelvin."

"I know," he said, a twinkle in his eye.

CHAPTER 17

Kelvin worked his own brand of magic and got Moana to agree to an appointment at Love Blooms at two in the afternoon. I made sure to arrive earlier than that to keep up with the charade of being Kelvin's florist partner.

Moana arrived at precisely two o'clock and appeared as radiant as before. She wore a yellow dress that made her seem like the sun itself, completing the look with a matching bright headband.

She rubbed her hands together in delight. "Thanks for fitting me in your schedule. Now show me the posy sprays."

"You were thinking about having a bouquet of the same flower. Ranunculus, right?" Kelvin said, as he reached into a refrigerator.

"Buttercups, yes."

"I wasn't sure if you wanted only one color, an exact match to your bridal floral theme, or a combo of shades." Kelvin brought out three options for Moana to ooh over. One bunch was pure white, another white and peach, and the third had pink and orange blooms.

"It's so hard to choose." She brushed the tips of her fingers against each of the bouquets. "Maybe pink and orange, to differentiate their flowers from mine. And remember, I want them hand-tied."

I jumped into the conversation. "Sounds perfect. Kelvin, I bought all those spools of ribbon the other day. They're in the back if you want to go through the colors."

He bobbed his head. "Ah, right. It might take me a few minutes to round up all the possible choices."

I figured he'd understand I was asking for a private chat with Moana. The benefits of best friendship. "Thanks, Kelvin."

He left, and I decided to start off with a compliment to loosen her tongue. "I love your sunshiney headband."

Moana touched it. "I like coordinating my outfits. And I'm picking out a pretty peach headband to match my wedding color theme."

"I'm sure it'll look lovely. And congrats again. It's so exciting that your special day is just around the corner, even though it'll be later than you had initially planned."

She rubbed her stomach. "There was no way I would have been able to go through the original ceremony without . . . repercussions."

I clicked my tongue in acknowledgment. "That must have been awful. I sure hope your lawsuit goes through without a hitch. Or did you say it was off for some reason?"

She crinkled her nose. "I'm not holding my breath. Every other suit of mine got dismissed, except the one against Charlie Gong. I went after him personally since he came up with the idea for their new glazed fortune cookies and experimented on me and my friends, but since he's gone now . . ."

"Actually, I heard from a reliable source that a claim continues even after someone dies."

"Really?" Moana whipped out her phone and seemed to look something up. "You're right. The case is still active."

I peeked at her screen. "You have access to the lawsuit info online?" Tech sure made life easier.

"Uh-huh. If you're a party in the lawsuit, you do." She pointed at her name listed in the "plaintiff" section.

Moana continued. "It's a good thing I can check because my lawyer rarely updates me. I guess a measly five thou payout isn't worth it to her."

She clicked back to the main page with its listed court records. I noticed she had access to a different file there as well.

"What's that?" I said, pointing at the other case.

Moana groaned. "It's Charlie's counterclaim. How ridiculous."

She tapped on it to show me, and I speed-read through it. Charlie had claimed he was a victim of emotional distress.

"Can you believe it?" Moana said. "Who's he kidding?"

I shifted my feet. Clearly she'd never heard not to speak ill of the dead. Although I did agree with her in theory.

How could Charlie have claimed emotional pain and suffering when Moana had been the one literally sick to her stomach? And he had been countersuing her for a larger amount.

Kelvin returned to us then with a number of ribbon spools in his hand. "Is this a good time?" he asked.

Even though he looked at Moana, I knew the question was meant for me. I gave him a subtle head nod, and he went off on a monologue about different ribbons, including grosgrain, satin, and tulle varieties.

I tuned the two of them out as my mind went over the court records. Had Moana thought that a lawsuit would end when someone died? Could that have been a reason for her to want Charlie dead—to permanently stop the counterclaim?

Also, she'd sued the man for $5,000, but he'd countered her with $10,000. If they'd both won their suits, she'd come out with a net loss of five thousand. Not a happy resolution. Although, was there any way Charlie really could have won his? But juries could be swayed, and the Fortune Cookie King title did have a certain cachet.

The name "Alma Paz" brought my attention back to Kelvin and Moana's current discussion. My best friend was going on about my godmother's unique candles. Good for him. We loved boosting each other's businesses in this cozy cul-de-sac.

Kelvin said, "She's just next door, Paz Illuminations—"

"Wait"—Moana held up her hand—"I know that name. I've ordered from their shop before."

Kelvin chuckled. "Here I am going about Alma's store when you already knew about it."

"It's okay," Moana said. "I want the very best candles for the new centerpieces I'm imagining."

Her face got all dreamy, and she looked so innocent. Could the blushing bride really be a killer?

I wondered if my godmother could shed some light on Moana's true character. Was she a regular customer? How long had it been since Moana last ordered from Paz Illuminations?

"Gonna take a quick break," I told Kelvin and Moana.

They waved me off, their heads bent over a pencil drawing Moana had made of her ideal table centerpieces.

* * *

At Paz Illuminations, I found my godmother behind the counter, working on her silver laptop, a typical pose for her. She closed the lid when she noticed my presence.

"What are you doing here?" Alma asked. She peered across the way at the bakery, where the lights were off. "Is everything okay? Why aren't you open?"

"Long story short, it has to do with the police investigation. Basically, Mom thinks I need some time to rest and not bake so much."

Alma pursed her lips. "Strength arrives in times of adversity."

I must be getting really strong if that were the case. Practically Wonder Woman at this point. "But I'm not here about me," I said. "I had questions about one of your customers. Moana Clark."

"Can you describe her?" That was my godmother for you: straight to the point, never mind why I had asked what some might call a bit of a strange question.

"She's in her early twenties," I said. "Has brown hair. Wears headbands that match her clothes."

She shook her head. "I think I would've recalled someone like that walking into my store."

Darn. I'd been hoping Moana might have visited the shop in person at least once, even if it had been long enough ago that she didn't remember the storefront.

"Maybe online then?" I asked, though I wasn't sure how much I could really learn about Moana's character from her Etsy orders.

My godmother did some clicking before asking, "What's the name again?"

I told her, even going so far as to spell it out.

"Bingo. She bought something from my online store.

Two scented candles in honey horchata and toasted coconut."

I licked my lips. "You're making me hungry."

"Good thing you're a baker," Alma said with a smile. "So what did you want to know about Moana? And why?"

It seemed Alma wanted more of an explanation than I'd hoped. "She's a new customer of Kelvin's. Basically, I'm curious about her character. I thought if you'd chatted with her in person, you could tell me more about her." I knew it was a weak explanation, and I was grasping at straws, but any info was better than none for an investigation, right?

"Hmmm . . ." Alma said, before seemingly deciding to bypass the fact that I was apparently vetting Kelvin's customers. "Let me check my notes to jog my memory. Well, she paid for her candles, and the funds went through, but . . ."

I moved closer to my godmother, who was frowning at her screen. "What is it?"

"There *is* something strange," Alma said. "Moana was supposed to stop by the store the other day. Messaged that she'd be in the area, but she never showed up."

"She bailed on you?" That wasn't a great quality trait, although it wouldn't qualify Moana as a murderer either.

"Ghosted me," my godmother said. "She didn't even apologize for missing the appointment. Here, you can see the messages for yourself."

I skimmed through the conversation on the Etsy site. Alma had summarized their interaction well. They'd set up a date and time to meet. And then nada. Why had Moana skipped the promised visit?

CHAPTER 18

Why had Moana set up an appointment to visit Paz Illuminations and then failed to show up? Did it mean anything, or was she just a preoccupied and slightly rude bride-to-be? I pondered this as I walked slowly back to Love Blooms.

Had she felt under the weather? Dragging my feet, another theory emerged. I double-checked the appointment date. It'd been the day Charlie died, so Moana might have been in the local area. And maybe she hadn't gone to Paz Illuminations because she'd been too busy—with murder.

I didn't want to confront Moana outright. She might lie to me. I might be new to the sleuthing game, but surely a killer wouldn't just admit to murder. And I couldn't predict how she'd react, whether she'd lash out at me.

When I marched back into the flower shop, though, I realized she'd already left. It looked like there'd be no confrontation of any kind today, and I couldn't help but be a little relieved.

"Where'd you rush off to?" Kelvin asked as he placed some flowers back inside the fridge.

"To Alma's. I thought she might give me some insight about Moana."

"Because Moana was one of her candle customers."

Kelvin put it together aloud as he righted a lopsided plant display. "What'd you find out?"

"Well, Alma only ever interacted with her through Etsy. But Moana did stand her up for an in-person meeting the day of the murder." I elaborated on how Moana had bailed on my godmother. "If only I could verify that she'd actually come this way or not. Like with camera footage?"

Kelvin shook his head. "No way. It's downtown Pixie."

"Yeah, I know," I grumbled. There was an ordinance that no shops in the quaint downtown area would put in surveillance systems. The mayor and city council had both agreed that it'd be a "bad look" for Pixie. They wanted that sweet small-town atmosphere to be on display for visitors.

To be fair, many residents felt the same way. People kept their windows open throughout the night. Some never locked their doors. Others even left out fruit or extra furniture for passersby to pick up on a whim. Until Charlie's murder, Pixie had felt like a peaceful oasis.

"Do *you* think it could be Moana?" I asked Kelvin. He'd interacted with her a few times already. Maybe he'd have a clearer perspective, or perhaps she had let something slip during their business conversations.

"I don't know, Lissa." He busied himself with smoothing the tulle ribbon on a spool. "She seems nice to me."

For sure, she'd looked like an angel while she'd been dreaming of centerpieces, but appearances could be deceiving. "Even nice people can get pushed too far," I said.

Niceness was Kelvin's Achilles' heel, made him overlook things. How many times had his mom said to him (and also to me) while we'd been growing up to "play nice" with others? To Kelvin, it was the most important character trait.

I continued. "But Moana does have a real motive. Lawsuits and money have influenced many people, even nice ones."

"Still . . ." Kelvin took a moment to walk to the back and put away the ribbon. When he returned, he picked up the conversation where we'd left off. "What about the others in Charlie's inner circle? They all have motives, right?"

I excluded the workers who'd punched in on their timecards at the fortune cookie factory (they had alibis) and put up three fingers. "So the top suspects are Cayla, Logan, and Michael."

Kelvin nodded. "Cayla is managing the factory now, and she's always wanted to be in charge."

"Perhaps. But would you kill your boss just to get a promotion? Unlikely. There are easier ways." I put down one finger. "How about Logan?"

Kelvin rubbed his chin. "He's probably strong enough to kill someone with just his bare hands. And he did get injured in the factory, so maybe he wanted payback."

"Yes, but like you said, he was injured. Could he have done it with a hurt hand?" I put down another finger. "And that leaves Michael. Who stopped using Charlie's fortune cookies—"

"And issued a disclaimer about them."

"Was killing Charlie the only way he could get out of their contract?"

"That's harsh," Kelvin said.

"We're just laying out possible motives," I said, a bit defensively as I paced around his store, dodging the various pots and vases scattered around the cozy space. "After all, Detective Sun suspects *me*, and I'd just met Charlie."

"They all have *sort of* motives," Kelvin said, echoing my own conclusion. "Ones that *could* have led them to murder, but then again, maybe not."

"If we don't have solid motives for any of them, how else can we figure out if they're involved?"

Kelvin glanced through the shop door toward Paz Illuminations. "How about the camera thing you brought up? We need to figure out which of them were even around here on that day, that evening?"

"If only we had trackers on them," I said.

"Ha, like Apple AirTags." Kelvin lifted his black iPhone in the air. "I never lose my keys anymore."

While staring at his cell, I went through the list of people in my head again. "You know what? We *can* use your phone for something."

"I was joking about the tracking devices."

"I meant we could use it to make a phone call."

He fake gasped. "Is that what this thing can do?"

"Joker. Just for mocking me, we'll split up the calls. Half for you, and half for me."

"What 'calls' are you talking about?" Kelvin said. "To whom?"

I mimed a splint around my left hand. "We're checking out Logan's story. The hospitals in the Fresno area. We can take, like, a twenty-mile radius around Smiley Fortunes."

"All righty then. Guess we got our work cut out for us."

Kelvin and I mapped out the area around the fortune cookie factory and checked the online listings for local hospitals. We took turns placing calls to split the workload. A couple of times over the afternoon, though, he got interrupted by a customer, so my tally was growing higher than his as we neared the final four prospects.

He called the last three and got a variation of non-answers we'd heard before. The information was confidential, or they'd never heard of a Logan Miller.

"Guess we'll have to loop back around to the ones unwilling to tell us anything over the phone," Kelvin said. "We could make a day trip of it on the weekend."

Though he said it a bit sarcastically, I knew he was being sincere. If I asked him to, he really would spend his free time touring the local hospitals. Not the most fun and relaxing weekend activity, that's for sure.

I pointed to the last hospital on our list. "Don't give up hope just yet." But, to be fair, I also felt drained and despondent.

Once I dialed, I steeled my nerves for a rejection. The person who answered sounded polite and kind, though, unlike the dismissive voices I'd been coming to expect. And I didn't even have to go through an automated message system to get to a live individual.

"How may I help you?" she asked.

Kelvin's mom had been right. Being nice meant everything. I gave my spiel about how I was searching for a friend. Was Logan Miller still at the hospital?

She hesitated. "Logan, huh?"

"Yes. Logan Miller. He injured his hand."

"I'm sorry, but he's not here."

That was a change from the typical reply. "Do you mean he was never there to begin with? Or that he'd been there previously?"

"He got discharged a while back. We sent him on home to recover."

Success! I'd finally reached the right hospital. "Oh, really? Do you know when he got out?"

"Give me a moment." I heard some typing over the

line, and then she told me the date and time he'd gone home. I thanked the woman but stumbled over my words.

Kelvin touched my arm. "Everything okay? You seem stunned."

I was gripping his phone in my hand, staring at it blankly. "Oh, yeah. I'm fine."

He eased his cell out of my grasp and waited me out.

I finally looked him in the eyes. "But guess what? Logan wasn't in the hospital when Charlie died. In fact, he'd been discharged the day before."

CHAPTER 19

I slammed my hand down on a nearby table in frustration. Why couldn't suspects stay put?

"Whoa, there." Kelvin rushed to my side, not to comfort me, but to rearrange a bucket of lilies I'd jostled.

"Sorry. I just wish we could nail down where people were that day."

"Too bad they're not plants, huh? Always calm and rooted."

Was that a metaphorical dig at me? "You and your precious greenery," I said, a little sharply.

"Come on, Lissa. You know I didn't mean—"

His words were cut short when a large group came inside the store. I spied their minivan parked at the curb, complete with Nevada license plates.

"This shop is adorable! What a cute little town," one of them exclaimed.

I left the now crowded space to let Kelvin attend to his customers. Besides, I needed to get some fresh air. To sort out my feelings, which were a combination of irritation at our afternoon of ineffective sleuthing and Kelvin's last comment.

Should I go home? But I didn't want to transfer my sour mood over to my mom. Where could I go to relax?

My footsteps took me automatically to Gold Bakery. I peered through the glass door. Maybe there were some treats left inside. I'd feel better with a delicious pastry in my tummy.

I unlocked the store and went in, and it seemed my luck had finally turned. There were multiple trays of left-over pastries for me to eat. I picked up a scrumptious egg tart and rested on the stool behind the counter, taking a moment just to admire the pastry. The beautiful golden color of the custard center. How had my mom perfected the cheery hue? It was the exact warm yellow of sunshine.

I ate the egg tart slowly, savoring the sweetness on my tongue. When I finished it, I licked the flaky crumbs off my fingers.

What had I been worried about again? It didn't seem worth the trouble anymore. As a member of the Jin family, Mom's food magic didn't work on me, but years of delightful bakery memories bubbled up to my consciousness, and I smiled. There was something to be said for the natural magic of a happy memory.

The shop door swished open. Oops, I must have forgotten to lock it.

"Oh goodie, you're still open." I recognized the woman before me. A regular customer. In her forties, with fiery red hair and splashes of freckles that made her appear younger. I'd nicknamed her Sweet Tooth Sally in my mind, and with her big heart, it worked on a number of levels.

"Actually," I said, "we *are* closed. Not sure if you know, but we're working reduced hours."

"I heard that rumor but decided to come anyway and found the door unlocked."

I stood up, brushing crumbs away from my shirt. "Just in here getting a snack."

"Shucks. I was really craving Angela's pineapple buns," Sally said. She always did.

It was only one customer. I could make an exception, especially for a regular. "We still have some in stock. How many do you need?"

Sometimes Sally came in to satisfy her own sugary cravings, but other times, she ordered in bulk. She had many connections in Pixie and came from a family who'd been settled in the area for generations. I knew she was on the PTA and participated on the boards of several local nonprofits.

She tapped her bottom lip with her index finger. "Maybe three dozen. I'd like to bring some by the tutoring center." Sally also volunteered a lot. I don't know how she juggled it all.

"Let me check that we have enough." I walked back into the kitchen. Counting the number there, I knew I needn't have worried about the supply. But now I had a different worry brewing: These reduced hours must have meant a decrease in customers and fewer pastries sold overall.

As I placed the buns gently into take-out containers, I asked, "How'd you first hear about our new hours?" It helped to understand whether we reached our customers better online or through word of mouth.

She waved her hand in the air. "It's Pixie." Of course, the small-town rumor mill.

I lowered my voice even though no one else was around to listen in on our conversation. That was the other thing about Sally—with her volunteering and connections, she ended up getting all the gossip. "What are people saying about Gold Bakery? And please, don't sugarcoat it."

She bit her bottom lip, not bothering to chuckle at my

pun. "People are concerned, naturally. But I figured you changed your hours for a good reason. Everyone's heard about the nearby murder. It must have been terrible for you and your mom."

I finished packing the buns in the containers and snapped them closed with more force than necessary. "Yes, it really was."

Sally seemed to loosen up a bit, warming to her theme. "Well I, for one, don't believe the gossips who say it's because of your baked goods. People will say anything, but I'm sure your fortune cookies aren't unlucky. And they certainly couldn't bring a murderer right to your back door. Gold Bakery's treats have never brought me anything but joy."

Really? That was what people in town were thinking—and not just thinking, but saying? I knew they didn't like change much, but fortune cookies that brought bad luck? Honestly, it was nice of Sally to defend us, but I noticed that even she wasn't clamoring to buy any today.

Sure, I'd always felt a little on the outside of things in Pixie, but everyone had seemed so happy to buy my new fortune cookies. My mood sunk again a bit, but my resolve stiffened. I absolutely had to find out who killed Charlie Gong.

She leaned in and opened wide her blue eyes. "Anything I can do to help? You know I'm a loyal customer."

Could she assist? I thought about Sally's extensive network. If she ever considered running for mayor, she'd be a shoo-in. "Since you know so many people, could you ask them if they saw anything that night? I mean, it'd be helpful to the police." And to me since I was under suspicion.

She barely kept the smirk off her face. "I heard the detective in charge is a Fresnan."

"I'm not sure where Detective Sun is from, but it's true she's currently working at the Fresno department."

"No wonder this case hasn't been solved yet," Sally said. "This is Pixie. Someone from Fresno just can't connect."

I'd seen this animosity toward our neighboring city appear sometimes. Many residents were fine with Fresnans, myself included, but others thought those from the larger urban region put on airs and acted snooty toward people in Pixie. Apparently, even Sweet Tooth Sally had a bit of a bite when it came to the town rivalry.

"You know, I think you may be right. People would be more willing to share with you, a true local." A well-known resident with roots (there was that word again) inspired trust in others. Roots, plants . . . I should apologize to Kelvin for my rash exit. It had been hard to learn what people were saying about my fortune cookies, but Sally's offer had reminded me why I loved Pixie so much, and Kelvin was a big part of it.

Sally misinterpreted my flushed face. "Don't worry, it's no hassle at all, Felicity. But I *am* going to need more treats for this to work."

"We've got plenty around, and I'll be sure to give you a decent discount." I placed more pineapple buns and egg tarts in containers for her but skipped the fortune cookies. Once the case was resolved, then people would realize for sure that my cookies were fine. Not bringers of bad luck. In fact—when I got a handle on my fortune-telling magic—I hoped they'd be the opposite. Until then, I didn't want to risk it.

I rang her up, and Sally left with a swagger to her steps. With a little convincing, she really would make a great mayor when the current one retired.

Before I left, I walked around the bakery again, wiping

things down and straightening stuff. I sighed as I stared at my abandoned fortune cookies. If people in town didn't want them, would I have to throw them away? It hurt my heart to have to dump my precious creations. All those hours of hard work.

Wait a minute. Did I need to sell them to only local people? There was a desire for my fortune cookies just one town over. I mean, I'd even entered into a recent partnership with Michael at Foo Fusion. Maybe it was time to visit my business partner to see if he needed a refill on baked goods. And while there, I could just maybe check his calendar for details on his recent whereabouts.

CHAPTER 20

I felt even more encouraged to visit Foo Fusion the next day when I analyzed our current customer base. The morning crowd at Gold Bakery had been thin. I wondered if people were upset about our dwindling hours or still alarmed about the murder that had happened in our back alley. Maybe Detective Sun had even asked enough prying questions of the residents that they knew I was a suspect in the case. Whatever the cause, even my mom wished me well as I left the shop, toting an abundant supply of fortune cookies, to head into Fresno. We really needed to up our orders.

I'd timed my arrival to coincide with a natural lull at the restaurant. Or at least so I hoped. Surely, Foo Fusion would have a few quiet moments after the lunch rush. I wanted to catch Michael when he wasn't running back and forth from the kitchen.

Luckily, I hit the conversational jackpot. When I arrived, there were only two tables of patrons in the place, and they were finishing their meals in leisure.

"Glad I caught you," I said to Michael, where he lounged at the register.

He laughed. "Hard to miss me. I'm here almost all the time."

We'd only just begun our chat and already he'd provided a possible alibi for himself. Would the restaurant even be able to run without him? If only I had X-ray vision as a superpower, I could look beyond the kitchen door to see how many workers he had. Did he have someone who might be able to cover for Michael when he needed to run out for an errand? Was there a way to find out?

"It's so hard being a business owner," I poured on the sympathy before taking a risk and venturing a white lie that would hopefully help determine his alibi. "My friend was here Tuesday night. She mentioned it when I shared that you were stocking my cookies, but said she didn't see you. But I know certain weeknights can be slow for restaurants, a great time to run errands." Like killing someone, maybe?

"Hmmm." He frowned a bit, thinking back. "There's always a chance I stepped out to the bank, but we had a large party that night so I was here until pretty late. I hope your friend enjoyed her meal."

"Oh, definitely. She can't wait to come back." I crossed my fingers mentally, hoping my fictional friend's taste buds would forgive me.

"What brings you here?" Michael asked. "It's kinda late for lunch."

I lifted the bag of fortune cookies up. "Came to check if you needed any restocking."

He smiled, showing off a crooked incisor. "Not yet. But I must say your cookies are *way better* than our previous ones."

Clearly, my lucky streak was continuing since Michael had given me the perfect in to talking about Charlie. "How long did you work with Smiley Fortunes, anyway?"

He scratched his balding head. "Not long. Maybe a month or two."

"How did you find them in the first place?"

"You've got it backwards. Charlie found *me*. Before we even opened." Michael pointed out the front door. "Or at least he found my car. There was a flyer under my windshield wiper from the factory, advertising bulk fortune cookies at a huge discount."

"Sounds like Charlie knew how to hustle." He must have really wanted to keep that Fortune Cookie King title. That must have been how Charlie had managed to hear of Gold Bakery so soon after I'd started fortune cookie making, by trying to spy on any rumblings of competition.

"Tenacious businessman, I'll give him that," Michael said. "But lousy cookies."

"You didn't realize earlier? Couldn't try a sample before you ordered?"

"Of course I did," he said. "The first batch was adequate. And so extremely cheap. Plus, locally made—thought that'd be a draw for customers."

"What happened after that? I know you eventually stopped giving out the fortune cookies." As Kelvin and I had experienced. He'd only relented and given us the cookies after issuing a warning.

"Business picked up for us." He placed a hand over his heart. "What a blessing. But then Charlie started having problems fulfilling my orders. I needed him to work faster, which he did. He met my deadlines, but only by taking shortcuts."

I glanced around the dining room, but the low murmur of conversation continued to flow. Nobody was paying any attention to us. "What did Charlie do?"

"I'm not sure . . ." Michael's mouth twisted. "But the new batches were horrible. People complained about toothaches after munching on them. It started driving customers away from Foo Fusion."

"Yeah, I can see how that would be bad for business."

"I actually blew up at Charlie about it." Michael hung his head. He did seem like a man who could be fierce if pushed hard enough. I remembered how he'd shooed away the mourners at his doorstep when they'd tried to erect that makeshift memorial marker.

We stayed in an awkward silence until I felt compelled to soothe him. I'd rather calm people through baked goods, but I guess I'd try words this time around. "Well, it definitely makes sense you'd be mad about the poor quality."

"I still feel bad about it, though. Yelling at a guy on his very last day on earth."

Wow. No wonder Michael felt guilty. But was he guilty of murder? I should put some more feelers out. "Maybe he wasn't such a great guy, easy to get mad at—is that accurate?"

He snapped his head up. "You're right. Nobody liked him. Not even the people at his factory."

"You've been there?"

"I visited to double-check standards. Wanted to figure out what was wrong with the cookies we got but didn't see anything odd. Even chatted with the employees to make sure, but they said none of their processes had changed. But they did share what they truly thought of their terrible boss."

A swoosh as the door opened behind me stopped our conversation. I could hear a family coming in, complete with a wailing baby and a toddler whining about how hungry he was.

"I'll have to take care of these new customers," Michael said, already pinning a polite smile on his face.

"Sure." I paused. "Do you want a fortune cookie? Might make you feel better."

"We still have some. I'll grab one from our own supply later." He glanced at the huge bag I'd brought over. "Your cookies are unique. Tasty. Why don't you try pitching at these other places while you're in the area?"

Michael scribbled something down on a server's pad, ripped the guest check off, and handed it over.

"Thanks," I said as I got out of the way of the hungry family and exited.

In the restaurant's parking lot, I read what Michael had written down. He'd suggested a few local groceries. Might as well try to drum up some extra business. Goodness knew that we could use more money coming in, particularly if Pixie residents continued to avoid our bakery.

I felt like a Girl Scout out selling Thin Mints, except I was hawking fortune cookies. Michael had put the names of two grocery stores on the guest check.

The first was an Asian mart and an easy sell. When I walked in, my nose tingled at the medicinal, herbal smell. It reminded me of ginseng roots and homeopathic healing. The silver-haired older lady, who introduced herself as Tala Santos, was only too willing to stock my cookies and wrote down my contact info in a paper receipt notebook. Guess she didn't believe in cash registers either, because I noticed an abacus sitting nearby.

Alight with success, I marched on—feeling a glow of pride at the idea of proving to my mom that I was fine, and bringing in some extra cash while I was at it. When I went to the second store, I didn't find any distinctive smells. It was a small grocery shop with only one international aisle. The shelves there were crammed with a variety of spices and condiments. I also noticed Hello Panda cookies, ube pastries, and mochi rice cakes.

I approached the man behind the counter. He was tall and slim, maybe in his late forties, with a groomed beard. His name was Jeremy Scott, and he had a penchant for inserting "like" into his sentences. When I asked him about displaying my cookies, he said, "We do, like, sell international stuff. But the aisle is already full." I could tell.

"There isn't anywhere else you can place them?"

He shrugged. "We already have almond cookies. Isn't that enough?"

"Those are totally different. And fortune cookies come with cool messages."

"I don't believe in those. Fortunes and such. I think horoscopes are, like, a waste of time."

Perhaps I'd better name-drop to get some traction. "Michael Fu recommended your store to me. Thought you might be interested in my fortune cookies."

The name, if anything, brought out a grimace on Jeremy's face. "Yeah, I know the guy. Tried to connect with me at his restaurant, but I'm not big on newcomers, especially those with subpar food."

Ouch. But I latched on to a word in the second part of his sentence. "'Newcomers'? So you must have lived here quite a while?"

"Only all my life." He grinned, showing a fine display of pearly whites. "And I always had a knack for business. Back at Roosevelt High, I had the sense to buy snacks in bulk, separate them out, and upcharge my peers."

I sidled nearer to him. "I'm a local, too." I could make that claim. Pixie was pretty close by.

Interest flickered in his face. "Really? I do reserve a

section for local small businesses. You don't make your cookies in a factory like some others around here, right?"

His gaze seemed rather searching as I answered. "No, we're a mom-and-pop shop—or rather, mother-and-daughter bakery."

I could see his initial resistance softening. Now to close in on the deal. "Want to try a sample cookie?"

"Okay, I'll bite." He chuckled at his own joke.

Once he unwrapped the fortune cookie and bit into it, I knew I had him. He even closed his eyes while chewing. "This is so good."

"Thank you. It's made with our family's special ingredient." Magic.

"I'll take two dozen to start. And will restock if needed."

Like with the other grocery store, we exchanged contact info on pieces of paper. I really should look into getting business cards, especially if Mom and I wanted to network and expand our business ties.

The owner waved merrily to me as I left. I felt so buoyed by his response that I thought I would try one of the bigger eating establishments in the area. Michael had only given me a list of local grocers and not Fresno restaurants. He probably didn't want to send my business to any of his rivals, but if I could make a deal with Foo Fusion, maybe I could top that with a well-respected restaurant.

Imperial Garden was a flagship dim sum eatery. My mom and I loved to visit on special occasions. We had a tradition of going there for our birthdays. Sometimes the wait could be extra long, with a line running out the door, but the food was worth it.

I passed through its entrance, wowed once more by its glass chandeliers and marble columns. Servers bustled around the dining area. The woman at the front register was on the phone, answering a question about the menu. After she hung up, I made my pitch.

Before I'd even gotten past the fact that I made fortune cookies, she stopped me. "Another fortune cookie vendor? No, thank you."

I tried to offer her a sample to taste, but she denied me again. "We already have a reliable supplier."

Defeated, I slunk out the door. Well, two out of three wasn't bad. Things might finally be looking up for my family's bakery. If only solving a murder were so simple.

CHAPTER 21

I invited Kelvin over to my home's small patio to share the good news that Fresno businesses were buying up my fortune cookies. It was a cramped concrete space with bushes lining the perimeter and a vinyl fence separating us from the next apartment. At least Mom and I had some outside space, though, because there were locations in Pixie that didn't offer any frills beyond four enclosed walls.

Kelvin and I sat around the mosaic bistro table with Whiskers at our feet. I was glad the bunny got to bask in the sunlight. That was the silver lining of having reduced hours at the bakery. Otherwise, we arrived home too late to let the bunny out in the daytime.

Kelvin leaned back in his chair, almost kicking me with his long legs. "Congrats, Lissa. Your fortune cookies are killing it."

I gave him a sharp glance. Was he making a pun? Because, too soon.

He held up his hands. "Sorry. Just put together why you were really in Fresno in the first place."

Kelvin knew that I was usually both a homebody and not a particularly avid marketer. "Fine, you got me. I may have stopped by Foo Fusion to find out a little more."

He shook his head. "I can't believe you went snooping without me."

I wasn't sure if he was sore about missing out on the action or if he was concerned I'd gone traipsing into a possible murderer's den alone.

"It wasn't a big deal," I said. "Didn't learn too much. Only that Michael works all the time at the restaurant, and he remembers being super busy with a large party that night, so maybe he didn't have a chance to confront Charlie."

"Owners, we do put in a lot of work."

"Yeah." I glanced through the clear patio doors to my mom inside the living room. She was binge-watching a TV series, but I wasn't sure if she was doing it out of enjoyment or to distract herself from our own slow-going business.

Kelvin snapped his fingers to get my attention. "Focus, Lissa. Does that mean we should cross Michael off the suspects list?"

"Let's say we lean away from him for now."

"What about Cayla? She probably works just as hard to manage a factory."

"You could be right about that." I paused. "That means we've cut our list in half, leaving Logan and Moana as the most likely culprits."

"I'm making some centerpieces and need Moana's approval on them," Kelvin said. "But they'll take a while before they're completed to her exacting standards. Can we work on Logan first?"

"You know what? I still have that business card he gave me during our 'job interview.' I'll contact him, maybe ask about his new position."

A knocking sounded on the patio door, a warning

signal, before Mom carried out a tray to us. She walked over, asking, "You kids hungry?"

I noticed that she was offering us pineapple buns and egg tarts. My heart sank a little. Was she taking leftovers home because we weren't selling enough at the shop?

Kelvin flashed a brilliant smile her way. "I'm always hungry for your treats, Mrs. Jin."

"Why, thank you, Kelvin." Mom put down the tray and positioned two small plates before us.

"Thanks, Mom," I said, infusing extra enthusiasm into my voice to make up for my worrying thoughts.

She left us alone after that, and Kelvin started scarfing down an egg tart. I took delicate bites of the pineapple bun and almost choked. Were these over a day old? They tasted stale or something.

"Are you all right?" Kelvin looked ready to bolt up and do the Heimlich on me.

"I'm fine, but"—I stared at the offending pineapple bun—"do you think there's something off with the taste?"

"Nope." Kelvin patted his stomach. Of course he'd gobble everything down without any complaint.

"It's different from Mom's usual high quality. Let me try an egg tart." I put down the nibbled pineapple bun and reached for the other pastry.

Again, after a few bites, I tasted something strange. I left the baked goods uneaten on my plate. Noticing Whiskers nudging my leg, I picked her up.

"What could be wrong with them?" I mused as I stroked her fur. Immediately, a vision flashed in my mind.

Mom. With her back bent over a tray. She wiped at her face. Did she get flour on it by accident? But, nope, a tear wound its way down her cheek.

She'd been crying while baking. A no-no. And it'd

transferred over. What I had tasted wasn't staleness, it was sadness.

I really needed to crack this case to bring order back to our lives. "Give me a moment. I'm going to hunt down that business card," I said to Kelvin.

"Right now? Are you sure you don't want to talk about . . . what's on your mind?" Leave it to Kelvin to pick up on my anxious feelings.

I shook my head. "No thanks, and trust me, we need to act fast." He knew better than to keep pestering me. I'd tell him when I was good and ready.

While he selected a fresh pineapple bun, I darted back into the apartment. The business card had to be somewhere on the dresser in my room. I figured I'd stashed it there or in one of the drawers.

Nothing on the desk's surface except for wrinkled receipts. I finally found it lodged in the corner of the bottom drawer. And my luck held. Not only had Logan put his email on it, but he'd also given me his phone number.

Waving the card triumphantly in the air, I ran back out to Kelvin. "Got it. Let's call him this instant."

Kelvin offered me his phone. I dialed and put the call on speaker so we could both hear.

Logan's voice rumbled out at us. "Who is this?"

I cleared my throat. "It's me, Felicity Jin, the fortune cookie shop owner." Well, daughter of the owner, technically. But "owner" sounded like it had more authority.

"Right. I remember meeting you near the Fresno water tower."

"Yeah, you gave me your business card, which was how I got your number. I was, um, wondering how your job search is going. We still have an op—"

"Thanks, but I don't need a position at your shop anymore." I could hear his smile even over the phone.

"Landed a cushy job at a furniture store in River Park. Right after meeting with you, in fact."

"You work at the mall?" I asked.

"It's actually known as an outdoor shopping experience," he said.

Okay, an outdoor mall, then. "Do you think I could swing by?"

"Why?" Suspicion tinted his voice.

What valid reason could I give? "You don't need a job, but I'd love to pick your brain about the factory. Our fortune cookie business might be expanding soon, and I'd love to get your take on the dos and don'ts if we decide to mass-produce." Which was partially true. I needed more info about the people who worked there . . . but my mother would never sully the Jin family legacy by crafting our baked goods on a factory floor.

"I'm not sure I can tell you too much," he said.

I played the novice card. "Anything would be great. I only started fortune cookie making recently, and it's a tough business."

"You seem to be doing all right," he said. "The fortune cookies are delicious and even your message was spot-on for me. In fact, I've been spreading the word about your custom fortunes. Tell you what, come by in an hour when I'm on break. If you bring by half a dozen fortune cookies—those things are addictive—you've got yourself a deal."

I hung up and gave Kelvin a high five. "The investigation is back on."

CHAPTER 22

River Park was an outdoor shopping center in Fresno off of Blackstone Avenue. At night, its lit signage stood out, even though it was surrounded by massive palm trees. The center sprawled across several streets and held multiple parking lots, and the area featured some well-known, upscale chains.

It took Kelvin and me a few laps of confused circling around a rotary to find the furniture shop where Logan worked. It was an elegant store, the outside painted in contrasting shades of black and white.

I let Kelvin go in first to wander around the place. After a space of ten minutes, I followed, but with a more determined purpose. Logan worked in the couches section of the store, but he said he'd be at the general information desk waiting for me.

Good thing he'd let me know where he was because I almost didn't recognize the man standing there wearing a white dress shirt and paisley tie. He seemed more teddy bear than grizzly bear—my initial impression upon meeting him—in this new line of work. He'd even slicked back his hair with some styling gel.

"Logan?"

"Yep. I clean up real nice, right?" He held his left hand out to me. Before we shook, I noticed faint pink markings scattered across his meaty palm. Burns from the factory, I bet.

"I've got fifteen minutes," he said. "What questions do you have for me?"

I'd ease into the interrogating. "Well, as you know, I do everything myself right now. It'd be great to have some extra hands, but I need to figure out how an assistant could help. What role did you have at the factory?"

"I did everything," he said. "We learn to do all the positions in case someone gets sick. Plus, I heard we used to have more workers years ago, but the company keeps downsizing."

"So you rotated roles among the employees?" I asked.

He nodded. "Honestly, it's not that bad. We only have three major stations: mixing, folding, and inspecting."

I remembered the woman who'd been stirring the vat of batter. "Do you get to go and buy the ingredients?"

"Nah." He mimed stirring. "All we do is mix. Rote stuff."

"I took a tour of the factory the other day." That woman had put something from a bottle into the mix. "Are you sure you don't get to add anything to the batter?" I asked.

"Charlie is—or was—in charge of the winning Smiley cookie formula. But sometimes you could make your own mark on it if there was extra vanilla or something like that lying around."

"Did the formula ever change?" I wanted to know what the chalky taste Moana had talked about could have been.

"Who knows what Charlie was up to? He always

pushed us to work harder, to make the cookies faster." Logan scowled.

"Is that how you burned yourself?" I asked gently.

"Yeah." He glanced down at his left hand. "Charlie wanted us to use our nimble, bare fingers to fold. Only I was having problems shaping the cookies fast enough for him. I took too long that day and burned my palm on the hot plate."

"Yikes. I'm sorry. Does it still hurt?"

He wiggled his fingers. "No, they're as good as new now."

"How long did it take to heal?"

"Pretty quick. I'm strong." He flexed his biceps, and I was afraid his dress shirt might rip.

I said, "Dakota told me you had to go to the hospital for the burn."

"He worries too much. I only stayed overnight."

"But didn't you get a good amount of time off work?"

His face reddened. "Um, I might have put my workers' comp to good use. To find another, more respectable job."

I glanced around the fancy furniture store, and hoped to put him at ease with a compliment. "Well, your effort seems to have paid off."

"You can say that again. I work on commission, and these couches practically sell themselves. Hey, you aren't in the market for a leather couch, are you?"

"Not on my baker's salary," I joked. "Speaking of which, here are your fortune cookies. Please, try one now. They taste better fresh."

"Don't mind if I do." He reached for the take-out container.

I made sure to make physical contact as I passed it over.

He broke open a cookie. "Empty, huh? I've got all the luck on my side now, so no need to give me another custom fortune."

Little did he know. My hand snaked around the mini notepad in my pocket. I cleared my mind and waited for an incoming revelation. But nothing happened.

Logan was munching on the fortune cookie, getting crumbs all over his white dress shirt. "Just as good as I remembered," he said.

Maybe he had to consume the whole cookie for the magic to work? He finished eating. Still nothing.

"Ah, my break's almost up," he said. "Maybe I can sneak in another cookie before I start working again. Thanks, Felicity."

"Er, sure. No problem." I stumbled away from him and the take-out box. I'd baked all of them without any messages so that no matter which cookie he decided to choose, I'd get a chance to write his fortune.

What was wrong with me? My fortune-telling magic seemed to have disappeared entirely. Then I remembered my mom, and how her magic had recently shifted from spreading happiness to heartbreak. Maybe bad things were happening to my entire family.

The next day, Kelvin had an appointment with Moana. He'd finished his floral-and-candle sample centerpieces and had invited her to come by the shop. I had my own duties that morning, but I thought I could swing by Love Blooms after replenishing our supply of fortune cookies.

Concerned about making the appointment, I finished my baking before Mom. I stocked our front display case like usual, but something felt off despite the bright morning light streaming through the window. Mom should have been busy in the back, but it was weirdly quiet.

I snuck into the kitchen and spotted her standing as if frozen. She looked at a loss for something to do.

"Hey, Mom, everything okay?" I asked.

"Huh? I'm fine. Yes, fine." She blinked at me and started moving. "Just a little slow today."

Mom poured ingredients into the mixing bowl and whisked stuff together. It seemed almost robotic the way she worked.

And it was strangely silent. Mom wasn't humming. Even though she always infused music into her baking.

After she put the batch of egg custards in the oven to bake, I went over to her and squeezed her shoulder. Had she shrunk this past year? I didn't realize until now that I'd gained two inches on her.

She turned and actually looked up at me, which was odd, almost like I was the adult and she was the child.

"It'll be okay, Mom," I said, trying to push actual belief into the words. But even with my (somewhat erratic) fortune-telling gift, I knew I couldn't predict our future for sure.

The timer dinged, and Mom slid the tray of egg tarts out. They looked fine. Perfectly round and ready for consumption. Maybe I was overthinking things.

The first customer rolled in a few minutes later and actually squealed over the treats. She ordered two dozen total: twelve pineapple buns and twelve egg tarts.

"Sorry, I just can't wait," she said as she bit into a tart. Then her face fell. "Did your eggs go bad?"

Mom rushed to her side. "What do you mean?"

"It just tastes . . . I don't know, rotten?"

My mom actually trembled. I don't think she'd ever heard a negative comment about one of her baked goods in her entire life. "I'm pretty sure I checked the dates on the carton."

"Maybe it's a fluke. But, just to be safe, can I get a refund?"

The customer is always right, I thought to myself, as I returned her money. After she left, the rejected egg tarts in their box lay on the counter accusing my mom and me.

Mom couldn't even look at them. She turned to me. "Can you throw them away?"

"She could've been wrong."

Mom's voice shook. "No. I've stopped humming. I must be losing my joy in baking."

"Can that even happen?"

"I didn't think so . . . until now."

Something my mom made up when I was young came to mind. "Hey, Mom, how do you spell Jin?"

"What?" She glanced at me in surprise.

I repeated my question.

"J-I-N," she said.

"No. You spell it J-O-Y."

She gave me a soft smile. "I'd forgotten about that joke."

It had always made me giggle as a kid. Plus, she'd give me a pineapple bun after, which made the whole routine even better.

"Let's start anew," I said, rolling up my sleeves. "And we'll do it together."

"As family. You're right." Mom stood straighter, and I realized I was only actually half an inch taller than her. Whew.

We got back in the kitchen and worked next to each other. She made a new batch of egg tarts, and even hummed something tuneless under her breath.

There was something beautiful about us putting out

treats together side by side in the oven. It was like they were meant to be near each other. As though Mom and I were meant be together, to support one another, always.

Of course, my fortune cookies needed less baking time and got done first. I shaped them with ease even while they were hot to the touch.

"You've sure made a lot," Mom said.

"I'm leaving a batch here and taking a few fortune cookies next door."

"For Kelvin?"

"Yeah. And another friend." Which was a stretch, but I didn't want to go into details about Moana to my mom.

"You know what?" Mom said. "Take the day off. I feel better now."

"Are you certain?" I said.

"Yes, go and hang out with your friends. You deserve more breaks anyway."

I let her return to Mom mode, shooing me out the door, so I could have "socialization" time. It was comforting to return to some of our usual routines.

As I walked out, I clenched the handle of the take-out box. I'd gotten extra fortune cookies for Moana, to test my powers on her. To make sure my magic still worked.

CHAPTER 23

I pushed open the door to Love Blooms, holding the box of fortune cookies out like the offering it was. "Hello? Feeling peckish, anyone?"

Kelvin and Moana were standing over a table cleared of everything except some candle displays. He raised his eyebrows at me.

Probably due to my awkward word choice. Who said *peckish* anymore? I blamed my nerves and tried again. "How is everything going?" I asked. "Get a lot done?"

I scrutinized Kelvin's expression, wanting to know how the investigation portion of his chat had gone. He gave a slight shoulder shrug, but Moana chimed in with plenty to say.

"There are some excellent samples here," she said. "But I've narrowed it down and am trying to decide between two setups."

Moana pointed at one version with a rounded mirror, scattered petals, and tealights. Then she gestured to another sample sans mirror, with slim pillar candles and a bouquet of peach roses at the center.

I chose my words carefully. "They're both *breathtaking*," I said, hoping for a sudden and candid reaction to my statement. After all, hadn't Charlie Gong died from suffocation? I'd predicted something like that in my fortune cookie message that Detective Sun had shown me.

Moana preened as though she'd made the bouquets herself. "Yeah, they're stunning, right?"

Since she was in such a good mood, I decided to ask, "And what happened with those lawsuits? Any update?"

Moana pouted. "Charlie's personal rep is a pain in the you-know-what."

"He's got his own representative? Someone the court assigned him?"

"I don't know, but Kay does not want my clearly rightful claim to go through and keeps talking about defamation."

Kay? Could she have meant Cayla? That woman did seem to like taking charge of things.

Moana continued. "Honestly, I just want things to wrap up before the wedding." She pivoted toward the centerpiece with the pillar candles. "I choose that one."

"Excellent pick," Kelvin said. "I'll send you the invoice soon."

"Whatever you want to charge is fine. I convinced my MIL to cover the flowers and the cake. Sky's the limit now."

Good for her. I passed Moana the box of fortune cookies, purposely brushing my hand against hers. "Want one? They're fresh from the bakery next door."

"Is that the place that gives out customized fortunes? I've been hearing about them." She plucked a fortune cookie out.

I readied myself and reached for the mini notepad in my pocket. It was time to see if I still had my predictive power. I could physically taste my overwhelming desire for the magic to appear; it was a sweet and tangy kind of longing.

She nibbled on the fortune cookie and closed her eyes for a moment, seeming to savor it. A faint rushing sounded in my ears, like the gentle hum of the ocean. Bright colors swam across my vision.

This time, though, I was grounded. I could see the lines but also Moana before me, eating the fortune cookie with delight.

I studied the rainbow colors in front of my eyes and selected green. Once I touched that, my hand itched toward the notepad, and I wrote down the words. The haze passed quicker than before, and I could even read my sentence before I handed the slip over to Moana.

"Your fortune," I told her, hoping she'd been too distracted with the eating to notice me scribbling. "It came in the box."

"Thanks." She looked at the prediction, and her eyes widened. "I really hope so. My man likes rewarding me for doing all this planning that he finds a chore, and I've been craving pasta recently."

I'd written "Your partner is preparing a romantic dinner of DiCicco's takeout."

Moana got a sudden text on her phone. " 'Save your appetite for tonight because you're pasta-tively amazing,' " she read out loud and winked at me. "Seems like that fortune cookie message was right."

I continued to beam even after she left the store. Turning to Kelvin, I said, "Did you hear that? My power is still working."

"That's wonderful, Lissa. And you seemed unfazed about it this time around."

"It's true. I made it through unscathed, with no dizziness."

"How?" he asked. "What did you do differently?"

I thought back to my emotions. "Maybe things worked

out better because I welcomed the power, wasn't fighting against the prediction. I even picked the color with care."

He gave me a strange look. "Say that again?"

I explained how when I received a fortune, I also saw colorful lines. "But why couldn't I predict something for Logan last time?"

"Could've been a fluke," Kelvin said. "Or maybe it's a one-and-done."

"A what?"

"Sometimes I make a special flower arrangement that's unique to the recipient, and I don't use it for anyone else."

"Are you saying I might be able to give out only *one* very personalized fortune to everyone I meet?"

"Would explain it, but who knows?" He gave me a thumbs-up. "Now that you're in tune with your skill, though, you've got plenty of time to explore all the possibilities."

I went home, humming. My skill would blossom, like Kelvin said. I knew I would be able to wield it with more confidence given enough time. And what better way to sharpen my talent than at my family's magical bakery? That was the best place to experiment, and I'd start when we opened in the morning.

Inside the apartment, it was dark, and the curtains were drawn even though it wasn't close to nighttime. "Mom, are you home?"

I noticed her in the living room, in the faux leather recliner. Her eyes looked puffy, and she dabbed at them with a tissue.

"Have you been binge-watching more dramas?" I asked.

She shook her head. In a voice cracked with pain, Mom said, "I can't do it anymore."

I laid a hand on her shoulder, towering above her since she was seated. "Do what anymore?"

"Bake."

I tightened my grip on her. Though I was frightened, she'd always been there for me before, and now I would be strong for her. "You've been baking all your life, Mom. You can't lose a talent like that."

"Felicity"—she removed my hand—"you don't understand. The joy has disappeared from my baking."

"How can that be?"

"I thought I was better, but except for that one batch I made with you by my side, everything else tasted awful." She continued. "We'll need to close the shop. Permanently."

It was as though the spark of false hope had backfired, making her close up her heart even more. I raised my hands, warding off her words. "Let's put a hold on that. I'm still bringing in some revenue, selling fortune cookies at businesses in Fresno."

"That's not the point," Mom said. "If I'm not giving my customers a taste of joy, it's all meaningless."

"Can't we wait a month or two? Until we restabilize?"

Mom sighed. "I think a week is all I have left in me. There's no music anymore with the baking. I can't sing, whistle, or hum."

"Actually I heard you sort of humming when we were baking together," I said.

She wrinkled her brow. "Was I? I didn't notice."

"You were," I said. "Even though there wasn't a melody. But that means things are looking up, right?"

And they'd be even better if I could solve the case soon. I didn't want Mom to even entertain the thought of shutting down the family business—and our Jin way of sharing magic. Moving around our apartment, I pulled open the curtains in our home to let in the light. There was still hope—for my mom, Gold Bakery, and me—to solve the murder.

I reflected further. What did I really know about Charlie Gong's homicide? Nothing. Although the detective seemed to think I knew more than I let on. Because of my fortune cookie message.

What *exactly* had I said again? I plopped down in a dining room chair, and Whiskers hopped closer to me.

"Any more magical answers?" I whispered to her. "I wish I had a better memory of the previous fortunes I'd predicted." I'd finally controlled my writing to some extent, but during those first few times, the thoughts had appeared like manic scribbles from someone else, and I couldn't quite recall their specifics.

The bunny twitched her nose at me. Would it help if I held her? She'd given me flashes of insight before.

I scooped Whiskers up and petted her. "Some assistance with Charlie Gong's fortune would be great."

My mom called out from the other room. "Who are you talking to? Kelvin?"

"Nope. Whiskers." But having my best friend over later might not be a bad idea. He always cheered my mom up.

I continued running my hand across Whiskers' fur in a smooth, hypnotic rhythm. The memory surfaced then.

Detective Sun's face appeared before me. Her voice echoed in my memory: "Too much concrete knowledge will surely suffocate you."

What had Charlie gotten evidence of? Something related to the businesses he'd been involved in? Or could it have been Moana's lawsuit? I didn't know enough about his personal or professional life to make any conjectures.

Maybe I could focus on the second part of that sentence. Suffocation. How many ways could a man suffocate? I tried to think back to the day we'd found the police swarming in the alley. I hadn't even seen the body at all, just the bag that they'd zipped him up in.

Why had he been found in the dumpster in the first place? Was it to get rid of his body, or had Charlie been walking around there—and someone had confronted him? Was his death a planned crime, or one of passion and opportunity?

I had a lot of questions, and I knew two heads were better than one. Besides, it'd been a while since Kelvin, my mom, and I had eaten dinner together.

CHAPTER 24

Kelvin had a longstanding tradition of eating quarterly dinners with my mom and me. It was a regularly scheduled chance for our trio to bond and catch up on one another's lives. The routine had started when we were younger, after Kelvin's mom had passed away and his dad had taken on more hours at the hospital.

Even though Mom considered Kelvin family, he always remembered to show up with a hostess gift for these dinners. He also took off his shoes without being asked, which Mom said was a sign of good manners.

Kelvin beamed at my mom tonight and offered her a sprig of yellow daisies. "Thanks again for opening up your home, Mrs. Jin."

"Of course. And these are lovely." Mom said that every time—except on the one occasion Kelvin had given her stargazer lilies. She'd dumped those blooms in the trash. They were the signature flowers that my father used to give her.

My mom placed the daisies in the already prepped crystal vase at the center of the dining table. "How is Ansel?" she asked Kelvin.

My best friend mumbled, "Dad's good. Same as usual—busy."

My only recollections of Mr. Love involved him running off in scrubs. He was a tall man with a closely shaved head and a trim goatee. When I was younger, I adored his smile, the way his eyes crinkled with warmth. But it was rare that he smiled after Mrs. Love passed away.

Kelvin turned to me. "Need some help in the kitchen tonight?"

"Very funny. It's a simple meal per tradition," I said, but then realized maybe he'd offered more for himself—to take his mind off his dad's constantly busy schedule. "Though I guess you can wash the celery and peel the carrots."

I was always in charge of the food for these quarterly get-togethers, and I opted for one-skillet meals. The fact that I could cook a little offered me solace for the many years I couldn't bake to save my life. I could even mess up a bit with the measurements while cooking and still salvage the meal.

Tonight, I'd decided on cashew chicken, which only required that the nuts, celery, carrots, and meat be tossed together with oyster sauce. It didn't require much work, and we got the table all set within half an hour.

Our dinner conversation consisted of the happy events in our lives. We skirted around heavier topics like murder, or failing magical baking abilities. Mom chatted about her latest TV series binge. I talked about my fortune cookie deals with the small grocery stores in Fresno. Kelvin discussed being featured in wedding magazines and various blogs for his floral arrangements.

Then Mom brought out the dessert. Usually, we had a carton of ice cream in our freezer at the ready. But this time, she gave us all egg tarts.

"Is this from the bakery?" I asked.

Mom sighed. "I made too much again. Guess I overestimated the amount of customers who'd be coming in."

"Maybe we should up our hours again. Get more people through the door."

My mom shook her head. "I don't know. My baking is still . . . Well, why don't you try one?"

Kelvin happily munched on an egg tart and gave her a thumbs-up.

I took my time to chew the pastry to analyze it. There was definitely something off. First, the technical aspects seemed wrong. The crust wasn't flaky enough, and the custard was almost runny. Then the underlying emotions were off. There was a swirl of sadness mixed in with the egg, and a touch of despair in the butter.

What if my mom was right about her baking troubles? Would this downturn in her happiness continue and ruin her inner magic? I hedged my words. "They taste mostly right. I'm sure the customers won't even notice."

Kelvin took another egg tart and gobbled it down. "Yeah, these are scrumptious."

My mom curled her hands into fists. "Not everyone is as kind as you, Kelvin. I can tell it's wrong, and I would hate giving my customers bad-tasting pastries."

I glanced at Kelvin, pleading for some help.

"You're probably too sensitive. I'm sure you still have top marks online," he said, pulling out his phone. "Let's check Yelp."

I couldn't help peeking over his shoulder and reading out loud. "The latest review says, 'I love the goodies from Gold Bakery . . .'" I didn't finish the rest of the sentence.

Mom noticed my pause. "Go on."

I stayed silent, and my mom appealed to Kelvin to

continue. She knew his weakness; he would comply, and he'd never been able to lie outright to her face.

"Well, the customer doesn't like the shorter hours. Said she's only able to come in after two p.m., so the new schedule is a bother."

That struck a familiar chord, and I checked the profile pic. "Can you click on the name?"

It was Sweet Tooth Sally. I was a little disappointed she'd felt the need to vent online even after we'd chatted face-to-face, but I put that aside and wondered if she'd gotten any leads since we'd last talked. "You know what, Mom? Why don't I add a few hours to our schedule? I can use the extra time to exclusively sell my fortune cookies. Once we, of course, sell out of your treats, people will have to try mine."

"I'm okay with that idea," Mom said. "It takes the pressure off, too. I'll make fewer pineapple buns and egg tarts from now on, so people will buy yours."

"Or maybe Lissa can take a shot at baking them," Kelvin said.

I almost reared back in my seat. "Not a good idea."

"Come on," Kelvin said. "You've practically perfected your fortune cookie recipe now. How hard could it be to graduate from that?"

Florists. They didn't know anything about baking.

Mom angled herself toward his phone. "What other comments have we gotten?"

Kelvin used his body to shield the phone, but Mom was quicker. She'd already read the next review and gasped.

She jabbed a finger at the screen. "This other customer actually said my pineapple bun made him cry. And not with happiness."

"Just someone trolling," Kelvin said.

"Do you get trolls on your account?" Mom asked.

"Um . . ."

She held her hand out for his phone, and he relented. Mom searched for Love Blooms and read from his latest Yelp review. "'Kelvin is a genius.' This Moana person goes on and on about your brilliance."

Kelvin started slouching in his chair, as though hiding from the compliments. "She just liked my idea for her wedding centerpieces, that's all. And most of the credit goes to Alma's amazing candles, which pair beautifully with my flowers."

"Paz Illuminations. I'll check them next," Mom said. If only she weren't so familiar with apps and phones.

Mom started listing all the wonderful comments people made about my godmother's shop. "There's only one semi-negative remark here," she said. "And it's from that same Moana gal."

"Really?" Kelvin and I said together.

We both scooted closer to the phone. Moana had made a comment about Alma's store. That it'd been closed when she'd gone there one afternoon.

Or at least, Moana had thought it'd been closed. Paz Illuminations' dark interior had fooled more than one customer before. When had her failed excursion to Paz Illuminations taken place? I checked the date of the post. It was the day of her missed appointment, the day of Charlie's murder.

CHAPTER 25

Mom did scale down her baking efforts, so much that when I went in the next day, I'd sold almost all her goodies by two in the afternoon. Exactly five minutes past the hour, Sweet Tooth Sally rushed in.

Her face was flushed red. "Finally," she said. "I caught you."

"Oh. Were you looking for me?"

"You, or Angela." Sally glanced around the store.

"Mom left early," I said, "but I'll be around during the afternoon hours in the interim for your shopping pleasure."

"Great, but this isn't about my taste buds. It concerns that murder case . . . I found an eyewitness," she said.

Thank goodness her network connections had paid off. "You're a lifesaver."

She beamed. "I try my best. And your treats did get people talking."

I leaned over the counter. "Who's the witness?"

"It's old Mrs. Spreckels."

The librarian at Pixie Public Library. She'd had strands of silver in her hair when I'd been growing up, and now she had a full head of white. More to the point, the library was right around the corner, on the only main street leading to the cul-de-sac of shops and the back alley where Charlie Gong had been found.

"What did she see?" I asked.

Sally chewed on her bottom lip. "Unfortunately, not a lot."

"That's unusual. Mrs. Spreckels is so observant." She noticed misshelved books or any sort of mischief in the stacks. I'd gotten a warning once or twice for just squeaking a chair at the library.

Sally continued. "Mrs. Spreckels didn't see much, but she had the door open to take in the evening breeze and heard something. A thumping noise and someone sprinting down the road."

My hands felt clammy against the countertop. "The murderer?"

"Could have been. When she finally got to the doorway, she only noticed a blurred running figure."

"She couldn't make out anything?"

Sally shrugged. "It was getting dark by then. But this person? They'd been bolting away from the direction of your cul-de-sac."

I wiped my sweaty palms against my jeans to dry them. "Why didn't Mrs. Spreckels say anything to the police about this?"

"She figured it was someone out for a jog." Sally hemmed. "Plus, she did get a speeding ticket in Fresno a few years back."

Mrs. Spreckels had a fine memory to go with her sharp eyes, I'd give her that. I guess she could also hold on to a grudge for a while. "Do you think she'll talk to the police now? To help us out?"

Sally's face softened. "For your mom and Gold Bakery? Yes, I think she would."

I rummaged through the store, looking on shelves and

in piles of paper before I dredged up the detective's business card. Then I made the call.

Detective Sun and I showed up that very same evening to the local library branch. Sally couldn't make it to the interview, and Mrs. Spreckels had insisted on having a third party to witness the conversation, so I obliged. The detective had reluctantly agreed to the old lady's demands in order to get her eyewitness statement.

Pixie Public Library's stately brick building, with its arched windows and doorway, really was an architectural marvel. It always made me feel minuscule in a soothing the-world-is-bigger-than-your-problems sort of way.

Something about the wealth of knowledge hidden inside the library, facts that I could obtain with a mere flip of the page, made me smile. I didn't go into the library as often as I would have liked because of the bakery's hours and my general exhaustion afterward, but whenever I did, it transported me to earlier, happier days.

I still loved the hush-hush sound (or, ideally, absence of noise) of the library. Mrs. Spreckels made sure a solemn silence reigned in her biblio-kingdom. The towering shelves of the library practically touched the ceiling, and sometimes I was afraid for the building if a big earthquake ever hit our town.

Mrs. Spreckels stood behind the curved circulation desk made of aged oak, peering at us through her horn-rimmed glasses. She gave the detective and me a curt nod and beckoned us toward the office behind the info desk.

I'd never been back there, but I imagined it was where they stocked all the new arrivals, saving the best for the librarians before releasing them to the public. But instead of a cave of literary wonders, I was disappointed to find a small space crammed with file folders, rolling step stools, and hard-backed chairs.

The librarian closed the door, leaving a small crack to peek through. Then she sat down, and I pulled another chair over to her side and followed suit.

Detective Sun stood, leaning her back against one of the crammed walls and said, "Thanks for making the time to see me, Mrs. Spreckels."

She pursed her lips. "I'm doing this as a favor to Sally, who's president of our Friends of the Library group. Otherwise, I might not have gone through the hassle."

Detective Sun slipped out her phone. "Okay if I record this?"

"I suppose so."

The detective tried to get further details out of Mrs. Spreckels on what she'd seen the night of the murder. The librarian repeated the story I'd heard from Sally about her witnessing someone running outside the building.

"When was this exactly?"

Mrs. Spreckels glanced at the schoolhouse clock on the wall. "Around six in the evening."

"And where were you standing at that time?"

Mrs. Spreckels motioned to the outside lobby. "There. Close to the top shelf next to the front door."

Detective Sun pointed at the librarian's spectacles. "Were you wearing those?"

"Yes, I was tidying up the books and needed my reading lenses." She touched the beaded-chain eyeglass holder looped around her neck.

"And what did you hear specifically?" the detective asked.

She tugged on her right earlobe and tsked. "Pounding steps. Which, sadly, disturbed the peace of the library."

"So you went to take a look and noticed . . ."

"A figure running."

"From the direction of the bakery?" Detective Sun said.

"Yes, that's right."

Detective Sun brought the phone closer to Mrs. Spreckels' mouth for clearer diction, I assumed. "Was it a man or a woman that you saw?"

"Honestly, it was kind of a blur," she said. "But if I had to wager—though I'm not a betting woman, mind you, not even the California lottery—I'd put my money on a man."

"Why's that?"

"From the heavy tread of the footsteps and the general broadness of the body," she said.

"Interesting. Anything else you recall?"

"Only their yellow running shoes. After they ran off, I lost interest and went back to work."

"You know," Detective Sun said, "I asked every business around here about that evening. Why didn't you mention this earlier?"

"Like I said, I thought it was someone out for a jog. They seemed harmless enough."

"We asked people to tell us everything they heard, saw, even smelled that evening."

Mrs. Spreckels pulled out a cloth from the pocket of her oversize cardigan and wiped her eyeglasses. "Guess I didn't want to inconvenience the Fresno police with tiny details that might not matter." She'd said "Fresno" with clear disdain.

Detective Sun raised her eyebrow, and I explained, "Sometimes Pixie residents find it, um, easier to speak to locals about things."

"The two towns are right next to each other. Aren't they local enough?"

Mrs. Spreckels put her glasses back on, and we exchanged a look.

"Fresno isn't the same as Pixie," I said. "Very different."

The detective's posture stiffened, but she didn't change the professional indifference etched across her face. "Well, I want to thank you for your time, Mrs. Spreckels."

After we left the library, I said to Detective Sun, "That was great. Since it was most likely a man whom Mrs. Spreckels saw, I'm surely off the hook?"

"Not quite," the detective said with her characteristic sternness. "I still think it's odd that she didn't step forward earlier."

"Pixie ways," I said.

"And it's extremely convenient that you happened to find an eyewitness whose testimony helps you out."

"She's just sharing what really happened that night. You will look into it, right?"

The detective tightened her ponytail with a quick tug. "I follow up on all the leads I get."

Excellent. It wasn't a total promise, but I was sure I could spin it to my mom in a way that made it seem like I'd moved down the suspect list. Maybe some encouraging news would finally boost her mood.

CHAPTER 26

I walked back to inform Mom about the positive turn of events, whistling along the way. Wait, what? Yes, I was actually whistling while walking. Maybe mirth did spread through music like my mom had always told me.

As I stepped into our cul-de-sac of shops, I noticed the door to Paz Illuminations yawning wide open. Sometimes my godmother propped it ajar, especially when a customer complained about the darkness inside.

At the counter, Alma was helping a woman wearing a purple jumpsuit with a matching headband in her brown hair. I halted. Could it be Moana in there? Who else matched their hair accessories to their clothes?

My godmother was ringing up the purchases, and the woman shifted, giving me a view of her profile. I edged closer and listened to her all-too-familiar voice.

"No, thank you. I have my own," Moana said. She dug into her purse, pulling out condiment packets before finding some plastic carryout bags.

At least she'd finally gone to visit the candle shop in person. They must have made amends about the missed appointment. Or maybe Moana was making up for it now through her copious purchases of candles for the wedding centerpieces and some extras I assumed were just for fun.

Go Alma, I thought. Not that she needed Moana's business. I'd never seen the Yelp ratings for Paz Illuminations dip below four stars. My happy mood soared a little higher.

When I reached home, I burst through the door and said, "I have good news, Mom."

"Really?" She got up from where she sat in the recliner, her hands half covering her face, and met me in the entryway.

"Talked to Detective Sun earlier," I said, "and she's on the lookout for new suspects."

"Why, that's wonderful." Mom's face appeared to pinken with delight.

Whiskers hopped over to celebrate with us. At least, that's what it seemed like. That bunny could tune in to our moods like nobody's business.

Mom bent over and scooped her up. "We should mark the occasion."

"How?" I asked.

After a few moments of petting Whiskers and thinking, Mom said, "What about some baking?"

Yes! She actually wanted to bake again. I felt like world had re-righted itself. "That would be wonderful, Mom."

"And I have a brilliant idea for more recipes."

My mom had kept to the family's traditional pineapple buns and egg tarts for as long as I could remember. "I'm so excited you're back to baking, *and* you want to expand our usual inventory."

"Make tiny variations to them," she said, easing Whiskers down to the ground.

"That does sound like fun," I admitted.

When the bunny paused near me, I stroked her ears, and said in a whisper, "Thanks for all your help."

She twitched her whiskers and hopped away.

Mom flung open the cupboards in the kitchen, rummaging through the shelves. "We can keep the traditional recipes but infuse a little extra something in them. How do you feel about adding coconut to the pineapple buns?"

"Mmm, sounds delicious."

She took out a bag of shredded coconut.

I rolled up my sleeves. "Let's do this," I said.

The hours passed by in a flash as we worked together in the kitchen. Mom hummed the whole time, and I even started murmuring during the process.

She caught my tuneful murmurs. "That's kind of musical sounding."

"Yeah, I guess you were right on that count. The whistling, humming. Happiness can be like an overflowing song."

By the time we'd gone through three batches, Mom had crafted a new tasty recipe that had incorporated the coconut. I still enjoyed our traditional family version, but this new kind had a nice spin on it.

I bit into one and said, "This reminds me of vacations and relaxation."

"Joy comes in many forms," my mom said, as she wiped a bit of flour off her forehead. "And we can discover different ways to get there."

Although Mom was still fixated on joy as the family purpose, she was stretching her baking philosophy on how that could be obtained. She didn't need to follow the recipes line by line from long ago. She could innovate and still adhere to the Jin ways.

I wanted to encourage her newfound flexibility and modern way of thinking. "Agreed, Mom. I think a whole new line of pineapple buns could be sold in the bakery. For example, we could add custard—"

"Good idea. I'm going to jot a few different flavors down," she said, grabbing a notepad off a nearby counter.

She started brainstorming and scribbling.

While she wrote, I spoke aloud, "You know, maybe I could have various fortune cookie flavors, too?"

"I'm sure the customers would love them," Mom said. "As well as those grocery stores you're partnering with in Fresno."

I was thrilled to hear she was finally fully supportive of the inroads I'd been making with other shops. I could supply the stores with multiple flavors, and who knows what might happen after? "We're going to be the talk of the town, of the state! With your extra pineapple bun flavors and my growing range of fortune cookies, we'll be unstoppable."

We spent time dreaming away of a future where our shop was the pastry-producing star of Pixie. Or maybe beyond. People would travel from afar and go to our small town to seek us out. Hey, hadn't others from Fresno come to visit Gold Bakery already? That was a small step on our path to culinary fame.

The next day, I thought I'd share my potential new fortune cookie flavors with people outside my immediate family. I figured I should poll the Fresno grocery stores to see if they'd be interested in stocking other cookies beyond the usual vanilla ones. Then I could tell if it'd be a wise business decision.

Mrs. Santos at the Asian grocery store appeared happy to see me again. "Welcome back. Your fortune cookies are a hit, dear."

"Great. That's a pleasure to hear." I paused, before

deciding to dive right in. "Do you think customers would like other flavors besides vanilla?"

She hesitated. "Maybe, but let's stick with the traditional taste for now."

"Should I deliver more of those to you?" I readied myself for price negotiations and some abacus clacking on her part.

"Not yet," she said. "Let me get rid of some of my older stock first. I overlooked a few boxes left in the storeroom. I'm hoping I can return them to Smiley Fortunes for a refund."

"Good luck." I wondered if the factory would even take them back. They seemed like they were struggling as it was without getting returned orders. "Call me if you need any more."

"I will," Mrs. Santos said.

I moved on to the second store, the one with the special section for local businesses. The same man I'd seen before greeted me. "Good to see you," Jeremy said.

"How's business?" I asked.

"Fine. Are you, like, just dropping in?"

"Actually, I'm here specifically to follow up. I hope the cookies are doing well?"

"Excellent," Jeremy said. "We're almost out of stock."

"Wonderful, because I have new flavors available."

His dark brown eyes widened with delight. "I'll take some. And, wow, what great customer service, checking in on me. Nothing like that other guy."

"Michael Fu?" I asked. He'd mentioned connecting with the Foo Fusion owner previously, and of course, Michael had been the one to give me the hot tip to reach out to him.

Jeremy stroked his beard. "Not him. This man also sold fortune cookies."

Could he mean the Fortune Cookie King? "Was it Charlie Gong?"

"I didn't catch the guy's name. He hadn't gotten around to introducing himself before he got a call in my shop. And he, like, had the nerve to take it right in front of me."

I suddenly remembered that Charlie had also been fidgeting with his cell the day he'd ordered a fortune cookie from us. "Did he have bangs? Long enough to cover what might be a receding hairline?"

"Uh-huh." Jeremy frowned. "I thought it was quite unprofessional for him to take the call while giving me a pitch about his products."

"It might have been an urgent matter," I hedged, trying to give the dead man the benefit of the doubt.

Jeremy shrugged. "The phone call definitely got under his skin. He started, like, pacing up and down the aisles. I could tell he was irritated because he almost sounded like he was wheezing as he spoke."

I tried to say my next words in a casual manner. "You happen to know what he was talking about?" The conversation might contain a clue to the murder or the killer.

"Something about a lawsuit and having gone in to court that morning. Still, that was no excuse to be rude to me."

I wondered when Charlie had visited the store. "Do you remember which day he came by?"

"Nah. Didn't write it down because I never ended up making a deal with him."

Too bad. "You decided you didn't want the fortune cookies he offered?"

"He didn't even give me a sample to try, unlike you. Just rushed out the door, mumbling about a rival baker."

A *rival baker*? Could those words have referred to me and Gold Bakery? I wondered if Charlie had visited the grocery store the day he'd sped over to our shop. The same day he'd died. And according to the overheard phone conversation, he'd already been to court that morning, no doubt dealing with Moana's lawsuit.

CHAPTER 27

Charlie Gong must have been dealing with a lot the day he died, I thought, as I left the Fresno grocery store. I'd gotten a new order for a dozen chocolate fortune cookies, which should have put me in a good mood. However, my mind was still mulling over Charlie's bad destiny.

He'd had to deal with a lawsuit, fortune cookie competition, and finally an attack all in one day. And who had decided to literally take his breath away? Well, at least according to Mrs. Spreckels, it was most likely a man.

Since I was already on my fortune cookie run, I decided to approach the restaurant owner Michael Fu. He'd be easy to track down at Foo Fusion. And he was a man. I dared to hope my suspect list was finally dwindling.

I found him behind the front register when I walked in, as usual. He smiled at me. Michael always seemed to be working—was it just him and the chef keeping the whole restaurant running? But right as I had that thought, someone popped out from the kitchen. It was a worker in a rumpled dress shirt with jeans. "Need a break, boss?" he asked.

Michael nodded, slipped a piece of paper into a pocket, and pulled me aside to an empty table. "Just the person I wanted to see."

"Really?" I thought I'd need to go into my prepared pitch as a cover for snooping.

"I need more fortune cookies," he said.

"Perfect. There are these new flavors I'm thinking of adding." I started listing them, but Michael interrupted me.

"Will they be cheap?" he asked.

"Excuse me?"

"Inexpensive," he said. "Cheaper than the ones I'm currently stocking."

I calculated in my mind. "No, probably more, because I'll need to put in the special ingredients."

"Uh-uh." He shook his head. "I need cheap and fast, not pricey and gourmet."

"For what?"

He pointed to a blank wall near us, a wide expanse of whiteness. What on earth was he trying to say?

"I'm not following you . . ."

"I need to drum up more business, make a bigger profit. And this will help," he said.

I blinked at the nothingness.

"It's the Fortune Cookie Wall of Fame," he said. "Imagine rows of customer photos adorning that space."

"And how do the fortune cookies fit in?"

His eyes sparkled. "It'll be a competition. All-you-can-eat fortune cookies. Brilliant, eh?"

"I've heard of eating challenges before . . . but don't you want to do it with your own dishes? Advertise the food here?"

"No, too much cost." He gave me a sly grin. "But your fortune cookies. I can fill up their tummies with those."

I wasn't sure if that was a compliment or not. Were my cookies delicious or just plain cheap? Then again, all you can eat would mean a lot of fortune cookies, a bulk order. "How many would you need?"

"Glad you asked." Michael extracted the paper he'd put in his pocket earlier. "I have a contract all ready for you to sign."

I perused the document. Whoa, he did need a lot of fortune cookies in a short amount of time. I also checked the per-cookie payment. "This is a ton of work. I think we should renegotiate the terms—"

He glared at me. "Take it or leave it. I'm through with troublemakers and cheats."

"What does that mean?" I asked.

"If someone can't handle the increased workload, they get cut. That's my new motto."

I snuck a glance at the employee covering the register and felt sorry for the guy. I'd hate to work for a boss like Michael.

"I'm going to have to think about it," I said.

"Go ahead. But don't take too long. People these days think too highly of themselves. Anyone is replaceable."

That almost sounded like a threat, and I shivered but pocketed the contract. "I'll be in touch."

"The sooner, the better." Michael got up from the table and headed toward the register.

I bristled. Michael seemed to always ask for more and more. Was this how it was partnering with him? Had Charlie felt the same way and tried to make trouble—only to eventually end up in trouble himself?

Michael Fu's offer did sound tempting in some ways. It'd definitely rake in more money for our bakery. But could Mom and I complete it without overworking ourselves?

To get a handle on our finances, I'd better check in

with Mom on how the day went at the bakery. It'd taken longer than I'd anticipated to do the entire Fresno run, so she was already back home when I returned from my surveying.

"How were sales?" I asked Mom, who stood in the middle of the kitchen with a vacant look on her face.

She shook her head. "Oh, they were fine."

"Did you sell any of those new coconut pineapple buns?"

"Maybe three or four." She flashed me a brief smile before returning to her previous distracted state.

"Everything all right?"

"How was your trip?" she asked as I put away my purse. I'd noticed she completely avoided my question to her, but decided to let it go for the moment.

I recounted my chats with the two store owners, leaving out the juicy investigative bits.

She put a hand on my shoulder. "An order for your new chocolate fortune cookies? You're on your way to making it big, Felicity."

"Hardly," I said, but at least I was perfecting my sales pitching. "There's also another opportunity available."

"Really?"

"I decided to drop by Foo Fusion while I was there." I pulled out the contract.

Mom slid on her reading glasses, and we both went through the paper together.

"I wish the terms were better," she said after a bout of silence.

"Me, too. But he was unwilling to negotiate."

She took off her glasses and placed them on top of the contract.

"He's asking for a ton of fortune cookies," I said.

Mom rubbed her eyes. "You know what I say about

quality over quantity but . . . it would be helpful to us financially." She pointed at a letter lying on the kitchen table.

"What's that?"

"It's from the landlord for downtown Pixie businesses. He's requesting an increase in our rent for the store space."

I'd forgotten that it was time to renew our lease. It never rained but it poured.

"Is it just a cost of living increase?"

"That, and more." She sighed.

As I knew only too well, we'd been operating at reduced hours recently. Even with my new contacts at the Fresno groceries and Mom selling a little more at the bakery with her latest recipes, I guessed that it wouldn't cover our higher rental rate.

I gripped Michael Fu's contract in my hand. "Don't worry, Mom. I can do this."

"Are you sure?" She looked deep into my eyes.

"Of course," I lied.

Mom stared at me.

"Okay, I might just need a tiny bit of help, so who can pitch in?"

Mom held her hands up. "Definitely not me. I tried to help my own mother before, and it was a total disaster. We were baking together, working on the same recipe, and while the pineapple bun looked okay on the outside, it was terrible to eat."

"I don't understand. Both you and Po Po are talented bakers." I paused. "Was something off with the ingredients?"

"It wasn't that. And we followed the directions exactly. They were just overly sweet. Inedible when finished, and those buns certainly didn't bring anyone joy. Maybe there was too much Jin-ness involved."

Too much magic or power to be contained in a pastry? I didn't know that was a thing. "Fine," I said. "I'll ask Kelvin."

She scrunched up her nose like she'd smelt burnt sugar. "No, that might be risky, too. Your, um, father tried to help me bake once. Got a massive headache and almost lost consciousness."

Geez. I didn't know pastry making could be so dangerous. Or maybe it was our magic affecting innocent bystanders. But could I make enough fortune cookies on my own?

Huh. Did it have to be human hands that helped me? We were in the twenty-first century after all. Couldn't I get a little technological assistance? I had an idea.

CHAPTER 28

At the fortune cookie factory, the door was unlocked and I decided to walk right in. Nobody greeted me. The two employees were focused on their jobs, probably doing extra duties now that they were one employee short. Cayla Jung, the manager, had her back turned to me, with her phone glued to her ear.

They wouldn't mind if I had a closer inspection of their equipment, right? I went up to the industrial stirrer. How many more batches of fortune cookies could I whip up if I wasn't churning the batter by hand?

Still unaware of me, Cayla's voice took on a pleading tone. "Are you sure you don't want any fortune cookies?" she asked. "We've reformulated things. They taste so much better now."

I moved farther away from her, toward the batter-dispensing station.

Cayla cursed and hung up with the caller. Then she spotted me and strode over. "What are you doing here?"

"Don't worry, I've come about a business proposition."

She put her hands on her hips. "Power hungry, anyone? I don't think you have enough money to buy us out."

"No, I'm wondering . . ." I gestured at the space

around me. "Could I rent this place when it's not being actively used?"

"Oh, do you have a crew now?" She looked over my shoulder, as though searching for the numerous employees lined up behind me.

"Actually—"

She grimaced. "Is it Logan? Did he defect over to you? I should give him a piece of my mind." Cayla tapped on her phone, perhaps searching through her contacts.

"Honestly, I don't have any new employees," I said. "It's just me and my mom. Always has been and always will be." Especially with the rules about the magical baking she'd just given me. No one else could help bake my special fortune cookies even if I wanted them to.

Cayla stuck her phone in her back pocket. "Anyway, renting our space is not an option. We keep this place constantly humming."

"I can tell," I said, hoping to placate her with a few compliments as the workers scrambled to and fro. "Everyone is working so hard."

"A good manager makes sure people use their talents."

She could've used that saying for a fortune cookie message. At the thought, I naturally glanced toward the pile of printed papers. The woman worker I'd seen before was slipping them inside the fortune cookies and then folding the hot discs over a rod. At least she had gloves on, unlike poor Logan.

Even that metal tool instead of the cup I used to shape a fortune cookie might speed up my production time. "Can I just buy something small from you? You won't even miss it. You've got a lot of equipment in here."

She shook her head. "Sorry, can't help you."

"At least tell me where you purch—"

Her phone rang, and she pulled it out of her pocket. "Hello?"

She didn't have time for me right now. Or maybe ever.

I exited the factory just as I heard Cayla say, "You've got the wrong number."

It was a sad twist of irony that nobody was currently happy at the Smiley Fortunes factory. Despite Cayla's wishes, I could tell they were in trouble if she was begging people for orders. Maybe it was better that Logan had finally moved on.

Now that I thought about it, he'd be a good person to ask about the equipment. After having worked with those very tools day in and out, he'd have a good sense of where to order them, right? Or at least he'd be aware of their brand name. Even better, it would give me a justification for another chat with Logan. If he let something slip about murder while talking, of course, that'd only be a bonus.

I liked to do many things with my best friend, but bickering with him ranked at the bottom of the list. Especially while parked in front of a busy furniture store.

"I still can't believe you didn't tell me earlier about your solo sleuthing efforts," Kelvin said in the car.

"I'm sure you were too busy at Love Blooms to tag along. By the way, congrats on all the hype for your floral work."

He gave me a death stare. "Compliments are not getting you out of this, Lissa. You talked to potentially dangerous people all alone. Suspects in a murder case."

"Actually, no." I pointed to the storefront. "That's why I brought you here."

"And what about Michael Fu?"

"The restaurant owner?" I snorted. "He's a balding middle-aged man."

Kelvin held up a warning finger. "Doesn't mean he's not dangerous."

"There were witnesses around."

"One of whom was in his pay. At least you didn't sign a new contract with the guy."

"Not yet, but it would help business at the bakery."

"Nope, nope, nope. You're not thinking straight." Kelvin squeezed the gear shift like it was a stress ball. "If it comes down to it, I'll float you and your mom a loan."

"Thanks, but no." In all our years of running the bakery, we'd never relied on anyone else's generosity. If we couldn't make it on our precious baked goods, we didn't deserve to survive. At least that was the kind of thinking that had been passed down from my great-great-grandmother.

"There's our guy now." Kelvin jutted his chin toward the windshield.

"Finally." I'd called the number on his business card, but it hadn't gone through. Then I'd tried the furniture store. He was still working at the place but hadn't started his shift for the day yet.

"Wow, he's doing some heavy lifting," Kelvin said.

True. Logan was carrying out a velvet recliner to a pickup truck in the parking lot. Although he didn't seem to be breaking a sweat. "Looks like he's truly recovered from his injury." There was no bandage or anything constricting his movements.

"All right, remember the plan," Kelvin said. "You talk to him about the fortune cookie stuff, and I'll try to get him to open up more about being in Pixie on that fateful day."

I poked him in the ribs. "Why do you get to do all the fun stuff?"

"In case he decides to come after one of us, I'd rather it be me than you." He puffed out his chest, in prime protection mode.

"Okay, bruh." Really, Kelvin could be over the top sometimes, like I was his baby sis to shield. Or was there a different kind of emotion guiding his protectiveness? That was too messy to explore right now, so I jumped into action to avoid thinking about it.

Without waiting for him, I left the car and moved toward the furniture store. He had to jog a little to catch up. Served him right. I left the satisfied smile on my face even once he was by my side as we walked inside the air-conditioned building.

I found Logan in the section he was in charge of: couches. His features tightened when he noticed Kelvin and me walking over, but he greeted us in a cordial voice.

All part of his new business persona, I suspected. I noticed that he wore another dress shirt, this time with a subtle striped tie.

"I've been trying to get ahold of you," I said, "but your number doesn't seem to be working."

"Changed it," he said. "I'm having a complete break from the past. No more factory work. This way, they won't be able to track me down." Logan straightened his tie.

"About that," I said, "I'm actually looking for some baking equipment. What brand did you use at Smiley Fortunes?"

He shrugged. "Beats me. I don't examine the machines."

"But you were there, day in and day out."

"Charlie would've known the name."

I cast my eyes down and let a moment of silent respect

pass. "So you don't know where I can buy some baking stuff?"

"Charlie stockpiled the equipment. Kept it all in the storeroom in the back for when we scaled up. He had a big vision of expanding. Wanted to exchange his Fortune Cookie King title for Fortune Cookie Emperor someday."

Cayla had been holding back on me. She definitely had extra machines that I could have rented or purchased. I bet she didn't want to help a rival baker, even though our recipes were totally different. Hers, for sure, lacked magic.

Logan waved his hand over a futon. "Did you actually want to buy any furniture today?"

"Just browsing," I said, "but I'll be sure to mention your name if I do get anything. If I remember right, you work on commission?"

He nodded and started turning away. I elbowed Kelvin and gave him a look of incredulity. When was he going to start the investigating bit?

Kelvin wrung his hands and called out to Logan's back: "Hey man, nice shoes. They look brand new."

Logan pivoted around, finally seeming engaged in the conversation. "The wingtips *are* new. I got them for this job. Not my usual style, but you gotta dress for success."

"I like my Docs," Kelvin said, showing off his footwear. Really, they were going to talk about shoes for the next twenty minutes?

My best friend kept going, sizing up Logan. "You look active. Into sports? Maybe track?"

"Basketball sometimes," Logan said. "And I love my yellow Adidas."

I stumbled and knocked over a floor lamp. Before it

could crash all the way onto the floor, Kelvin caught it. "Whoa, there."

Logan raised an eyebrow at me. "You break it, you pay for it."

I checked the price tag. Five hundred dollars for a light? Not on my measly fortune-cookie-making salary.

An associate of Logan's, also in a dress shirt and tie, flagged him down. "You got a call on line one, man."

"Who is it?"

"A lady. Name of Rylan Sun."

So the detective had figured out Logan's current place of employment. Good. Maybe talking to Logan would get her off my back once and for all.

Taking that as our cue, Kelvin and I excused ourselves. In the car, he asked, "Lissa, are you really okay? Back there in the store, did you have one of your headaches again?"

"No. It was because of what Logan said."

"But he's not into track. He isn't a runner, like the person Mrs. Spreckels saw." Kelvin thumped the wheel with the heel of his hand.

"Yes, but Logan does wear sporty shoes."

Kelvin frowned. "A lot of people wear sneakers."

"Not yellow ones, and that's what Mrs. Spreckels remembered from the person who'd been fleeing."

Kelvin whistled. "Great, our job's done then."

"After we report it to the authorities," I said. "Although Detective Sun might have gotten that info out of Logan already with her current call."

"Still, we did good back there."

"Yeah, we're a great team." I gave him a fist bump.

But part of me was unsure. Could it really be so simple? Logan had admitted to owning yellow sneakers, but did that necessarily mean he was the killer? Still, passing the information on to Detective Sun couldn't hurt.

As Kelvin left his parking spot, I spied Logan coming out of the furniture store. He seemed slightly bent over, with his hand to his back, as though he were in pain. I craned my neck and watched as Logan slowly straightened up. Weird.

At the entrance to the shopping center, Kelvin paused, watching for incoming traffic before attempting to turn onto the main road. He grumbled at the new vehicle darting into the lot. "Someone's in a rush."

I glanced at the vehicle, then looked again. It wasn't just anybody in a hurry. "That was Detective Sun."

"Guess she decided to talk to him in person," Kelvin said as he turned on to the main street.

"Wonderful," I said. "At this rate, things will be wrapped up by tomorrow morning."

Justice would get served, and I'd finally have my life back on track.

CHAPTER 29

Things were not wrapped up the next day. In fact, everything got much worse.

"And it's all your fault," Detective Sun said, pacing back and forth in Gold Bakery.

My mom was sitting behind the register, and she alternated between giving both the cop and me gruff looks. It was seven in the morning, and none of us were at our best.

I held my hands up. "Logan and I were merely having a casual conversation."

"What exactly did you say to him?"

"We were talking about fortune cookies."

The detective stopped before me. "That wouldn't have tipped him off."

The door to the bakery sprang open, and Kelvin rushed in.

"I got the message to meet you here," he said.

Detective Sun now aimed her annoyance at him. "That's right. You're also involved. Because the other employee described the *both* of you as the last people to talk to Logan before he made his escape."

"What employee? Who are we talking about now?"

Kelvin said. My friend's brain did not work well this early in the day.

My mind, on the other hand, had apparently now gotten used to being up in the middle of the night to bake, so I could follow along the conversation. "Detective Sun is talking about Logan . . . who fled the furniture store right after we talked to him."

"What do you mean?" Kelvin scrunched his forehead. "The guy was right in front of the store when we left. And the detective was driving into the lot as we pulled out."

Detective Sun narrowed her eyes. "Logan decided to suddenly leave when I showed up. Hopped on his motorcycle and took off."

That might explain the back pain routine I'd witnessed. It'd be a valid excuse for him to leave work early and then make a run for it. I shuffled my feet, and Kelvin stuffed his hands in his pockets.

"Why would he do that? Leave so quickly?" the detective asked. "All I said was I wanted to have a friendly chat with him."

Kelvin held back a snort. I don't think he'd ever had a "friendly chat" with a police officer.

I jumped into the conversation. "When we last talked with Logan, he seemed fine."

"Not on edge at all?" the detective said, trying to read our faces.

"Um, I don't know. We were there to buy furniture," I said, "not talk about his feelings." A little white lie, but couldn't the police fine us for obstruction of justice? Mom and I really couldn't afford any more fees on top of the newly increased hike in rent.

"But you didn't buy anything at the store," Detective Sun pointed out.

Kelvin looped his arm around my shoulder, and I

felt braver. I doubled down on the lie. "We were there browsing."

"And all you talked about was furniture and fortune cookies?"

Kelvin's hand jerked on my shoulder. He was cracking. Why did he always buckle under pressure? "We might have talked about shoes, too."

"Shoes?" Detective Sun repeated.

"Yeah, about what he usually wore. On his feet."

She continued to stare Kelvin down until he blurted, "Which are yellow basketball shoes. The same kind that the eyewitness saw on the runner."

The detective's mouth tightened.

"Can't you put an APB out and find him?" I asked.

"How many resources do you think we have?" she said. "I was only going in for a chat, not a deep interrogation. We certainly don't have enough on him to call in the big guns."

Kelvin pulled his arm off me and wrung his hands. "But what about now that you know about his shoes—is that enough?"

"Especially if you get a search warrant and find those sneakers," I added.

The detective silenced me with a look. "Perhaps you should stick to baking."

"If I can keep our shop open," I murmured under my breath.

"What's that?" she said.

"I said I'll try."

"Try really hard," the detective said. "Logan seems impulsive at the very least. The worst case scenario, he could be unhinged, armed and dangerous."

I didn't know if she'd said that last part to scare me off the sleuthing. Logan had never been anything but polite to me, but he sure had a lot of strength in his arms. Enough to carry a recliner across a parking lot. Or maybe drop a body into a dumpster, I now thought.

Could he have done that with only one good arm? Or perhaps he had already healed by then. Hadn't he told me himself that he'd tried to milk the disability leave? I knew he'd already been discharged from the hospital by the day Charlie had died.

Detective Sun nodded at my best friend and me. "Stay out of trouble," she said, "the both of you."

"Of course," I said while Kelvin nodded.

Mom added, with her typical desire to get authority figures on her side, "Thank you for keeping our community safe."

"Just doing my job," the detective said, but her lips lifted in a smile for a brief moment.

My mom waited until both the detective and Kelvin had left before she confronted me. "What's this about you investigating things? After I specifically told you I didn't think it was a good idea?"

"We wanted to help move the case along," I said. "Red tape and all that. Besides, the Fresno police department probably has enough on their plate without branching into Pixie territory. Really, Mom, we haven't done much at all." Okay, so it was stretching the truth, but I comforted myself with the thought that I was doing this to clear my name and get the bakery back on track. If Logan really was the killer, I'd done the whole community a service by tracking him down and telling Detective Sun. Mom didn't need to know *everything* I did for the shop . . .

"I trust the authorities, as should you," Mom said, in a tone that I knew meant the discussion was over. "Okay, enough with the distractions. Let's get to work. We've got a long day ahead of us."

I glanced at the handmade sign still pinned to our glass door advertising our temporarily reduced hours. "It won't be that long."

Mom sniffed. "You can take that flyer down now."

And that's how I knew my mom felt safe again. She wanted to revert to our normal business hours, and I was more than happy to support her in that. I ripped the paper down with glee, and the two of us immersed ourselves in flour and sugar while prepping for the day, the detective's bad mood entirely forgotten.

It felt as though our fortunes had started reversing. We had a small trickle of customers and then longer lines as word spread that we were fully back in business. I wondered if the rumor mill had already spread the news that the police were chasing after a solid culprit in the Charlie Gong murder case. One who had nothing to do with Gold Bakery.

By that evening, we'd sold completely out of many of our goods, including some specialty treats. It appeared that my chocolate-dipped fortune cookies were a hit.

The final person to walk through our door was Michael Fu. I hadn't expected to see him turn up at the bakery. Even though he wore a breezy polo shirt with shorts, he mopped his forehead with a handkerchief.

"Can we help you?" my mom asked in a polite tone from behind the register.

"It's about the contract." Michael turned to me. "Are you ready to sign it?"

"I'm still not sure I should."

He stuck his handkerchief in his back pocket. "I really want to start up the AYCE fortune cookie idea," he said.

I bit my lip. "It'll be a lot of work. I'm still not sure we can handle the supply."

My mom came out from behind the counter. "All you

can eat?" she said. "How many fortune cookies would that take? We at Gold Bakery pride ourselves on quality, not quantity."

Of course, I hadn't mentioned the all-you-can-eat specifics when I'd been giving her the rundown of my successes the day before. Oops.

Michael stared at the few pastries left in the case and licked his lips, as though he could taste their goodness through the glass.

My mom caught him gazing with yearning and said, "They don't just look good. We put a lot of special love in every bite."

She meant they were each lovingly magicked, not that she could say that outright. But either way, hopefully he'd get the point.

Michael turned his attention to me. "We can renegotiate. Up the price for each fortune cookie. Would that help?"

Now he was talking. It was tempting, especially since we had the increased rent to pay. Would it be worth being an exclusive supplier to his fusion restaurant? He'd been helpful in some ways, but hard to handle in others. I still couldn't be sure about entering a long-term, high-quantity partnership with him. "How about we do a trial run?" I said. "I have some stock in the back. You can pay for all of those . . . at a reasonable price."

He nodded eagerly. Despite his previous threat, he probably didn't have that many fortune cookie companies to fall back on besides our bakery.

I went to the back and rounded up all the cookies I could find. When I returned, I said, "Let's find out how fast these go. Once we figure out the demand, then I can determine whether or not I can work with you on the all-you-can-eat proposal."

"Fair enough," Michael said.

I rang him up, figuring in an increased price per fortune cookie.

He didn't balk at the total calculated sum.

"Good doing business with you," I said.

"Same. And hopefully, there will be more of it soon. I'll be sure to draw up a new contract with the increased payment rate."

We'd see. I didn't want to promise anything, especially since my two hands could only bake so much. But at least he was now open to working on my terms.

Michael left with his haul of fortune cookies, and my mom grinned at me.

"What?" I said.

"You're doing it. Being a savvy businesswoman while not sacrificing our ideals."

I smiled back at her. Really, I was triumphing. I could bake the Jin way *and* make a profit. At least enough to keep our modest shop running for the present.

CHAPTER 30

Of course I wanted to share the good news with Kelvin. What were best friends for if not to celebrate the ups in life?

My mom gave me the go-ahead to slip out for a minute while she finished closing up, and I walked next door to find him still busy. Our stores closed up around the same time, but he wasn't a stickler for schedules. Sometimes he'd let a few last-minute customers sneak in.

With what I considered extreme patience, I waited for the woman wearing a pink headband to finish talking to him. When she shifted to peer at some flowers Kelvin was showing her, I realized I knew her.

"Moana?"

She turned around. "I didn't see you in the shop earlier. Figured you weren't working today."

That's right. She still thought Kelvin and I were business partners. Guess she'd never bothered to peer inside the neighboring bakery.

I shrugged, keeping up the charade. "I had to run some errands."

"Kelvin here is showing me these gorgeous flowers. I told him we wanted edible ones to put on our cake."

"Like I said before"—Kelvin held up the beautiful

specimens—"these are all organically grown. And I think we can narrow down the choices to the pansies, begonias, or roses."

Moana touched the soft petals of the flowers with her fingers. "What are their taste profiles again?"

"The violets may have a slight minty flavor."

Moana shook her head.

He continued. "Begonias offer a taste of citrus."

She pursed her lips.

"And roses have a subtle sweetness to them."

"Those would be perfect," she said.

"A classic choice." Kelvin wrote her choice on a piece of paper. He loved jotting things down on scraps as reminders. "I'll make sure to save plenty of them. We'll need quite a few for a five-tier wedding cake."

She smiled, her lip gloss shining bright under the shop lights. "Guess everything's coming up roses for me now."

"So true. You must be excited for your upcoming wedding," I said.

"That too, but I'm talking about finally squaring away this lawsuit business with the Cookie Prince."

"Fortune Cookie King," I corrected, but I'd seen him referred as "prince" somewhere else before. The note at the makeshift memorial. Could she have written that? I recalled Moana's plastic bags and her condiment packets. "So your suit went through, and you got the money?"

"Well, Charlie's personal rep and I had a deep moment of connection."

I scrambled in my mind for Moana's last reference to her. "I thought you said she was a pain."

"It takes a person in pain to give out pain."

That'd make a good fortune cookie saying, if a somewhat disheartening one. Maybe I should start writing things down like Kelvin.

"What happened?" Kelvin asked, finished with his note taking and now fully focused on our conversation.

"We bonded over our hatred of the same guy," Moana said. "I got so mad about that counter lawsuit, I once wrote a nasty note about him using sweet-and-sour sauce. But at least I didn't date the guy in the past. That's how she got roped into repping, just for old time's sake."

"That's too bad."

"Anyway," she said, "we both agreed to drop our suits."

"She didn't mind?" I asked.

"Nah, Kay was doing it out of obligation. Plus, I said I would offer her a settlement out of court." She tossed her head. "That way my name doesn't get muddied before I tie the knot."

I wondered how much she was willing to pay to make the case go away. "Glad it worked out," I said.

"Yeah." Kelvin nodded and started putting away his precious flowers with care.

"Way cheaper than letting things drag on in the legal system," Moana said. "I've got better things to do—like plan a wedding!"

Kelvin and I congratulated Moana once again on her forthcoming nuptials.

"The day will be perfect now. Those flowers on the cake were my very last detail," she said and walked out with a bounce to her step.

"Wow, she's gonna buy out your whole store," I told Kelvin.

"Hardly, but I'm proud I'll be contributing to the wedding of her dreams."

"Even if it did start off as an investigative ploy."

"About that." He leaned toward me. "Are you okay that the detective dropped by for a visit?"

"It was better with you there," I admitted. "Less intimidating. And it seems like she's finally moved on from me. I still can't quite believe Logan did it."

"Maybe we should stick to flowers and fortune cookies."

"Good idea. Speaking of which . . ." I proceeded to share with Kelvin the negotiations with Michael Fu and how I hadn't backed down from my principles. I'd even gotten a higher profit margin.

He high-fived me. "Way to go, Lissa. Good job standing up for yourself and your treats. After all, they're definitely one of a kind."

After Kelvin and I had finished our chat, I returned to Gold Bakery, which had been already locked up in my absence. My mom was waiting for me outside.

"Ready to go?" she said, looping her arm around mine.

"Yes." I marveled at the quietness of the night as we strolled along the street. Already I felt safer walking around Pixie knowing the police were hunting down Logan.

"I'm glad they have that bad man in custody," my mom said.

She always thought in such stark terms. People were either all good—or not. Take my biological dad . . . I shook my head to clear it and to correct the details of her previous statement. "Actually, Mom, they're still chasing him."

She stopped short on the pavement. "Not anymore. While you were gone, Sweet Tooth Sally came in with an update."

"And?"

"That Detective Sun did a fine job." Mom beamed with pride as though the cop was a relative of ours. "Caught him for sure. He's should be at the Fresno police station right now."

I whistled. "That was quick."

My mom sighed with satisfaction. "Finally, things are all good."

We arrived at our apartment, and as she let me in, Mom said, "Felicity, I've been meaning to say: I love how your mind is always bursting with creativity. Experimenting with flavors, reaching out to stores and restaurants, expanding the business."

"Thanks," I said. Those words meant so much to me, but I couldn't help wondering what was coming next. She fiddled with the keys in her hand, pausing before she began again.

"I also want to say . . . you don't have to be like me. Stay in a small town, live in a tiny space." She gestured around her.

The apartment was cozy, and I quite liked our mismatched furniture. Every item had a story behind it. The desk my eyes landed on as I mulled over her words had been gifted by a neighbor who had repurposed an old sewing machine table. "Our place is comfy and always has been."

"I just wanted you to know. If it's not enough, you can always spread your wings." She took a deep breath. "You know, put down roots elsewhere."

She was mixing her metaphors, but I got her gist. "I've never asked to move, Mom."

"And I know you wouldn't. You've always been content to tag along behind me. Not even asking to leave when your best friend went away to college."

I had felt a twinge of jealousy when Kelvin had gone

to UC Merced. Emails and texts didn't quite make up for the loss of face-to-face contact, but he'd swing by on the weekends, so it hadn't been awful. Plus, I'd been focused on chipping in at the bakery and finding my personal Jin magic. "I wanted to be here, Mom. With you."

"To help me and the bakery." She put the keys away in our scuffed koa wood bowl (from an appreciative customer) and couldn't quite meet my gaze.

"I wanted to stay. Truly. I still do." I squeezed her hand, and she looked up at me.

"I'm grateful for that, each and every day."

Whiskers hopped into the scene and added to our number. I patted her on the head. "We're appreciative of you, too. The Jin family always stays together, no matter what."

CHAPTER 31

Our sense of peace and unity was shattered the next day. Kelvin banged on the door of the apartment very early in the morning. I'd just changed out of my pajamas when Mom let him in.

"Why all the ruckus?" she said.

He bobbed his head. "Sorry, Mrs. Jin. I need to talk to Lissa, and it's urgent."

I yawned and poured myself a bowl of cereal. "Seriously? It couldn't have waited until I got some food in my system?"

Kelvin plopped himself on a kitchen chair next to me and waited until I'd taken a few spoonfuls before speaking to me—in a whisper.

Thank goodness my mom was distracted, running around getting food for Whiskers, because he said, "Logan called me."

I dropped my spoon into the bowl. A little bit of milk splashed out. I ignored it. "What? How did he get your number?"

"Well." Kelvin gave a soft chuckle. "That was *your* doing. Since we called him on my phone to set up that first meeting at the furniture store."

Whoops.

"Anyway," Kelvin continued, "the guy got released . . . and the first person he wanted to reach out to was me."

"You? How come?" My brain caught up with me. "And he was let go already?"

He shrugged. "I don't know why. On both counts."

I thought about the situation. "If Logan was released, that means the police don't have enough evidence to arrest him. Yet."

"Right." Kelvin wiggled in his chair. "So the thing is, Lissa, I heard him out when he called me."

Uh-oh. I didn't like where this was going. Kelvin was a softie. He always listened to every solicitor and spammer before giving a polite reply. Sometimes the call ended with him buying junk he didn't like or need. Was Kelvin's love of being "nice" about to strike again? "What'd you tell him?"

"That I would meet him at my shop in twenty minutes."

I blinked at Kelvin. "You invited a potential murderer to meet with you alone in your store?"

"Hey, he *was* released. I'm sure it'll be fine."

There Kelvin went giving everyone the benefit of the doubt. "I'm coming with you," I said. Two people were better than one in a scuffle. "And I'm gonna have my mom watch out for us and have the phone ready just in case."

"I don't know why you're so worried. Besides, it's a busy street. Lots of people coming and going."

Maybe in the middle of the day. But not in the early morning. Or in the evening, at least not at the time when Charlie had truly needed someone as an eyewitness.

"Just wait for me." I cleaned the milk spill but abandoned my bowl of cereal. After asking Mom to keep an eye out on us from the bakery, I followed Kelvin out the door.

* * *

Honestly, Logan looked out of place at Love Blooms. If he'd been in a majestic forest instead of a flower shop with his big bear size, it might have been more fitting. He kept batting at the fronds around him and bumping into the vases. Thankfully, nothing had actually broken . . . so far.

Kelvin did not have any giant shears lying around—my first weapon of choice—but I'd equipped myself with a wicked-looking forged fork. I hid it behind my back as Logan blubbered on about his gratitude for Kelvin at arranging this meeting. I felt slightly ridiculous but comforted myself with the thought that it was better to be safe than sorry.

"I appreciate the kindness," Logan said once he'd made it safely to a more open area of the shop. "The cops were not so compassionate."

Come to think of it, the man did have bags under his eyes. He must have gone through a lot. If he wasn't a murderer, I would feel bad for him. But was he really one or not?

"I'm here to listen, serve as your sounding board," Kelvin said. "So they released you . . . ?"

"Of course they did. Because I wasn't answering any of their questions, or at least not in the way they wanted. I know the cops were trying to trap me." He thumped his chest with a closed fist. "But I'm innocent."

I raised my eyebrows at Kelvin, and he studiously avoided me. Logan, though, caught my doubtful expression.

"What, you don't believe me? I've got proof." His fingers flew over his phone. "I'll send you something." A ding came from Kelvin's pocket, which he ignored.

"I don't need to see anything. Tell me why you had them chase you down," Kelvin said, without any condemnation, only curiosity.

Logan focused his gaze on a nearby fern. "I don't have the best history with cops. I panicked. Especially once I saw her holster."

Kelvin nodded. "I feel you."

Logan licked his lips. "Yeah, I appreciate that. And your tip-off."

Kelvin cocked his head to the side.

"You know, at the store. When you asked about my running shoes. It made me realize that the cops must've misinterpreted things." Logan looked straight into Kelvin's eyes. "Thanks, man. I wanted to tell you that in person."

I leaned over the counter and checked out Logan's current shoes. No more wingtips. Yellow basketball ones instead. I gripped the huge fork in my hand tighter. "Pixie's a small place, Logan," I said. "I know the witness who saw someone running away from the alley. Someone wearing yellow shoes. If that was you, what's the story?"

He glanced down at his shoes, as though surprised he was wearing that particular pair. Maybe he'd put them on in the morning out of rote habit. "Well, the truth is, it *was* me. And I was scared."

"Of what?" I asked.

"I'd just met up with Charlie near some shops, thinking he was ready to apologize and reconcile. Instead he exploded on me."

"And you ran away because he was yelling?" The reasoning seemed flimsy. Logan could probably hold his own in any argument.

"No, not only that. After getting riled up, Charlie started breathing hard. His face was turning red, and I just didn't want to stick around if anyone else showed up and got the wrong idea. Like I said, I don't have the best history with the police."

Kelvin jumped in. "Oh no. Was he having some sort of medical emergency?"

Logan glanced to the side, at a display of pansies. Fitting. "Um, Charlie brought out some sort of round disc and started breathing into it, so I figured he'd be all right."

Something rang false about his story, but I wasn't about to confront the man right now, especially with only a gardening tool to protect me.

Kelvin, on the other hand, appeared to believe the tale. "Well, if the police don't have any solid evidence of you actually being near Charlie when he died, it should turn out fine."

"Yeah . . . you're right. I'm sure it'll all work out. Thanks again for the warning. Let me get out of your hair." He glanced again at his shoes and mumbled a goodbye to us.

"What'd you think?" I asked Kelvin after Logan had gone.

"The police couldn't hold him, so . . ."

"That doesn't mean anything," I said. "They could still issue a warrant for his arrest later."

"But if the guy was there while Charlie was still breathing . . ."

Just barely. Suddenly, I realized: Logan had witnessed Charlie having difficulty breathing. The fortune cookie I'd written had talked about suffocation. Could it have been referring to a respiratory issue? Was this not a murder case at all? What if the cause of death wasn't a pillow smothering but a fatal breathing problem? Then again, why would a man who'd died of natural causes end up in a dumpster? "What if Charlie wasn't really fine when Logan left?" I asked. "People do lie."

"Then he won't be able to outrun the evidence and the police." Kelvin glanced out the door and flinched. "Um, why is your mom trying to flag you down?"

CHAPTER 32

I peeked outside. My mom appeared to be jumping up and down and waving me over to the bakery. They didn't seem like distraught jumps, but I hurried anyway.

She held a phone near her ear and covered the receiver with her hand. "It's that Michael Fu. He keeps on ringing the store."

What now? I took the call, so Mom could concentrate on actually running the shop.

I moved to the corner of the bakery, trying to get more privacy for my conversation. "Hi, this is Felicity. How can I help you?"

A rush of breath came at me. "Oh, finally. I've been calling and calling."

I grimaced but made my tone polite. "Yes. For what reason?"

"Cookies. I need all of your fortune cookies."

I couldn't help from smiling. "People ate them already?"

"Yes, we're getting really low on our supply. This contest idea has been a huge hit. Please, I'll take as many as you can make. If you can bring them tonight, I'll make sure to pay you well." He named a hefty sum.

"Okay, I'll come by after the bakery closes."

"Thank you." I heard a babble of voices from the other end of the line. "A lot of customers are here for the challenge. See you soon."

While Mom managed the rest of the bakery, I snuck into the back to craft an avalanche of fortune cookies. Flexing my hands, I got to work.

Though I started out with a will and plenty of joyful purpose, the repetitive motion of rolling out of each disc, slipping a paper in, and molding them into the correct shape started to bore me after a while. Worse, my fingers started cramping up.

I shifted them this way and that, stretching them out. I even cracked my knuckles. Nothing doing. They still hurt.

My mom checked on me now and then. Noticing my grimaces, she kept asking if I needed to take a break.

"No, I've got to finish these as fast as possible." I even blew through lunch, though my stomach got mad at me.

As I put in slip after slip of paper, the words started blurring before my eyes. I thought my vision had seriously succumbed to the heat of the kitchen. I blinked to clear my head and felt wetness trailing down my cheek. Was I crying? Why?

The answer came to me within seconds. I felt like a machine. Fortune cookie making was no longer fun. Was this how it felt to work in a factory? To have worked at Smiley Fortunes?

For maybe the first time, I fully empathized with the workers there. Which of course led me to thinking about one of them in particular. Could Logan have built up layers of anger at the repetitive work over time, enough to unleash them on Charlie that fated day? The first portion of my fortune message had talked about knowledge. Was it the understanding of the intense labor and the poor treatment—I mean, Logan *had* gotten his hand burned, no matter how quickly it had healed—that had led to his boss's demise? How much of what Logan had told us before had been the truth? And if Logan really hadn't killed Charlie . . . who had?

No, I needed to stop with this line of thinking. Investigating wasn't my job, I reminded myself. Baking was my duty. I'd done as much sleuthing as I could, and whether or not Logan was the killer, I seemed to be moving down Detective Sun's list of suspects. I focused on the fortune cooking making before me. But these mass cookies . . . Were the customers really going to enjoy them?

Truth be told, people who entered all-you-can-eat contests weren't savoring the food. I bet they were scarfing down my fortune cookies, possibly not even chewing them completely but swallowing them almost whole to save on time.

Baked treats were meant to be relished. Especially ones from my family's bakery. We were in charmed and privileged roles as magical bakers. My mom had always told me that, making sure to impart both the responsibility and the power of our positions.

And I remembered again: My magic extended beyond the physical cookie, to that of true fortune-telling as well. I glared at the pile of printed generic fortunes before me and crumpled them up. Why was I wasting my time making subpar cookies with fortunes that meant nothing?

I stopped baking. These would be all that Michael Fu would get, and I'd bow out gracefully from his proposition. I wasn't going to mass-produce any more fortune cookies. The long-held Jin truism was right: We were meant to provide quality over quantity.

Of course, that didn't mean I couldn't experiment. I could do tweaks, add in extra flavors and personalize my baked goods. A combination of what my family had always done, and my own take on baking—maybe that was the solution I'd been looking for all along.

I stared at the collection of discarded fortunes before me. Could I tweak other things, too? Might I be able to change up my magic, modify it in subtle ways? I'd already started to do so, hadn't I? My gift had expanded from baking into something new: predicting the future.

Still, when a Jin made a promise, she had to follow through on it. That's how I found myself hauling the bags of fortune cookies I'd made before my epiphany into Foo Fusion later that evening.

Michael had done a stellar job of advertising the fortune cookie challenge. Maybe too stellar. It was hard to miss even from the exterior, where someone had painted a giant fortune cookie paired with the words "All You Can Eat" on the glass storefront. Inside, flyers seemed to be taped on every available surface, marketing the contest.

I noticed that one customer near the front had taken on the challenge. There was a rapidly diminishing mound of fortune cookies on that eater's plate. It actually sickened my stomach to watch the gorging. Not a flicker of a smile or any sign of enjoyment crossed the customer's face as he shoved in one cookie after another.

Turning my attention to the register, where Michael was busy talking on the phone, I dropped my bags on the counter. His eyes brightened at my arrival, and he finished up the call after sharing the restaurant's operating hours with the person on the other end.

"Things are booming," he said with a wide smile at me. "Not least because of your fortune cookies."

"Thanks, but—"

He reached below the counter and came up with an envelope. "And here's your money."

"There's something I need to tell you . . ." How could

I explain that I wasn't planning to move forward with his business venture? It felt like the most awkward kind of breakup.

Before I could formulate a few professional but gentle words, he'd already left for the kitchen, carrying my fortune cookies, giving me time to rethink my decision. Was I making a mistake? The thick envelope filled with cash seemed to reproach me.

No, this wasn't about money and what it could buy. Although I was a little hungry. That's what I got for skipping lunch.

When a worker bustled out of the kitchen and took over the cashier duties, I did decide to place an order. I'd tried quite a few of Foo Fusion's other options but hadn't eaten their doughnuts yet.

I opted for a dozen: six of the glazed kind and six of a curry version. Croquettes, they were called.

It only took ten minutes to get them. I'd ordered them for takeout, but the fragrance coming from the bag was too enticing.

I decided to seat myself at a two-top and take a few bites before I left. My stomach would be pleased with me.

The glazed doughnut was pleasant, sweet but not overly so. And the croquette was . . . revelatory.

I'd never had a croquette before, and it seemed like a better, puffier doughnut, deliciously embellished with bread crumbs. Upon first bite, I discovered an astounding curry combination of savory meat and potato. I should've ordered a dozen of the curry version alone.

Maybe it was because I'd been blindsided by my enlightened taste buds, but I didn't notice the newcomer in the restaurant until she emitted a sharp wail.

"What do you mean you won't take my fortune cookies?"

It was Cayla, her voice starting to rise with anger.

"Aren't you holding an all-you-can-eat competition?" she said. "And Smiley Fortunes is your usual supplier."

The worker at the register pulled at his shirt's collar. "I think we're switching companies. Um, I mean we *have* switched."

"To whom?" Cayla tapped her sharp nails on the counter in frustration.

"Some bakery in Pixie."

I gulped and shrank in my seat, thankful I'd picked a dim corner of the restaurant.

The worker cleared his throat. "Sorry."

"Oh no, your boss can't do this to me. I want to speak to him right now."

"Hold on a moment." The worker fled into the kitchen, and Michael soon came out.

He had a grim face when he approached Cayla. "Like I told you before, our formal contract was not with Smiley Fortunes factory but with Charlie Gong, the individual."

She spluttered. "I'm, like, Charlie Gong's rep. You have to deal with me."

"Read the fine print. I don't," he said. "Besides, we've had customer complaints about the poor quality from Smiley Fortunes, remember?"

"We've changed the recipe." She pointed at a hand cart beside her. It was loaded with boxes upon boxes of fortune cookies. "These are better-tasting. And I've got plenty of them for your new all-you-can-eat challenge."

He eyed them with distrust. "I don't know . . ."

"I'll leave a box for you out of good will. I'm sure you'll change your mind." Cayla gave a brisk nod goodbye and wheeled her cart out of Foo Fusion.

CHAPTER 33

I needed to rectify this situation. Maybe if I talked to Michael and clarified my stance, it would help both Cayla and me.

Michael still stood at the counter, his hands curled into fists before him.

I sidled up close. "Hi, there."

"What?" His answer came out as a bark, but then he softened his tone once he saw me. "Oh, it's you."

I held up my take-out bag. "These curry croquettes are amazing."

His fingers relaxed. "Yeah, they use our special secret recipe."

"Well, they're great," I said and then took a deep breath. "I'm so sorry to tell you this, but I can't do it anymore. Make that many batches of fortune cookies, I mean."

A loud belch sounded in the air. I peeked over to the table where the competitive eater sat, looking queasy. I shook my head. "It's too much strain on our small family business."

"No, no," Michael said. "You just need more confidence in your skills. Take us as an example. I have a small staff, and we can still churn out Chinese food, hamburgers, and doughnuts."

Of which only one cuisine was any good. I kept my opinions to myself and gave him a sad smile. "I couldn't help overhearing your conversation with Cayla. Maybe you could send some business their way? They've got the factory space and multiple workers ready to handle your bulk orders."

"No way. I've been down that road before."

"People deserve second chances."

"It's not just that." Michael ran his hand over his bald head. "There are rumors of curses involved."

I widened my eyes. "What?"

"It's been said that Charlie was fated to die a bad death. That he was cursed. In fact, the whole company is cursed."

"That can't possibly be true," I said, hoping my terrible fortune for Charlie hadn't started this rumor.

"I know someone who knows someone who knows someone in the Fresno police department. In the evidence locker, they kept the fortune cookie message telling Charlie of his demise."

Oh. I felt my body temperature rise.

Michael traced the twisted branches of the potted money tree on the counter. "I need to keep making good luck, not bad. And those cookies from Smiley Fortunes must be cursed."

"Fortune cookies are just food. They can't do anything." I hid my crossed fingers behind my back.

"No? Then how did Charlie die after eating one of his own cookies?"

I didn't correct Michael. He clearly hadn't put two and two together that Charlie had died in Pixie, close to our bakery. Michael thought the ill-fated fortune cookie came from the Smiley factory, not my family's business.

He gestured me closer then lowered his voice. "And you know what? I'm spreading the word about the danger.

Letting others know about those wretched unlucky cookies."

I mumbled something unintelligible and fled the restaurant as quickly as I reasonably could. If the people of Fresno and Pixie put their heads together, they'd soon realize that those supposedly unlucky fortune cookies came from Gold Bakery. If customers were already wary of entering a business where someone had died in the back alley, they would be terrified of a place that had actually sold the fated cookie.

I believed deep down that my magical powers weren't a curse, but maybe I needed to concentrate on them more, to influence the predictions. I had to make sure I never crafted evil fortunes for people.

The problem with testing my fortune-predicting skills was that I needed volunteer eaters. Reflecting on my past experiences, it seemed clear it had to be someone I hadn't known for a while, someone who was practically a stranger to me. And, as Kelvin had theorized, I could only predict an individual's fortune one time, as my attempts with Logan had proven.

Also, I'd culled a list of tips to enhance my ability while not creating health problems for myself. To ward off headaches and dizziness, I needed to embrace my talent and be prepared for the messaging.

What better way to test out my ability than to use it on unsuspecting customers? I couldn't make a batch of hollow cookies sans fortunes to pass out. Nothing irritated a customer more than not getting what they expected, and fortune cookies without messages seemed . . . well, empty.

On my way back to Pixie, though, I brainstormed, and came up with what I hoped would be a method to help expand my baked offerings and test my magic at the same time.

* * *

When morning rolled around, I knew what I had to do. I'd offer people free tastes. Scrumptious Samples, I'd call them. Custom-made, fresh on the spot. This way I'd get to try out various flavors, and I'd be able to construct personalized fortunes all in one go.

I'd chosen the classic Neapolitan trio as pleasant options for my first go-round: chocolate, vanilla, and strawberry. But I'd also added two unique flavors: pandan and ube. I'd gotten tiny bottles of their extracts on sale at the grocery store recently and couldn't wait to try them out.

The first customer who agreed to a strawberry sample and a free personalized fortune was a woman with a clutch of scratch-off tickets in her hand. "Please," she begged, "I really want a good fortune."

Her frizzy hair stuck out like a corona around her head, and I hoped I could help her out with my magic. I touched the stack of tickets, managing to brush her palm in the process.

"Let's see." I gave in to my head space and followed the dazzling lines of color. Still reflecting on the lotto tickets, my heart steered me toward the red line. I plucked it in my mind and let the message form inside me.

Then I wrote it down carefully on a slip of paper: "Lucky lady, you will soon accumulate riches of two thousand dollars."

The customer hopped up and down in glee when I handed her the note. "I've got to try my luck right now."

She pulled out a tarnished penny and managed to scratch off every single ticket. Repeated yeses flew out of her mouth as she continued to rake in the winnings. All to the total of $2,000. "You've sure got a gift," she said.

I waved it off. "Nope, I'm just good at guessing."

But I knew in my heart it was more than that. I was harnessing my gift, and I wasn't experiencing any headaches or pain. In fact, diving into things fully had made accessing the magic easier, and I relished the smoother, happy process of fortune-predicting.

Over the course of the day, I managed to give out dozens of sample flavors. Only a few customers agreed to personalized fortunes, though. Guess everyone else was too busy or hungry to hang around and wait for a customized message.

The unaware volunteers helped me figure out that the different-colored lines corresponded to unique categories. I'd already started mapping out the connections between hues and types of fortunes—red for finances, yellow for travel, blue for career, and so on—when the last customer walked in before closing.

An older gentleman, he wore a trilby hat and carried a chestnut cane with brass trim. "I'll sample the ube flavor," he said.

"Certainly, sir." While coming up with his message, I concentrated in my mind on the purple line, the only untested color left.

I discovered the prediction had to do with health. As soon as I received the message, a bitterness arose in my throat. This was the first unfortunate fortune I'd gotten today. The rest of them had involved a joyous reunion with a lost pet (right outside on our cul-de-sac), an exciting vacation (a surprise call about a tropical island destination), and even receiving mail (a text about an important package).

The message I'd unveiled for my current customer read "The heat will sag your spirits." I pocketed the unhappy fortune without giving it to him.

It was true that the local summer weather harbored on horrible. Temperatures could easily reach the triple digits. Even though we hadn't actually entered the sunny season, we'd been hit with an unusually warm week.

Gold Bakery had its air-conditioning running on full blast. The old man ate the ube fortune cookie and declared it delicious, but within five minutes, he appeared faint and lethargic.

He leaned on his cane and said, "I think I might need to sit for a spell."

Yikes. What the older gentleman needed was to rehydrate, I thought. I darted to my mom for help, and we scampered around the kitchen, creating a homemade electrolyte drink. We threw together strawberries, lemon juice, water, honey, and a pinch of salt.

He gingerly sipped at our brew until he felt better. Mom even escorted him to a paratransit vehicle waiting to take the man home and made sure he got on safely.

I flipped our sign to CLOSED after the harrowing activity and swallowed hard.

When my mom returned, she said, "You look pale, Felicity."

The shop was empty, and I was too tired to say anything besides the honest truth. "I really wanted him to be okay. I can't handle being involved in another death, or even a sickness."

My mom placed her arms on my shoulders and leaned her forehead against mine for a moment. It felt good, like she was transferring over some of her confidence and power.

She stepped back and looked into my eyes. "Felicity, you predict the future, not tragedy."

"Are you sure about that? I'd say prophesizing one man's suffocation and another one's illness were pretty bad things."

"Let's think through this together," Mom said. "What

happened after you wrote the fortune for this man, today?"

"He felt ill, faint."

"And then?"

"The guy sat down."

"Which was helpful to him, right?" Mom said. "What else?"

"I got scared . . ."

"And?"

"Then you and I ran around getting ingredients for a drink."

"Exactly." She turned in a circle as though taking in her surroundings for the first time. "You made this bakery a safe haven for him. Without your fortune, he wouldn't have been in tune with his body or its needs. Maybe he wouldn't have sat down when he needed to."

I caught on to my mom's train of thought. "And for sure, he wouldn't have gotten our homemade drink."

"Which revived him. And I escorted him safely to his waiting transportation," she said. "You *predict* the future, you do not *cause* it, Felicity."

Mom was right. I could predict fortunes, which only indicated possible futures. Not definite ones. And even with the sad ones, it didn't mean they had to spell doom. This time, we'd reacted quickly enough.

And we'd had enough time to do so. I thought back on my prepared fortunes from today. That was another common factor in all my predictions. The messages seemed to come true within a short amount of time. I'd say within about half an hour.

Fascinating. I felt like I was finally getting a handle on my magical abilities. I gave myself a mental pat on the back, but my buoyant state soon fled—when Kelvin burst, worried, into the bakery.

CHAPTER 34

Kelvin ran through the door and over to me—pulling out his cell phone without any preamble. He found the message thread from Logan, scrolling past old texts and a screenshot, and clicked on the recent video he'd received. It was of a police vehicle passing by Logan's home at an abnormally glacial speed.

In the short clip, Logan had pinched back the curtain of the window and filmed the patrol car through the pane.

"This is the fourth time they've circled around." His voice quivered. "What do they want from me?"

"What are you two watching?" Mom asked. She was sweeping the floor again even though it was already tidy.

"Nothing," I said right as Kelvin replied, "It's a video of the police patrolling a neighborhood."

Mom nodded a few times and clicked the broom into place. It was one of those nifty sweepers with a long dustpan that could attach to the broom's handle. She'd gotten it at an Asian grocery store a few years back, and the standing dustpan was a lifesaver on her back. "You know, Felicity, you should go over there."

"Go over where?"

"To visit the police. Give them our thanks for watching over us all the time." She paused. "And encourage

Detective Sun about the case. It wouldn't hurt to apologize for trying to undermine her investigation as well. I'm sure she'll solve it in no time."

How often had I heard the same advice from my mom? All about trusting and relying on the authorities. She'd drilled into my head tales of stranger danger, making sure to note that I should always turn to someone in a uniform (cop, security guard, postal officer) for help. If I ever got seriously threatened—which had yet to happen in Pixie—I figured I could handle things well enough on my own. I stood up straighter, ready to rebuke her.

Then Mom added, "Besides, it'd make me feel better. And get us back into the good graces of the local cops."

I couldn't help pointing out the error in her logic. "Detective Sun works at the Fresno police department, not Pixie."

"That may be true, but she's in our community now and wrapping up a case here."

Mom had a point, and I didn't like refusing her requests, especially if it was a small thing I could easily do to bring her more happiness. "Of course I'll go," I said, holding up my hands in surrender. I'd found following Mom's way to be the path of least resistance my entire life. She'd bent tradition more than I'd ever expected her to in the past few days and weeks, but her respect for authority wasn't something that would change so easily.

Mom could finish cleaning up here while I would head to the police as a filial ending to my workday.

"Wanna come?" I asked Kelvin, who'd been seemingly focused on his phone while my mom and I talked—though I had no doubt he'd overheard the entire conversation.

"Can't," he said. "I've still got to do some things at the shop."

I'd be flying solo, then.

"Don't forget the oranges," Mom called out as I exited the shop.

I turned so she could see me through the glass door and gave her a thumbs-up.

What was with Mom and her love of oranges? Okay, in some ways I got it. Chinese people thought the fruit was lucky. They were placed in front of altars, on tombstones, and given out during the Lunar New Year. Also, the word for the smaller mandarin oranges sounded like "gold" in the Cantonese dialect, same as our last name. Guess the fruit kind of served as a calling card from our family. But still, the amount of them we consumed seemed excessive.

I picked up the fruit at a WinCo along the way to the detective's lair (my snarky nickname for her office). Fresno was a big enough city that it had police stations in several different neighborhoods, and I'd actually had to call each one to verify which location the detective worked at. Apparently, she was stationed at the tiniest branch. The station flanked a main street, but if I hadn't been keeping a close lookout, I might have missed it with its unassuming brown exterior.

Inside, the building was modernized with a ballistic glass shield surrounding the information booth. The guy manning it had to ask me again who I wanted to see, as though I was playing a prank on him.

"I want to talk to Detective Sun," I repeated. "Rylan Sun."

"Sure, got it." The man motioned me away, but I stood there, waiting. Maybe if I remained in his sight, he'd act quicker.

I was close enough to the glass that I could see his

smirk as he connected to the detective over the phone. I could also hear his words: "Hey, Miss Sun-shine, you got a visitor. A family member."

I had to bite my tongue. *Of course* he assumed we were related. East Asian ethnicity and all.

He hung up, and upon finding me there, issued me a frown. Then he pointed to a bench behind me. "Have a seat, I insist."

The bench was the same dull brown as the outside of the building. And hard. I sure wasn't going to have a picnic on it anytime soon.

I was still trying to make myself comfortable when a dark shadow loomed over me.

The detective had arrived. Her voice was slush cold when she spoke. "*Cousin* Felicity, how may I help you?"

"Whoa," I said, "it wasn't me. I didn't claim to be family. The guy just assumed."

Detective Sun held back a snort. "At least he finally remembered I worked here." Wow, she'd broken out of her typical professional demeanor. That was definitely progress in our relationship.

I decided to press my advantage and said, "Um, thanks for working on the Pixie murder case."

She blinked at me, maybe uncertain of my motives. Or perhaps thinking I wanted to extract more information from her.

I proffered the bag of oranges and quickly muttered a jam-packed sentence: "Andsorryforinvestigatingonmyown."

She took the fruit offering, and a gleam entered her eyes. "Ah, I think I get it. Your mom made you come."

I started to protest, but she waved her hand at me to stop.

"My mother would've asked me to do the same," the detective said. "Save face, make guanxi—good connections—with the police. Obligation either way. But I would've done it because, you know, it was my mother . . ."

So she did understand my position. Maybe better than most others would. I cracked a small smile, but Detective Sun was no longer looking at me. She murmured, not quite under her breath, "I wish she were still here."

"I'm so sorry," I said, and I meant it. It'd been my mom and me for as long as I could remember. If she were gone—I sucked in my breath. My mind couldn't even go there. Maybe our magic could preserve her? She didn't seem to age, customers often said. Perhaps she could live forever, like the lady in the moon. But that was truly magical thinking.

Detective Sun's voice was soft when she finally responded. "I appreciate that. It's been ten years, so you'd think I'd be okay by now, but . . ."

"We all grieve differently. And a loss like that never entirely goes away," I said. My dad had disappeared from my life when I was a baby, but sometimes I still longed for him and grieved for the childhood I never had.

The detective looked vulnerable, her eyes hooded. She seemed less cop-like than ever even though we were, ironically, chatting at the police station.

"Tell your mom not to worry," she said. "We're homing in on a suspect, and I'm sure he'll break soon."

Logan. It must be. I pictured the alley scene on the day of the crime and imagined how the situation might have gone sideways for the two men. Even at Gold Bakery, while waiting for my fortune cookie, Charlie had been grumpy. Impatient and distracted by his phone.

He'd probably continued with his foul mood when he met up with Logan. And Logan, in turn, had responded poorly. Very poorly.

Something about this particular train of thought brought with it a sense of unease. I could almost grasp the wrongness—

"Thanks for the oranges," Detective Sun said.

I refocused on the present moment. "Uh, sure, no problem."

"And say hello to your mother for me." I wondered if the heartbroken detective saw my mom as some kind of new maternal figure in her life.

"Will do," I said with great gentleness.

CHAPTER 35

Mom and I both woke up early the next day, even before our usual start time. I'd tossed and turned after my intimate conversation with Detective Sun. Mom, on the other hand, woke up brimming with hope, trusting that my police visit would lead to a string of good things.

At the bakery, I yawned as I went through the starting tasks. By the time the grinding of wheels down the back alley sounded, I'd already decided to take a stretch break.

Since the garbage collector was around, I might as well go say hi. Besides, he'd been the one to find Charlie Gong and start the formal investigation—maybe he'd know something.

I recognized the man in the baseball cap by sight. He'd been assigned our route for so many years that I'd seen his scruffy brown beard turn gray over time. I waited until he'd lifted the dumpster, emptied it, and placed it back down before I approached the vehicle.

Waving my arms, I flagged his attention, and he turned off the truck. He stuck his head out the window. "Everything all right, miss?"

"Sorry to disturb you," I said. "I'm Felicity, I work at Gold Bakery. I wanted to introduce myself."

He nodded, seemingly familiar with our business.

"I know you were the one to find the body of Charlie Gong. And I wanted to thank you for reporting it, for allowing justice to be served."

He messed with the brim of his cap. "Naw, it wasn't all that special."

"But if you hadn't spotted him . . ."

The man cleared his throat. "Easy 'nuff with the Serevent in his hand. Or salmeterol. A prescription med. It comes in a round container."

The disc Logan had spoken of finally made sense. "Ah, right."

The man tugged on his unkempt beard. "It's too bad the poor soul didn't reach for his albuterol instead."

"His what? I don't follow," I said.

The man sniffed. "I've got asthma myself. Albuterol's what you turn to when you get an attack. Serevent's only for long-term control."

Would Charlie have survived whatever had happened to him if he'd taken the right medicine? My mind went back to the older gentleman with the cane whom we'd served. Mom and I had helped him to rehydrate, and the fortune I'd predicted had seemingly shifted slightly. I thought back to what my mom had made us realize: Without my magical foreknowledge, things could have ended much differently for him.

If I had known on that fateful day . . . If I hadn't been so dizzy, had managed to remember Charlie's fortune, might I have been able to jump in and save his life like I'd done with the recent customer? Could I have done more to change the course of destiny?

The garbage truck started up, and the driver summarized, "The whole thing's a darn shame."

I nodded as he reversed out of the alley with an insistent beeping of his vehicle. It was true, what he'd said.

But I wasn't sure if I thought the shame was on the situation or on me.

As Mom and I worked on our respective dough-making, I decided to broach the topic of "destiny." It was better having a conversation while immersed in a parallel task, less awkward this way.

"Do you think you can outrun fate, Mom?" I asked.

She paused in mixing the dough for her pineapple buns. Even though I'd suggested buying a stand mixer more than once, she said her hands had to be involved in every step of the creating and baking process for the joy to come through. "What makes you ask such a thing?"

I sighed. "It's about . . . my predictions and my power. Do you think there's any chance I can actually change fate?"

She pounded the dough, once, twice. "Your father"—her nostrils flared—"he believed that fate was set, couldn't be changed."

"You don't think so?" I added a touch of pandan to my batter, avoiding the reference to my father in favor of more information.

She molded her dough into a ball, placed it in a silver bowl, and covered it with a damp towel. It would need time to rise. "I bake magical goods. And I do believe these pastries bring more happiness to people, change their lives for the better."

I rolled out my dough into round discs, the shape reminding me again of Charlie's last breath. "If fate can be altered, then couldn't I have changed Charlie Gong's? Or was I unleashing his doomed destiny with my fortune cookie?"

"Felicity, you can't think that way." Mom started

on the sugar crumble topping for the pineapple buns. "Your talent, besides giving joy, appears to be *predicting* futures."

"Exactly," I said. "If I'd never predicted his death . . ."

She held up a finger. "First off, you didn't predict he would die, right?"

I thought back on my fortune. The message had only read that he'd have problems with breathing. "Not technically, I guess."

"Second," she continued, "a man makes his own fate. You can only predict it, which means you get to give someone a momentary glimpse into their future. And—maybe—a chance to change it."

Finished with my dough circles now, I placed them into the oven to bake while my mom created an egg wash. She'd use it to baste each pineapple bun so the sugar crumble would adhere better to the bread.

I pulled out the slips of paper from the apron tied around my waist. "What if I could write people nicer messages? Tweak the magic to create better outcomes?"

Mom tilted her head at me. "I don't know, Felicity. I breathe love into every pineapple bun. And the customers come and eat them, but even I'm not sure whether they'll keep that happiness for a day, a month, or a year."

Is the magic dependent on the customer then, so personalized that we only enhanced whatever was already there? Maybe. The more I dove deeper into my magic, *our* magic, the more mysteries I discovered it held.

The timer dinged, and I pulled out the baked discs. At least for this batch, I could plant some positive fortunes. I slipped in the preprinted messages, all cheery and bright future-focused. I tried adopting the same optimistic attitude as I continued baking with my mom.

About twenty minutes before opening, we had everything cooling on racks of silver trays. The entire kitchen smelled like sweet success.

So it came as a shock when a sudden crash sounded from the front of the bakery. We peeked out of the kitchen, and my mom scrambled to the doorway first. She held her arm out to bar me from moving forward, like she'd done every time we hit a pothole when I was younger and riding in the passenger side of her car.

I lowered her arm and gazed at our front door, which now had a sizeable hole in it and a cracked spiderweb lining. What had just happened?

My mom stood in shock while I staggered closer. I stopped short of the door, which had an array of sharp glass all around it. A rock the size of my fist lay in the pile of debris. It was a jagged cold gray lump but textured with bumps.

Was it even a rock? I began stooping down to examine it when my mom cried out.

"Don't, Felicity! I'm calling the police right now."

Oh yeah. This was now a crime scene. I should step back.

I returned behind the counter with my mom while she dialed the cops. Pixie was small enough that a patrol officer arrived within minutes. He jotted down the information we provided, and per my mom's request, took the rock with him.

"Heavier than it looks," he said. "But I'll take care of it."

Mom and I thanked him. As he made to leave, I asked, "Will you be able to find out who did this?"

"We'll try, but sometimes these are one-off pranks. Could be a teen—from Fresno, clearly."

Of course. The implication was that Pixie teens wouldn't have dared do the damage. I know it'd been drilled into me many times what being a resident of our small town required: civility. That principle—and the fact that everyone would've found out too quickly—kept many of us law-abiding citizens even when bending the rules a bit might have felt easier in the moment.

I turned back to the gaping hole. An eyesore. And I wasn't so sure our insurance covered acts of vandalism.

After the police left, I went to get the broom, but Mom beat me to it. She brushed me aside. "No, I will do it. Clean. Make everything better."

As she began sweeping, the first customer of the day stopped before our broken doorway. "Oh my. Let me make a phone call."

Uh-oh. Who was she going to tell? Word would spread, and then what? Would people start shunning our bakery?

But I was wrong. A swath of Pixie residents *did* gather around, but it wasn't to gawk or gossip.

I recognized the familiar faces, including Sweet Tooth Sally. The group set to work, cleaning the floor and boarding up the glass. The slapped-on-a-wood-board look wasn't the most aesthetic decor, but it was safe and allowed us to keep the bakery open.

Mom and I rewarded all the wonderful volunteers with free baked goods. Sometimes I did love living in a small town. Times like this reminded me why.

Not only that, but they ended up urging their friends and acquaintances to drop by. More customers, paying ones, flocked to us. Some declared they wanted to help a local business that had been hit hard (literally).

What had been planned as an act of destruction transformed instead into something beautiful and productive. But as I thought again about the act of vandalism, I glanced at the board on the door with worry. Who had thrown a rock at us? And had it really been an adolescent prankster from Fresno?

CHAPTER 36

The prank didn't seem so innocuous and one-off when our bad fortunes continued. In the late afternoon, an anonymous package was delivered to our shop.

"Are you expecting a delivery, Mom?" I asked.

"No." She waved me to the side as she continued to help bakery customers.

"Be back in a moment," I said, carrying the brown box into the kitchen.

It wasn't heavy, and maybe I was being overly paranoid, but I bent my ear close to the box. No ticking noises, so that was a good sign.

Unsealing it carefully, I found . . . my own fortune cookies staring back at me. They were the same ones I'd recently delivered to the Fresno grocery store with the local goods display.

A small note taped to the bag of the fortune cookies signed by Jeremy Scott read "Sorry it's not working out."

What had happened? Why would Jeremy write that? Perhaps Pixie wasn't local enough for him.

Could the rivalry between towns extend in both directions? I'd always felt it was one-sided, but maybe Fresnans didn't want to buy things made in our Pixie community.

Or maybe the owner himself had decided to choose handmade pastries only from Fresno proper.

My mom peered into the kitchen. "More help in the front, please."

I shoved the returned fortune cookies into a dark corner—and the thought of them to the back of my mind—and hustled to assist her.

We continued to be so busy that I'd almost forgotten about the return until I got a phone call at the end of the day.

"May I speak to Felicity Jin?" The voice on the other end sounded familiar.

"That's me."

"Good thing I kept your number in my receipt book. This is Tala Santos."

The older lady who ran the Asian grocery store in Fresno. "How can I help you?"

"Well, I've been thinking about things." Her voice shook. "It felt mean throwing away your goods, and I can't afford to mail them back to you. I have a small operation, so can you pick up your fortune cookies instead?"

I echoed her. "Pick them up?" What was wrong with them? And why this sudden decision?

"Wonderful," she said, mistaking my repetition for agreement. "We're open 'til seven tonight. Bye." She clicked off.

"What was that all about?" my mom asked.

I stared at the phone in my hand. "I'm not sure." I glanced back into the kitchen where the other unwanted fortune cookies sat. "Honestly, I don't know what's happening. But I'm going to find out."

* * *

Later that evening, I dropped by the Asian mart. I timed it near their closing, as I wanted to get the owner alone to talk to her in depth. I hoped there weren't any lingering last-minute shoppers. Or if there were, maybe I could chat with her as she closed up shop. I could even lend a hand to make things easier for her as she tidied up—perhaps that would get us back in her good graces.

I needn't have worried. She was alone behind the counter when I walked into her store. "Everything okay?" I asked as I approached. "Was something wrong with that last batch of fortune cookies?"

Her eyes crinkled in confusion. "No, but I want to say I understand where you're coming from. My little grocery store doesn't get a whole lot of customers."

"I'm sorry?" I didn't know what she was talking about. Had she gotten the wrong impression somehow? I didn't look down on her store.

"Myself, I don't need a lot of profit," she said. "I just want to have a quaint environment where people can buy the Asian goodies they enjoy."

"I'm not sure I understand. Do you think I don't want to sell fortune cookies at your place anymore?"

She nodded, a resigned expression on her face.

"Why would you think I'd cut off ties with you?"

"Your associate, dear. Said you wanted to focus on supplying to restaurants instead."

Like Foo Fusion? My eyes narrowed. Michael was a staunch businessman. He'd given me the grocery store names in the first place. Could he now be taking away my connections to punish me?

Thinking of punishments, my mind wandered to the rock thrown at our door. Could Michael have acted out of retribution? Thinking that the threats might force my hand to return to him and supply his eating challenge?

The store owner cleared her throat. "Do you want to pick up the cookies now?"

"I apologize. There must have been a mix-up. I don't want to stop working with you. We'd love for you to keep on selling our fortune cookies, please."

Her sun-spotted hand fluttered around her throat. "Oh, well, that's wonderful. My loyal customers do so enjoy them. And I eat them for a snack now and again, too."

"I'm glad about that," I said.

But there was someone who wouldn't be glad to see me. When I showed up at their restaurant and gave them a piece of my mind.

At Foo Fusion, I wanted to barge right up to Michael, but there was a crowd in front of me blocking my way. How long did his dinner rush last? Or maybe the eating contest had gone viral; I heard more than a few customers asking to try the new fortune cookie challenge.

I got in line (having been taught not to cut) and idly wondered if the diners were still eating Gold Bakery fortune cookies or some poorer substitute.

When I reached the register, Michael appeared frazzled. A sheen of sweat covered his forehead.

"Next," he called without even looking at me.

"It's Felicity," I said, "and I won't be buying a single thing from you tonight. I don't appreciate you trying to take my business away from the local grocery stores."

He gave me a blank stare. "I'm not sure—"

"Or the rock thrown through my window."

He wiped his glistening skin with the back of his hand.

"Well, door. But you know what I mean."

"Actually, I don't."

"I'm out of our deal," I said, "and you're never gonna change my mind."

He glanced at the long line snaking out the door, seemingly unconcerned by what I'd just said. "Sure, whatever you want."

"Hurry up already," the person behind me said, their voice sounding quite close to my ear. I felt the crowd jostling.

Michael pulled out a sheet of paper from under the counter and flashed it at me. Our revised contract. He ripped it in two. "Done. It's all over. Satisfied?" he said before depositing the scraps in my hands.

Well, that was easy. I marched out of the restaurant with my head held high. A slight twinge of regret swirled around me—or maybe that was the fragrance of the curry doughnuts wafting in the air. I'd cut off ties, but I would sure miss those croquettes.

CHAPTER 37

Honestly, I felt kind of bad for leaving Michael in the lurch. I'd broken our agreement, and that wasn't the Jin way.

The remorse didn't last too long, though. Because when I returned to the apartment, I found Mom making phone calls in desperation. She was looking for a repairman to permanently fix our bakery's glass door.

It took her about an hour of calling before securing a friend of a friend of a friend to come in. Thankfully, this person could do the job on short notice and show up tomorrow morning. Again, small-town living had its perks.

It had all been a business agreement with Michael, so he probably wouldn't be too broken-hearted. Besides, my bowing out meant riches for another. Smiley Fortunes, for example, could use a boost. I believed in second chances. Wasn't that what had happened with me and my baking?

Perhaps I should give Cayla a call and let her know about the possibility of more business from Foo Fusion. With Whiskers snuggled up next to me, I looked up the company in the phone book and dialed. I knew it was late, so I wasn't surprised when I got their answering machine.

"Hey, Cayla," I said. "It's Felicity from Gold Bakery.

I wanted to let you know about a business opportunity that would be a great fit for Smiley—"

Beep.

I hated those voicemail services that cut you off after a certain amount of time. Or maybe Cayla couldn't be bothered with listening to long messages and had customized it to record only for a short while.

Oh, well. I would take care of it tomorrow. Maybe I'd call again and speak faster. Or drop by after work when I had more spare time to tell her in person.

Turned out I didn't need to do either. Cayla beat me to it.

The next day, about twenty minutes after we opened, Cayla showed up at Gold Bakery. She wore a black power suit with dark purple clay earrings, her hair pinned back by sparkling diamond barrettes, and exuded managerial authority, although she wasn't carrying her usual clipboard.

Cayla waited until I'd served the other customers before springing on me. "What's this about a business proposition?"

"Had to pull out of a deal recently," I said, explaining how'd I decided to break ties with Foo Fusion. Of course I didn't mention the damage to the bakery's glass door (though she'd no doubt seen it coming in) or how Michael had tried to sabotage my connections with the Fresno grocery stores.

She frowned. "You think Michael would want us back? After what happened?" I assumed she meant the demise of the Fortune Cookie King (and the contract) along with the poor quality of their products.

I thought about it. "I'm pretty sure he would. Out of

necessity. He needs a lot of fortune cookies, and I know Smiley can keep up with the high manufacturing rate."

She brushed off some imaginary dust from her lapel. "We do work quickly. Fast laborers and precise machines. A winning combo."

"Yeah, that's not really our style." I pointed to our small kitchen, where Mom was shuffling around. "This is strictly a mother-daughter shop, and I'd like to keep it that way."

"Good. So we shouldn't have any more problems with each other." She held her hand out, and I shook it.

A hint of rancid milk floated in the air, like her stress personified.

"Do you want a fortune cookie?" I asked on a whim. "I can make you a fresh one."

"That's actually very kind of you." I don't know why, but she seemed taken aback by my generosity.

"It's not a problem." I rushed to the kitchen, popping the batter in the oven.

On the counter, I'd already set out piles of printed generic fortunes, and I rummaged through them to find an encouraging saying for Cayla. Maybe something about her being financially secure.

I slipped in a prediction of abundant wealth and gave her the sweet treat. She murmured her thanks and bit into the fortune cookie.

The nausea started for me then. I couldn't believe the magic was still happening, even with a preprinted message already inside the cookie.

I'd forgotten that Cayla and I had shaken hands, and my fingers longed to create a customized fortune for her. My magical ability must be tied to the physical act of writing down a prediction, and printed messages didn't appear to block the magic from flowing.

While I was trying to stabilize the swirling colors in my mind, Cayla kept on talking. It was like hearing her through a fog. The words drifted to me in a haze: her deep concern about how the door to our shop had been broken.

I gave a curt nod, hoping it wouldn't increase my wooziness. If only she'd leave, so I could take a break and rest.

She said something about how it must've been a huge rock that had been thrown at the glass to cause it to shatter. I tried to smile at her, but maybe it came off as a grimace in my pain because she excused herself and backed away.

When she left, the boarded door closed with a thud, and I stared at it. Wait a minute. How had Cayla known it was a rock that had done the damage? She wasn't part of the Pixie grapevine. For all she knew, any object could've slammed through our door. A baseball, a brick . . .

I started slumping at the counter, and my mom hurried to my side.

"What's wrong, Felicity?"

"I'm trying to keep the fortune in," I whispered through gritted teeth.

"No, that's not good for you." Mom quickly brought over paper and pencil.

I picked a color, scribbled down the fortune as fast as I could, jammed it in my pocket without a glance, and ran out the door. Sure enough, a car peeled down the road, Cayla behind the wheel. It seemed like she couldn't wait to get away from me. My hunch had been right.

I called out a quick "Gotta go" to my mom and jumped into her Corolla. I'd need to hurry to chase after the fleeing Cayla. I turned the key in the engine, but the old car spluttered at me. "Come on," I urged it. "Please work."

What a time for the car to conk out on me. I gave it

two more attempts, but it still didn't start. Ugh. I'd never trail her now. But wait a minute, I'd written her fortune down. My magical skill might come to the rescue. I'd chosen the yellow line for Cayla, the color connected to imminent travel.

I checked the message I'd predicted about Cayla. It read "You will take a much-needed trip to where cookie smiles vanish."

The combination of "cookie" and "smiles" made me think of the factory. I turned the key again. This time it started, and I raced off to Smiley Fortunes.

When I arrived at the fortune cookie factory, something seemed amiss. The car Cayla had been driving was parked crooked. I stumbled on the unevenly paved sidewalk as I approached the vehicle. I soon realized the engine was still running. She must be in a hurry. But I didn't spy Cayla in the driver's seat. Through the windows, I checked all the seats, but they were vacant.

Then I went around to the back of the car and found the trunk slightly open. I bent to peek through the crack but couldn't make out anything in the dim interior. I lifted the trunk lid up.

Empty in there. Well, almost. There was something stuck in the far rear corner. What was it?

My balance teetered as I shifted forward to get to the inner recesses. I reached for the cylindrical plastic piece. An inhaler. I realized that right before my legs wobbled and a blackness enveloped me.

CHAPTER 38

I woke up to a small penlight shining in my eyes. The paramedics hovering around me assessed my vitals. Then they fired a bunch of questions to check on my present state.

After taking a deep gulp of air to center myself, I gave them the answers they wanted. My name is Felicity Jin. I'm twenty-eight years old. I live in Pixie, California. I'm currently at Smiley Fortunes cookie factory. I don't know what happened after my arrival.

Technically, I was sitting on the pavement near the ramshackle factory, not actually inside it, but they seemed satisfied with my responses. Once the medical professionals backed away, a familiar figure swooped in.

Detective Sun. I'd recognize her high ponytail anywhere.

My throat felt parched, and I gave her a raspy hello.

She motioned to the paramedics and got me a bottled water.

I yanked off the cap and took a deep drink. Ah, much better.

The detective crouched down to my level. "Want to tell me what happened?"

I skipped over the fact that I'd predicted Cayla's

location magically and went straight to: "I was following Cayla."

"And why were you following her?"

"She acted funny at the bakery."

The detective nodded, unsurprised by this tidbit of info. "Okay, and what do you remember happening when you got here?"

I squinted as though trying hard to spot something in the distance. "Her car was here. Parked."

Something about the car was vital. I tried remembering, but it set off a sharp throbbing in my head.

"How did you end up on the ground?" she asked.

"I was where?" I touched the back of my head, and it stung. A large bump was forming there.

A paramedic crept up on us and passed me a cold compress. I mumbled my thanks and iced my injury. The paramedic retreated, leaving us to our conversation.

"You definitely hit your head," the detective said. "How?"

"I, um, don't remember." It had to do with a car. The trunk somehow? I shook my head—and regretted it.

Detective Sun noticed my grimace. "Hey, take it easy. You bumped your head. Maybe you tripped on construction debris. It's not smoothly paved around here."

"There's something I need to tell you." I focused on visualizing a trunk. It had been open. I'd seen an important item. "The inhaler."

"What's that?" The detective leaned closer.

"In Cayla's car, she had an inhaler."

"I'm not following you."

"What if she had something to do with Charlie's death? Why else would she run away from me?"

Detective Sun glanced at the fortune cookie factory. The lights were off, and it must had closed for the day already. "You know, Cayla was the one who phoned this in."

"Excuse me?"

"She got flustered, saw my card on the desk, and called to tell us you'd had an accident. Wanted to make sure you got proper medical attention."

It didn't make sense. Why would she give me help? Especially if she wanted me silenced. She could've left me to fend for myself, and with the painful throbbing in my head, there was every chance that wouldn't have ended so well for me.

Detective Sun tightened her ponytail. "You know, Cayla told me she felt bad about the whole thing. Said she got spooked at the bakery."

"Why?"

"She could tell by the expression on your face that you realized she'd thrown the rock."

I *had* come to that conclusion, though I hadn't even wanted to think it to myself.

"Cayla admitted she broke your door out of jealousy. Apparently, she regrets it and wants to pay for any damage."

I couldn't care less about the door at this point. Was the detective absolving Cayla of any guilt for the murder? But I'd seen the inhaler. Unless it was Cayla's . . . but who puts a spare in their trunk? Wouldn't a glove compartment be a better choice? Not that I was an asthma sufferer and knew enough about it. I wished I'd gotten a closer look before I'd blacked out.

I knew I sounded like a broken record, but I stated it once more. "The inhaler, Detective."

She sighed. "I've already got a homicide suspect in mind. Once we compile more evidence, we'll bring him in."

"Detective—"

Her voice turned sharp. "May I make a suggestion, Felicity?"

"Of course."

"Let it go," she said. "Go back to baking. Focus on your relationship with your mom. Time is precious."

The detective had a good point. I'd injured my head, somehow. Maybe by tripping and falling hard, though I still couldn't quite believe that. Either way, it was probably time for me to relax and recuperate.

After refusing any more medical attention, I did as Detective Sun suggested. She dropped me off at home while another officer parked Mom's car in front of our complex. Once I entered the apartment, three figures rushed at me—okay, one of them hopped toward me.

The humans, of course, were Mom and Kelvin. I checked the clock. "Did you two take the rest of the day off?"

"Detective Sun called your mom," Kelvin said. "We both closed up shop."

"I was so worried about you." Mom had grabbed me as soon as I stepped through the door, and she held me tighter and tighter until I wiggled in her arms, and she had to release me. "The way you ran off like that . . ."

"I had to go after Cayla." I gritted my teeth. "After she threw that rock and damaged our bakery—tried to destroy our business—I had to say something."

"You looked so concerned, I sent Kelvin after you."

He gave me a sheepish grin. "But you were too quick. I couldn't chase after you."

Whiskers hopped up and down near me. I scooped her in for a cuddle. "I drove to the fortune cookie factory . . . where I was unconscious for a bit. The details are fuzzy."

Mom gasped, and Kelvin was shocked into silence.

"The detective only told me she knew where you were." Mom hurried into motion, placing a hand on my forehead. "Is it the fortune-telling? Maybe it's making you go weak again. At random times, now?"

"No, I don't think so." I rubbed the top of Whiskers' head. "Besides, the paramedics cleared me."

"Detective Sun assured me she was close to making an arrest. I can't wait to put all this drama behind us." Mom's eyes misted.

"Right." I took my time rubbing the bunny's head until my mom excused herself to freshen up in the bathroom.

Kelvin crept over to me. "What aren't you telling us?"

"I didn't faint," I said, reaching for the tender spot at the back of my head.

Kelvin examined the bump, and his voice grew rough. "Did someone hurt you, Lissa?"

"I'm not sure, but I did find something interesting in the trunk of Cayla's car." I filled my best friend in on how I'd discovered an inhaler, and my theory that Cayla might be tied to the murder.

"That's a direct connection," Kelvin said. "Did you tell the cops?"

"I tried to, but Detective Sun didn't believe me. She dismissed the idea. Said the inhaler might be Cayla's. Even thought that I might've tripped on the pavement and knocked myself out."

"I wonder why."

"Cayla was acting like a good Samaritan. According to Detective Sun, she was the one who called for medical help for me."

Kelvin's eyes narrowed. "To cover her tracks?"

"Could be," I said, but sighed. "The detective's not willing to consider her a suspect right now. Especially since she's keen on her current choice of a culprit."

"Logan Miller." Kelvin bit his lip. Maybe he was remembering the police cruising outside of Logan's home.

"What if the guy's innocent?" I said. "I'd feel horrible if I didn't do anything to help him, especially since—if he's not the killer—I got him into this situation in the first place."

"I can call him," Kelvin said.

We stopped speaking as my mom stepped into the room.

"What are you two scheming over?" she asked.

"Nothing. Just our plans for tonight," I said, not wanting to worry her any more than she already was.

"What? You two are going out?" Her forehead wrinkled with concern. "Is that too soon, Felicity?"

"I just need some fresh air," I said, motioning for Kelvin to go ahead and make the call.

He moved outside for privacy and returned with a smile. "I've found the perfect place for us to go, Lissa."

We exited the apartment, and I made sure I was out of Mom's earshot and line of sight before I spoke. "Did you get ahold of Logan, then?"

"No, I got an automated response that he was driving."

"But that's not helpful." I started trudging back to the apartment door.

Kelvin stopped me. "It is when his Do Not Disturb message is customized. Said he's off to the underground gardens."

CHAPTER 39

If you didn't already know about the Forestiere Underground Gardens, you might drive right past it. It looked like an unassuming building paired with a small grove of citrus trees, but the place was a California Historic Landmark, the brainchild of an Italian immigrant. The gardens boasted subterranean pathways, structures, and plants.

Most important, the temperature underground was at least ten degrees lower than at the surface level. I didn't know about Kelvin, but I sure wished for that coolness as we entered the main lobby.

The ceiling fans above me whirred, but they only circulated the warm air. When we asked, one of the employees told us that the current tour was already underway, and we were too late to join it.

I sat at a bench, waiting for the tour's end, while Kelvin strolled around. He explored the large lobby, stopping to read informational displays about Baldassare Forestiere, his Sicilian heritage, and the elaborate idea that had resulted in an underground garden.

About thirty minutes later, the loud thumping of footsteps alerted us to the returning visitors. Logan trailed at the end of the tour group, glancing behind him toward the stairs leading down to the gardens, as though he wanted to prolong his visit. I didn't blame the guy for wanting to stay a few minutes longer in the cooler environment.

After fanning myself with my hand, I got up from my seat and called his name. He started at my presence. "What are you doing here?"

"Kelvin called and got your automated driving response. We wanted to check on you, see how things were going." And ask a few questions about Cayla along the way, I added to myself.

I beckoned for Logan to follow me, away from the crowded merchandise section to the nearby vast and empty hall. I liked the comforting feel of being below the high rafters and the sight of solid brick walls surrounding me. Nothing bad could happen in such a grounded space.

Kelvin also stopped browsing and joined us.

"Did you enjoy your tour?" I asked Logan.

"It's so nice. Like a whole different world underground. I only wish I could stay longer." He motioned to the other room in the building, where I could spy a few wheelbarrows on display. "You know, the gardens are on the National Register of Historic Places."

Huh. Guess it'd been recognized both statewide and nationally. If we had one of these places in Pixie, we could bring in more tourists . . . and subsequently, bakery customers.

Logan continued. "I'm trying to go through my bucket list of spots to visit. Make the most of the time I have left."

"'Time left'? Is everything okay?" I asked.

"It's the police," he said. "They won't leave me alone. I've started having trouble sleeping at night." Now that he mentioned it, I noticed the dark circles under his eyes.

"I can't believe they're bothering you," I said, then dropped what I hoped would be an irresistible statement, "because I know you're innocent."

"You do?" He seemed flabbergasted.

I placed my hand over my heart. "For sure." Steering the conversation in a direction that might shed light on what I'd seen in her car, I said, "Cayla, for one, could be a possible suspect."

Logan shook his head. "Nah. She and Charlie were close, dating even."

They'd been a couple? That might explain the inhaler, then. Even if it had been Charlie's, a supportive girlfriend might keep a spare in her car.

Kelvin piped up. "What happened to your other shoes?"

Logan shuffled his feet. He was no longer wearing his yellow treads but simple white sneakers. "I got rid of them. Put them in the trash. They reminded me too much of that night . . ."

He'd wanted to dump the memories. I understood. But he couldn't so easily erase people's eyewitness accounts of him running away from the direction of the crime scene. No matter what I'd said to him, I still wasn't entirely sure who to think was responsible for Charlie's demise.

I tried to insert genuine concern into my voice to get him to open up. "What really happened between you and Charlie? I won't judge."

Logan began to move his mouth, but then doubt crept across his face, and he seemed to stop himself. "It's complicated. Anyway, thanks for checking in on me. But maybe I'm stressing for no reason, and everything will turn out fine."

He didn't seem convinced of his own words, and I wasn't so certain either, given Detective Sun's desire to close the case quickly.

My sense of unease only deepened the next day. It didn't help that I woke up in the dim light of pre-dawn with a pounding headache. On the other hand, I'd finally gotten used to regular baking hours. Didn't need an alarm clock to wake me.

I touched the back of my head and winced. The bump I'd received hadn't gone down in size, and it still hurt. I hoped the headache would go away once I started the usual morning routine.

Mom and I didn't talk as we made our way to the bakery, although she kept glancing over at me.

"Why are you looking at me like that?" I asked finally.

"Are you okay, Felicity?"

"Yeah, why?"

"Because you're making little groans."

I hadn't even noticed. "I'm fine, Mom," I said. We'd reached the shop by that time, and I began busying myself in the kitchen.

"Maybe take it easy today," Mom said.

"I will." Instead of pulling out loads of ingredients, I opted to streamline the selection of fortune cookies. I wouldn't be exploring the full range of flavors today. I'd stick to simple batches of vanilla cookies.

Mom also stayed with the staples: the traditional egg tarts and pineapple buns. In the same amount of time, she ended up making three times more pastries than I had. Then again, I kept on taking water breaks. I wasn't sure if I did it for my own health or to appease my mom.

Anyway, it wouldn't matter how many fortune cookies I made. Despite the pity bump in sales from the broken door, I figured people weren't clamoring for our goods again yet. Not with a murderer still on the loose.

Happily, I was proven wrong. Ten minutes before opening, there was a line already waiting patiently before the locked door. When Mom saw the people outside, she clapped her hands in glee.

"This community," she said almost under her breath. "I'm so glad we live here. It's such a safe, loving place."

Customers wanted to buy multiples of items, and we were selling out of our goodies fast. People couldn't wait to munch on the pastries, and some started eating them right in the shop (after paying for the items, of course).

One impatient customer couldn't even wait for that and started munching on my fortune cookie before I could ring up his purchase.

"Hmm," he said. "I remember it tasting better before."

Really? I kept a fake smile pasted on my face. One negative response didn't mean anything, right?

Besides, he still paid me for a varied collection of baked goods.

I soon noticed that Mom's baked items were selling at a faster pace than mine, but I didn't care. My fortune cookies were still relatively new to the lineup. It'd take time for customers to appreciate them.

As the day went on, I did eventually sell the entire batch of cookies I'd baked. The generic fortunes I'd preprinted had also run out.

I hurried off to make a new batch. To ward off any potential complaints, like with the previous impatient individual, I made a few flat ones to offer as samples, so people could try before committing to buy. Most customers accepted the freebies and ate them with delight.

Several, though, mumbled that the fortune cookies tasted "off" or were "a little stale."

They're freshly baked, I wanted to tell the critics. Was something off with my magic again? Still, I made a new batch and distracted myself with the next customer, a little boy waiting for piping-hot fortune cookies.

I'd give him an extra-special treat by writing a customized fortune for him. Maybe I'd predict good grades or a new bike or a warm puppy . . .

"It won't take long," I told the boy and his guardian. "Be back soon." I lifted my hand up for him to high-five, and he complied, giving it a loud thwack.

When I went to write his fortune down, though, nothing appeared to me. It was like my brain had been silenced. My mind became a blank space, with no colorful lines appearing. I waited a few more moments. Nothing.

Maybe my fortunes didn't apply to little kids? I wrote up a cheerful and happy message for the boy. It could be that younger folks didn't have their fates set yet.

I continued crafting more fortune cookies and selling them, but my failure stayed with me. Was something actually wrong?

When we had less of a rush, I focused my attention on a woman wearing a bright orange cardigan. I'd customize a fortune for her.

I went through the usual process of making physical contact before offering the cookie. Nothing happened the second time around, and this woman was a stranger and an adult. A void remained in my head, and my hands didn't itch to write down a message.

What was going on? I motioned for my mom to take over my spot at the register and moved into the kitchen. Standing next to a metal table, I stared at my hands.

I flexed my fingers. They seemed to be working fine.

From a cooling tray, I plucked a beautiful fortune cookie. The right color and shape. I tasted it. There was sugar, vanilla, all the right ingredients, but something was off.

That impatient customer had been right. The cookies were edible but not pleasurable. They didn't have that special hint of happiness.

And the fortunes? I could only make up pretend predictions, not actual personalized messages.

The chattering of customers from out front reached me in the kitchen. Would I be okay continuing to serve them plain cookies with bland fortunes?

No. That wasn't my destiny. It couldn't be. I leaned over the metal prep table, tracing the character of my surname into the leftover flour.

At least I'd lived up to the Jin name for a little while when I'd discovered my fated fortune cookie recipe. I had belonged for a moment in time. And now?

The knock on my head had upset the balance. Just as I thought that, my head seemed to bang—in a different way than the headache that had been plaguing me all day.

What was happening? The tempo of the sound shifted. That wasn't from inside my head. It was knocking, a pounding on the back door. I went over and opened it.

CHAPTER 40

Kelvin barged through the back door of Gold Bakery. His words came out in a rush: "There was a long line, so I came through the alley to avoid the crowd, and there's something import—Lissa, what's wrong?"

He stepped close to me and put his hands on my shoulders.

"My powers are gone," I said. "All of them. The joy-baking kind *and* the fortune-telling ability." I pushed his hands away from me.

Kelvin glanced at my head. "You did get a nasty bump recently. Maybe it has something to do with your injury."

I turned toward the counter and erased the Jin character on the metal table I'd drawn in the flour with a swipe of my hand. I'd been able to hold in my emotions when I was alone but with Kelvin, they all came spilling out. "You could be right, and it might have affected me permanently. What will I do if that's what happened? I just found my magic—I'd hate to lose it so soon."

"Lissa, look at me," Kelvin said.

I turned back toward him.

He gazed into my eyes. I could feel the kindness flowing from him. "Your powers, they don't really matter."

"Tell that to my ancestors," I joked darkly.

He raised an eyebrow. "You've never been at ease with yourself just as you are. When will you find your own joy and not bake it for others?"

"Gee, such wisdom. You should be writing the fortunes, not me."

"I'm serious. People who care about you, we love you for who you are, unconditionally."

I made a noncommittal murmur.

"Think about it," he said. "If I didn't have my flower power, you'd still appreciate me, right?"

"Well . . ."

He chuckled. "Okay, bad example."

The back door of the bakery swayed in the breeze, and I moved to close it, which reminded me that Kelvin had come here for a reason. "But you didn't come here to comfort me. Unless you suddenly developed ESP?"

"Sadly, no. But I come bearing news—about Logan. Posted earlier this morning on the *Courier*'s website."

I tamped down my own troubles, which I couldn't solve right now anyway, and focused on the murder case. "Tell me the details."

"I'll show you instead." He pulled out his phone and gave it to me.

The title of the article was "Fresno man arrested in Fortune Cookie King murder case." That was the hook? It was biased news, a smattering of facts but with a heavy emphasis that *of course, murderers came from Fresno and not Pixie.*

There wasn't much information beyond Logan's name and the charges against him.

"What could have happened?" I said as I returned the phone.

"Maybe the police got more evidence somehow?"

Then it hit me. They had. And it hinged on what

Logan had told us yesterday. "He threw away his shoes," I said.

Kelvin followed my train of thinking. "The police could've gotten forensic evidence off of them."

I thought for a moment.

"Hmm, let's take a walk."

"Right now?" Kelvin said.

"It won't be far." I ushered him through the back door. "Let's do an experiment."

I marched over to the dumpster and studied the lid. To open it, I saw how I had to position my body.

I yanked open the top. It was heavier than I'd expected but doable. "Need your help, Kelvin."

"Uh, how?"

I sized my best friend up. He was way taller than Charlie Gong and probably heavier, but he'd serve as a good estimate.

Without warning, I wrapped my arms around Kelvin's waist. He felt comforting, like good memories and fresh baked bread.

Kelvin squirmed a little in my grip. "Lissa, what are you doing?"

I tried lifting him up. It took a few tries, but I managed to raise Kelvin off the ground a couple of inches. But certainly not over my head. No way could I have thrown someone his size into a dumpster.

"Are you reenacting the crime?" he asked.

I hushed Kelvin but gave up on the lifting. Instead, I walked around the perimeter of the dumpster, studying the area.

As usual, the ground wasn't even close to immaculate. There were fast-food wrappers, grease-stained bags, smeared ketchup marks.

A memory flashed in my mind. When I'd taken out

the bakery trash the night of Charlie's death, I'd spied open condiment packets near the dumpster.

I crouched down to study the smears.

"Did you find a new clue?" Kelvin asked.

"No, but I think this is how the police finally got their arrest."

"By looking at the ground?"

"By matching Logan's footprints to the scene of the crime." Readily so, since he'd probably stepped into some sauce and provided a perfect partial imprint.

Kelvin offered a hand to me to help me stand even though I didn't need it. I appreciated the gesture because talking about crime scenes wasn't in the typical Jin conversation repertoire. My mom and I always tried to focus on the light and cheery. It meant we didn't talk a lot about the news. This whole investigation had been a break from tradition, and—as the bump on my head proved—it was starting to wear on me.

After I got to my feet, Kelvin said, "But aren't Logan's shoes his private property?"

"They were," I said, "up until he chucked them in the trash. Detective Sun probably didn't even need a search warrant to get them. The shoes were out there for anyone to take."

"Kinda smart of her," Kelvin said.

I closed my eyes and replayed a potential alley scene in my head. Charlie and Logan had had an argument out here. Then, if Logan's word could be counted on, Charlie started having breathing problems. An asthma attack? He reached for his medication and . . . what? It didn't work? How did Cayla fit into this scenario? Or did she at all?

I opened my eyes, frustrated. Nothing here except for this dumpster. Staring at it, I grew even more puzzled.

Logan could very well have pitched Charlie's body into the dumpster. He had the strength for it. Was he not so innocent after all? I rubbed at my aching temples.

Mom stuck her head out the back door, gave Kelvin a quick hello, and said, "Felicity, we've got some customers."

"Some customers" was an understatement. All of a sudden, people were swarming our shop. It was like the floodgates had opened after that *Pixie Courier* article. Plus, word had spread from our sales earlier in the day. I didn't even get to say goodbye to Kelvin as he snuck off while I dealt with the crowd.

Perhaps Pixie residents had been waiting, holding off their appetites, until we were totally in the clear. Then they rushed to the bakery in a feeding frenzy.

We kept on selling without pause until we'd cleaned out the entire bakery. And it happened before closing time.

For the rest of the customers, we had to write vouchers on the spot, promising them goods for the next day. We'd definitely have to come in even earlier tomorrow to bake enough treats, though I wasn't complaining. The murder might not yet be solved but maybe our financial problems would be over.

CHAPTER 41

My headache didn't diminish the next day, and it didn't help that Mom and I had gotten up even earlier to fulfill our promised pre-orders. In the kitchen of the bakery, I made batches and batches of fortune cookies, but they still tasted not quite right. There was a lingering hint of saltiness to them. My mom put it this way: "They taste like tears."

It was true. Maybe I hadn't openly cried while folding them, but there was a deep sadness residing in my soul. I cried internally for Logan.

The guilt gnawed at me, especially after how grateful he had seemed at the underground gardens when I said I'd believed in his innocence. And now he'd been taken into custody and charged with murder.

"Quit moping, why don't you?" my mom said as she maneuvered around me and slid a tray of egg tarts out of the oven. "You'll be of no use baking when you're so sad. On second thought, take the whole day off."

"But, Mom, the crowd—"

She snorted and motioned to our trove of pastries. We had woken up and baked a lot this morning. She could, for sure, sell her goodies. Mine might be passable in a pinch, though I wasn't sure Mom would stoop to giving out inferior fortune cookies.

"I think the bakery will be fine, Felicity. But you won't be fine stuck here. Go and clear your head."

"Thanks, Mom." I put away my apron and walked out into the crisp air.

I continued down the cul-de-sac, my steps automatically taking me to Kelvin's shop. For solace.

He was busy with a few early bird customers, so I waited until the store emptied out. Then I spilled my guts about my guilty feelings.

"Whoa there, Lissa," he said.

I rubbed my eyes, which had started to itch like I was on the verge of tears.

"It's not your fault, you know."

"I'd feel a lot of better if I could see Logan face-to-face," I said, "and he confessed that he really *was* the murderer." I gave a half-hearted laugh. "Case solved. Then I could put all this behind me, and believe this is justice and not a mistake."

"That's not a bad idea. Why not go and see Logan?"

"What?"

"We could visit him in jail," Kelvin said. "It's a secure place if he's a danger, and they do allow visitors."

"But what do you mean by 'we'?" I waved my hand at all his plants. "Who's going to run your shop?"

"The thing is, I've got a very nice boss, and he'll give me a long lunch break." He winked at me. "Besides, you look like you need a nap right now. Meet me back here at noon."

It'd been a while since I'd done some self-care. And Kelvin was right (as usual). I dozed off as soon as my head hit the pillow. Good thing I'd set my alarm to wake me up for Kelvin's lunch hour.

It seemed like barely any time had passed before I found myself back in front of Love Blooms. Once Kelvin saw me loitering on the sidewalk in front of his shop, he put up his WE'LL BE BACK sign and locked up.

It was a quick trip to get to the imposing gray building where Logan was being held. In the lobby, we made our request to visit him, but the woman in charge tut-tutted at us.

"New rules," she said. "Only one visitor per inmate."

Oh, great. Would we have to rock-paper-scissors it? I made eye contact with Kelvin, but he said, "You go in. I'll wait out here in the lobby."

The woman spoke up again. "Nope, not in the lobby, but you're free to wait outside the building."

Kelvin agreed. "I'll be right by the front door when you're done."

The security processing to access the interior went by in an anxious blur. I'd never been to a jail before, and my nerves were rattled. I had to show them my ID and even do a temperature check.

Security asked me to leave behind my belongings, so I had to drop off my purse. Then they made me pass through a metal detector.

The actual visiting area was like a scene from the movies. A row of windows separated the visitors and the inmates. Telephones attached to the walls appeared in each plexiglass partitioned space.

When he approached the window, Logan looked different. The standard-issue bright red garb didn't fit him well. He also appeared drained of energy and sat down with a slump. I perched across from him on a metal stool and picked up the phone.

His voice crackled down the line. "Don't know why you're here. It's game over for me."

"Not yet, Logan. Hey, were you able to get a good lawyer?"

"Can't afford one, but I'll have a public defender."

"I have a serious question for you." I licked my lips. "Are you innocent?"

He stared at me through the window, his gaze never leaving mine. "Yes, I am."

"Then you'll be set free."

He ran his hand through his hair. "If only it were that easy."

"If you'll tell me the truth"—I lowered my voice—"I can try and help."

His eyes flicked to the camera set in the corner of the tight space and then back to me. "Guess it can't get any worse than this. What do you want to know?"

"Your shoes," I said. "I'm making an educated guess here, but did they find your footprints at the scene of the crime?"

He hung his head. "Yeah, 'cuz I was there."

"But what were you doing in the alley?" I said. "Thought you were meeting near the shops."

"Charlie started getting riled up, so we moved somewhere quieter. The back street, to not disturb local businesses."

I continued. "And before, you told me you ran away as soon as Charlie started having breathing problems."

He tugged at the cord of his phone. "So that part wasn't entirely true."

I trained a sharp gaze on him. "Well, you can tell me what really happened now."

"Okay, okay. I saw the whole asthma attack. Charlie tried to use his inhaler thing, but that made it worse. He really had it bad—started drooling, turning pale. Then he collapsed . . . It all happened so quickly. He was gone before I could even reach for my phone."

I shivered. "What'd you do when you realized that?"

His voice turned emotionless. "I decided to help myself at that point."

"How?" I gently asked.

"By placing . . . his body . . . in the dumpster."

I suppressed a gasp at what he'd admitted to me.

Logan continued. "Charlie was gone by then. Lifeless. I mean, I didn't kill him, not really. But I wasn't thinking straight either. Out of sight, out of mind. I just . . . panicked."

This was a real-life case of sticking your head in the sand, and he had literally run away from the situation. But I still felt like I was missing a key piece of info.

"What I don't get is why you were in Pixie in the first place," I said. Our bakery wasn't anywhere near the Fresno border. And I doubted he'd been out for a jog in downtown Pixie like Mrs. Spreckels had originally assumed.

"Because I got a text from my boss," he said, "about wanting to apologize in person and saying we should meet up."

I blinked at him. Really? Had Charlie wanted Logan to return to the factory? I searched my memory bank. Charlie *had* mentioned being short-staffed—almost complaining about it—in our bakery. And he had seemed pressed for time, like he was on his way to a meeting.

"Anything else you want to add?" I said.

"I wished I hadn't worn those yellow sneaks. Too eye-catching." Logan's mouth twitched, and he hung up the phone with a firm shove.

The visit was over, but something troubled me about our conversation. If the Fortune Cookie King had wanted to reconcile, why couldn't he meet in Fresno instead of Pixie? Something was off about this whole thing.

CHAPTER 42

Why hadn't Charlie and Logan reconciled in a place closer to home? I left the jail, confused, and found Kelvin patiently waiting outside the entrance like he'd promised.

While we walked back to the car, I shared my thoughts with him. "I don't get it. Why would Charlie send that text? The meeting location doesn't make any sense."

Kelvin took two huge steps. "Maybe he deliberately chose to have Logan end up in a secluded spot."

I hurried my pace to match my best friend's stride. "Why? To get into an argument with him? He could yell at Logan all he wanted to in Fresno."

"Could it be the opposite of what we thought in the beginning? Maybe we have the culprit and victim reversed. Instead of Logan wanting to attack Charlie, the Fortune Cookie King had wanted to get rid of Logan."

We arrived at the car, and I tugged open my door. Could the police have gotten things so wrong? "But Charlie didn't have a weapon on him, remember?"

Kelvin situated himself in the driver's seat, and I buckled myself in next to him.

"That the police found," he said. "But do you think

they had time to check the entire dumpster? Maybe they just figured everything in there was trash and overlooked it."

"I'd give the cops more credit than that," I said. They had, after all, eventually matched Logan's footprints to the crime scene. Which reminded me. "Maybe it was about the lighting."

"What's that?" Kelvin turned to face me.

"The alley. It gets dark back there, especially in the evening. Charlie would've had the element of surprise on his side." Still, something about this reverse theory rang false. "But Logan would be stronger. In a fight between him and Charlie, I'd definitely bet on Logan."

Kelvin wiggled his hands before me. "Did you think about the injury? Logan's hand was still damaged then. That would have given Charlie more of an advantage."

"True, but Logan had been released from the hospital. He'd healed enough by then." I shook my head. "The pieces just don't fit together. Logan was already on workers' comp and making plans to leave. Charlie wouldn't have needed to take such drastic measures to get Logan out of his factory."

"That's if it was a work issue. There might have been a more personal motive at play."

"I think you're really reaching," I said.

Kelvin drummed his fingers on the steering wheel. "Well, if I'm wrong, then it's back to Detective Sun's theory," he said. "That Logan was the killer."

"You wouldn't think so if you'd seen him in there." I pointed in the direction of the building I'd just visited. "He told me the whole truth, even the ugly parts. His shoes were taken as evidence because his footprints had been found near the dumpster. And for a solid reason." I told Kelvin about Logan dumping Charlie's body out of sheer panic.

"I don't know." Kelvin started up the car. "Moving a body seems sketchy. And pretty deliberate."

I mulled over the coordinated meeting as Kelvin stopped at a traffic light. If only I had a copy of that text message. It would give me more insight into the entire situation. Digging behind the actual words might allow me to figure out Charlie's subtext and motivation. I slapped the dashboard with the palm of my hand in frustration.

"Hey, please don't damage Dahlia," Kelvin said.

"Your precious," I muttered but said in a louder voice, "If only we could get ahold of Logan's phone . . ."

"Why do we need his phone?"

"I want to see that text message from Charlie for myself."

Kelvin's brow furrowed. "But we already have it."

"We do?"

"Sure, he gave me a screenshot of it a while ago." A vague memory surfaced in my mind. During one of our previous conversations, Logan had mentioned texting Kelvin something that would prove his innocence. I'd even skimmed past the shot when I'd been watching that video of the cop car circling his place.

"What did the message say again?" I said. "Do you remember?"

"Not much," Kelvin said. "It was a quick text signed by Charlie, asking Logan to meet up in the alley at a certain time that day."

My heart sank. "Wait a sec. Did you say it was signed by Charlie?"

"Uh-huh."

"Where's your cell?"

Kelvin tilted his head toward the cup holder with his phone nestled in one of the slots. I grabbed it, thankful that my thumbprint was already stored in the settings and gave me complete access.

I opened the messages app and checked the thread with Logan's name. Charlie had signed it, but . . .

"Make a U-turn," I told Kelvin. "We've got more snooping to do."

Although Kelvin followed my directions, he asked, "Where are we going again?"

"To Smiley Fortunes."

"Why?"

I held up his phone. "Hear me out. What if Charlie didn't set up this meeting?"

"I don't understand." Kelvin hit the gas pedal as the light turned green.

"Maybe someone else arranged it. Why would Charlie need to sign a text? Does anybody even put their names on their messages?"

"Not usually."

"No, they don't. Unless it's the very first text, as a kind of intro. Maybe because Logan didn't already have the number in his contacts. Who's friends with their boss anyway?"

Kelvin grinned. "I'm really close to mine."

I ignored him. "This screenshot shows that *someone* texted Logan saying they were Charlie, but maybe it wasn't actually Charlie. But it was a person with a Fresno area code."

"And you think it's someone from the factory."

"Makes sense, doesn't it? People were upset about the working conditions there," I said. "From the lowly employees all the way up to the current manager."

Kelvin checked the clock on his car dashboard. "Well, guess I'm taking an extended lunch today. Somebody's got to make sure you don't end up with another head injury."

"Don't worry. We'll just be making one little phone call to find out who picks up." It would be easy-peasy, I hoped.

A bold idea popped up in my head. If I was really lucky, I could even snatch the phone that had sent the text while everybody was busy working. They'd have to put it down sometime, right? And it might just happen to have a history of incriminating text messages on it.

We arrived at the ramshackle fortune cookie factory, and I noticed Cayla's car right away on the street. She'd done a better job of parking it this time. Probably because she hadn't been in as much of a rush.

Lucky break. We could grab an extra piece of evidence while here. "That's Cayla's car," I told Kelvin. "And the inhaler's in the trunk. It could be helpful to the investigation."

I examined our surroundings. No Cayla outside. I checked the nearby building, and the door to the factory was open. Even from this distance, I could hear some sort of commotion.

"I'm going inside," I told Kelvin.

"Hold up. You're changing our plans at the last minute? I thought we were making a safe and simple phone call from out here."

"I want to visually see who picks up when you dial, to make sure. Come on, it'll be quick."

"Fine," he said, grumbling a bit but tagging along.

The voices inside were talking over one another. Nobody even noticed as I entered the room and took a spot in a dark corner near the exit.

I figured if I needed to make a quick getaway, it'd be an optimal location. Ideally after I borrowed—that sounded better than "stole"—the incriminating phone.

Anyway, wasn't the factory considered open to the public for fortune cookie sales? Someone could've dropped their phone on the floor, and I might just happen to find it. At least that's what I would tell the police when I turned in the evidence.

Kelvin hovered in the doorway, seemingly uncertain about stepping inside. I motioned for him to make the call to the unknown Fresno number.

I wondered who would pick up. He dialed, but I didn't hear any immediate ringing. Could the employees have tucked their phones away in a storage unit? I might not hear the muffled sounds then. Or had they turned their phones on silent?

I turned to Kelvin. "Anything?"

He shook his head. "No one's picking up, and no customized voicemail either. Just a digital recording with the digits of their phone number."

Drat. "Okay, strike one. At least you can go and grab the inhaler real quick."

"Me?" He raised his eyebrows. "What are you planning on doing?"

"I'm gonna stay here for a bit. Something interesting is happening." The mood at Smiley Fortunes felt strange, and I noticed the workers out on the main floor. They weren't positioned at their typical stations as they had been on my last few visits.

"Wish me luck," Kelvin said. "Maybe Cayla left her car unlocked."

I waved him off as the door to the office in the

warehouse opened. Cayla came out with her sleek hair tied back, her clay geometric earrings swinging as she rushed to center stage.

"Are you ready for the big announcement, everyone?" She flashed a sickly sweet smile.

No wonder nobody was working. Anticipation filled the air. What news would she share?

Cayla made a broad sweeping motion with her hand. "Take a look around you. This dream came from a single man, Charlie Gong."

The employees nodded as she spoke.

Cayla continued. "The Fortune Cookie King, as he was called. Smiley Fortunes was actually a play on the phrase that fortune will smile down on us."

A worker chuckled.

"Charlie opened this factory with its extensive equipment with the backing of—"

An alarm blared from outside, shrill and insistent. "My car," she said. "Someone's breaking into it." Cayla sprinted past me through the door.

Kelvin. Guess the trunk hadn't been unlocked. I hoped he had time to hide.

A few chirps soon sounded. The blaring disappeared.

Cayla returned, her face flushed. "First, spam callers. Now, car alarms. When will I get through this announcement?" she muttered, head down as she tapped at her phone.

She moved past my hiding spot and on to her office. Through the glass window, I could see her lay down her phone and pick up a clipboard.

Then she went back to the main floor and claimed the attention of the workers again. "Sorry for that interruption. False alarm."

Cayla started droning on about the origin story of

Smiley Fortunes and the backing of a generous anonymous donor who'd provided the initial capital. Maybe I could sneak into the office and rummage through it while they were still having their meeting? The warehouse's overall dim lighting would cover my movements.

But then I heard my name whispered from outside. I poked my head around the doorframe.

Kelvin held up his phone, his hand covering the mic. "It's Moana, sounding frantic," he said. "She's practically breaking down the door to my shop, and I can't convince her to leave over the phone. Let's go. Do this another time."

I considered it. Could the inhaler be a compelling-enough piece of evidence? I pointed in the direction of Cayla's car. "You got it, right?"

He shook his head. "Sorry."

Inside the factory, Cayla was still talking about the original mission of Smiley Fortunes. She sounded like she could talk forever on the subject.

Cayla had passed me, mentioning a spam caller—could that have been our staged call? Possibly. I snuck another peek at her office.

"Go," I whispered to Kelvin. "I think it was Cayla's number, and she's clearly occupied. This is my chance. She doesn't have her phone on her, and I know where she put it."

Kelvin hesitated. Moana's voice continued speaking in the background, muffled by his hand.

"There are other people in there," I said. "Even if she did catch me, I can make an excuse for visiting the factory. She won't do anything with her employees around."

"Fine, but I'll be back as soon as I can," Kelvin said. "And if there's any sign of trouble, drop everything and get out of there."

I gave him a thumbs-up, and he ran off to his car.

A collective gasp made me turn my attention back to the gathered employees in the factory. What had been said?

They seemed in distress now, crying or shaking their fists in the air.

Cayla spoke over them. "This will be effective immediately. Pack your bags and go." She glanced at her clipboard and checked something off.

The employees scattered to their cubbyholes and started collecting their sparse belongings. I'd lost my chance to sneak into Cayla's office unseen.

As they approached the exit, I flattened myself in the corner so the workers wouldn't notice my hiding spot, but they were too upset to pay any attention to me anyway. I caught a snippet of a conversation as they passed by.

"Can't believe she fired us," said Dakota.

"Laid us off, technically," the woman walking next to him corrected. "Too much competition. Along with the money problems. She even had to dig into the cashbox the other day."

"To pay off a fine, she said."

"Something about vandalism. But I guess it's her money to use." The two of them brushed by me.

They must have been talking about the damage that had been done to Gold Bakery. Could Cayla have been getting the cash to help our family?

I was so lost in my thoughts that I didn't hear the footsteps until they were upon me. A moment later, someone grabbed my arm.

CHAPTER 43

Cayla dragged me farther into the factory, but I didn't put up a fight. She held on to my arm with one hand, but the other gripped a familiar-looking inhaler. Maybe I could snatch it away without her noticing if I acted docile.

Just as I went to reach for it, Cayla let go of me, and I wobbled. She lifted up the inhaler. "Were you looking for this? Because I know my car alarm didn't go off by accident."

I squinted at the label on the inhaler, trying to read the name on it. "I think that belongs to Charlie."

She didn't deny it. "Why couldn't you stop with your snooping?"

"A man died behind our bakery," I said. "With a fortune of mine found on him. I felt compelled to investigate."

"Instead of a cookie, it's too bad he didn't have this inhaler on him during his asthma attack," she said with a smile.

"You took it away from Charlie," I said. "When he needed it the most."

She shrugged. "What can I say? I'm a planner."

But why? What could Cayla's motive have been?

Something one of the workers had said as they'd left the factory came to mind. The idea that the cashbox belonged to Cayla, that it was her money. "Did you kill Charlie for his money? To get this factory?"

She shook her head, hard, and her clay earrings whipped with the movement. "It was never *his* money in the beginning. This whole factory was built on my art fund. I was the anonymous donor, the person who provided the capital."

"'Art fund'?" I echoed, my thoughts snagging on the term.

She self-consciously traced an edge of her earring.

"Your jewelry," I said. "It's beautiful." It was. I hadn't noticed it before, but there were subtle elegant black ridges on them.

That seemed to loosen her tongue. "This is my favorite medium. They're made from polymer clay. Versatile, lots of colors, and dries quickly."

I continued probing. "What was your art fund for, specifically?"

"To attend classes, buy supplies. I knew I'd eventually get my name out there." She emitted a soft sigh. "Charlie used to encourage me about my art all the time back in high school."

"You two were high school sweethearts?" Logan had mentioned they'd been dating, but I hadn't realized how long.

"Two years' difference, my sophomore to his senior. I thought he was my Prince Charming come to life. Believed he'd whisk me away from a family who couldn't understand my love for art." Her eyes narrowed. "I was a fool."

Something had gone very wrong in their relationship. "What happened between you two?" I asked.

She huffed. "He used me, to chase after his silly fortune cookie dreams."

Did the hate stem from that first financial investment? "How much did you put into the factory?"

"Everything. My life savings. He said I'd soon double my investment." Her voice grew rough. "Not only did he steal my money, but he sucked away my time. I started working here at the factory for no pay."

I glanced at the machines before me and remembered the toiling workers, who didn't get any breaks.

"It's tough, repetitive labor," I said. At least the way Charlie did things. "And very different from art." I could relate to Cayla's need for a creative outlet. My mom and I also made art, but of the food variety. Maybe that's why I was eventually opposed to mass-producing my fortune cookies. On the other hand, I'd never arranged someone's death because I was feeling creatively unfulfilled.

"Business was slow even from the beginning," Cayla said. "We weren't making enough money after investing in all of the pricey equipment, so Charlie figured we could lower our expenses. Take shortcuts, everything from slashing the staff to skipping protective gloves." She glanced down at her own delicate hands. They gripped the inhaler, her fingers wrapped around the tiny warning label.

She continued speaking, her face growing redder—and I didn't think it was from the heat of the nearby oven. "Later on, Charlie started taking my art supplies for his stupid cookies. Because my clay is nontoxic."

I had a terrible thought. "No. Tell me he didn't put it in the food."

"Sure he did. He figured why not? Clay hardens quicker, makes the cookies crunchier, and helps them last longer on the shelf."

I made an involuntary choking noise.

"Yeah, that's what I thought, too. Even told him to stop, but he didn't listen to me. Never does—er, did. He was always saying, 'Aw, you worry too much, Cay.'"

Cay, or Kay. My earlier suspicion had been right. "You're Charlie's rep in court," I said.

She rolled her eyes. "That annoying lawsuit. Didn't help the money situation any, I tell you. Thank goodness I convinced Moana to settle. I'll get the money soon and then I can start over."

I imagined Cayla with her clipboard, checking that particular to-do item off her list. "The money. Is it so you can reboot the factory?"

"This dump? No way," Cayla said. "I've wanted out for a while, especially when Charlie started using the cement."

"Huh? What cement? Like the hard stuff on the ground?"

She cocked her head at me. "You didn't know? That's why Foo Fusion wanted to break ties with us. The cookies were getting too crunchy because of our, uh, special ingredient."

I could feel my throat tighten. I'd eaten those fortune cookies. Or had tried to. No wonder they were inedible. "Where did he even get that idea?"

"Outside." Cayla's eyes flicked toward the exit. "Our broken sidewalk that had to be fixed. Easy to pilfer supplies whenever the crew took a break."

I guess moving from clay to cement wasn't that huge of a jump for him. How could any proclaimed Fortune Cookie King do that to his customers? My voice sharpened. "Why didn't you stop him then? If you knew all about it?"

Her hand clenched the inhaler. "Oh, but I did."

I gasped. The inhaler she held. It must be the missing link. I was willing to bet she'd put something deadly in it. A poison that Charlie had inhaled.

She wriggled the inhaler in the air. "Think you got it all figured out now, huh?"

Cayla had negotiated with Moana. They'd been able to make a deal. Maybe I could do the same. We could compromise. "Now that you've told me your story, why don't you give me the inhaler? I can tell the police you were under pressure. Extenuating circumstances."

She snorted. "I don't think they'll see it that way. They might even believe I was the one who started the mess. It was my supply of clay, after all. That was the threat Charlie held over my head every day."

"I get it," I said, trying to appeal to her feelings. "You needed out of a toxic relationship and to leave a failing factory, all so you could pursue your artistic dream, your passion. I know what it's like to want something really badly and face almost insurmountable obstacles."

I also had a lifelong dream, except mine involved baking, not art. She must've heard my honesty and seen the truth written on my face.

"You're right," Cayla said. "All I need is a fresh start. So here . . ."

She bent down and slid the inhaler across the smooth factory floor. I watched it lodge right under the base of the oven, close to me but not close enough. Blue flames heated the hot plates, empty of their usual servings of batter, as they rolled along the conveyor belt.

No problem, it was just a bad throw. I could still reach it from here. Turning my back to Cayla, I focused on the inhaler. I swooped down and picked it up—right as a resounding clank sounded above my head.

CHAPTER 44

Cayla cursed. "Can't believe I missed!"

I stood back up and noticed her arms raised above her head, a solid chunk of concrete cradled in her hands.

She cooed at me. "Turn around again like a good girl."

I blanched. "What? Why?"

"It'll look better on the autopsy report if the blow lands in the same spot as before. Fewer questions asked if it's just a previous injury getting reopened."

Still shaking, I said, "But we had a deal."

She arched an eyebrow. "Did we?"

"Yes. You give me the inhaler. I talk to the police, tell them all about how things got to this point, and you get a fresh start."

"In jail, I bet," she said. "No thanks. But if I take care of you now, then you won't give me any more trouble, and I can hit the reset button completely." Cayla moved a step forward.

"No. Stop right there!" I held out the inhaler in front of me. Too bad I didn't know how to release the poison Cayla had put in it. "I've got a dangerous weapon in my hand."

She lowered her arms and laughed in my face. "Go

back to baking, Felicity. You're much better at it than detecting. That's a regular inhaler you're holding."

"It is?" My shoulders slumped. "But you took it away from Charlie. I figured it was deadly, and you didn't want the police to have it."

"Yeah, I did move it so that Charlie couldn't find it," she said. "Then all I had to do was set up the perfect stressful day to induce an asthma attack." Cayla switched her grip, grasping the concrete chunk with one hand and counting off on the fingers of her other. "One, he already had his court date set for the lawsuit. Two, he had to go begging at local businesses, hoping someone would carry his inventory."

I nodded, remembering the Fresno grocer who'd mentioned Charlie's distracting wheezing. His breathing problems had already started by that point.

"Three, I told him about your little bakery." Her eyes glittered here. "A sudden competitor from out of the blue, ready to dethrone him from his fortune cookie kingdom. A great source of stress. And, finally, the straw that broke the camel's back—I added Logan to the mix."

"You knew they wouldn't get along if they met up," I said.

"That's right." Cayla stalked forward while I edged backward. "Charlie wanted him out for good. Never once thought about taking him back, especially since Logan was using up all of that precious compensated medical leave and not showing up to work."

"You planned it so the two of them would talk to each other, argue even," I said.

"They're both so stubborn," Cayla said, "I knew it would end in an argument. And I figured it'd be better if they clashed far away from the factory . . . and me."

That way Cayla would be emotionally detached and

geographically distanced from the situation. Plus, she'd have an alibi by being at work.

I imagined the rising tempers of the arguing men in the alleyway and Charlie's already anxious state. He would've reached for his inhaler for certain. "You left him with the wrong kind," I said. "The disc instead of what he usually took for an asthma attack." Hadn't the garbage collector told me so? Charlie had only had the Serevent, the long-term preventative medication on him—not the kind that would quickly help in an emergency—when his body had been discovered.

"Whoops," she said.

"But there's more. You did something to it." A bad asthma attack wouldn't have explained what Logan had witnessed in the alley. Charlie had been drooling, turning pale.

"Sure, I supplemented the usual powder. With cement dust."

I choked myself, thinking of the fine silica that had probably clogged Charlie's lungs. The cement dust must have wrecked his breathing, worsening his typical asthma until he died.

Before me, Cayla shrugged. "Was it really my fault if he physically did it to himself?" Maybe that's how she'd justified things in her head. Or perhaps her resentment had grown so huge over the years that she viewed Charlie as an enemy to be taken care of. Another task on her to-do list.

She came nearer, and I retreated even closer to the oven. I could feel the heat of the open flames warming my back.

"You know," Cayla said, "that's how you die, too."

I gulped. "Um, how exactly?"

"By your own doing. Falling on the sidewalk again." She tsked. "How very clumsy of you."

"Nobody will believe that. Not my family, friends, or the police."

"Really?" She gave me a wicked grin. "They believed it when I caught you snooping around my car and knocked you upside the head. Poor Felicity stumbling on the pavement."

My headache. I knew I hadn't tripped. She'd snuck up on me while I'd been distracted by the inhaler. But Cayla had not only hurt me, she'd taken away my powers somehow, my family gift. I gritted my teeth.

She said, "It would've been better, more neatly resolved, if I added to the bump on the back of your head, but oh well. I guess you could also fall on your front. They did a horrible job fixing that pavement outside—must have been the shortage of construction supplies."

She gripped the concrete chunk in both hands again, her hold now menacing.

I needed to find a weapon to defend myself—and fast. But all I had was this lousy inhaler in this vast factory filled with all sorts of machinery. Maybe I could block her blow with it. Repositioning it in my hand, I noticed the warning label again.

Cayla raised the concrete in the air, and I sure hoped the fine print on the inhaler was right. She angled her arms to better aim for my head, and I took that moment to twist away.

I also tossed the inhaler into the flames. *Bang!* I dove away.

The sudden explosion threw sparks in the air. Cayla startled, dropping the concrete chunk on her own foot. She yelped out in pain while I made a run for it.

I sprinted for the exit and ran smack into Kelvin, who'd just opened the door. He steadied me and tucked his phone away.

"I heard the boom," he said. "Are you okay?"

I nodded.

"I also called the detective. She's on her way."

He opened his arms, and I almost rushed into them for comfort. But then I paused, distracted by the odd pink color on his head. "What's in your hair?"

"Oh, that's petal confetti. Moana came by to—" Suddenly, he darted around me and took up a wide stance, arms up, as though ready to block.

What was he doing? Then I spied Cayla. She was hobbling along but still holding that chunky rock in her hand. The woman just wouldn't give up.

Kelvin glanced over his shoulder at me. "Don't worry, Lissa—"

"I've got this," a new voice added. "Step aside." Detective Sun slid by Kelvin and me.

She unholstered her gun and trained it on Cayla. At the sight of the weapon, Cayla froze. She dropped the concrete and held her hands up.

Everything happened in a rush after that. Police officers swarmed into the factory. Emergency medical technicians entered the building to check on me.

Then there was the questioning. I had to recount what happened to me several times to set the record straight. Finally, exhausted, I was cleared to leave.

Kelvin steered me out of the building, his warm hand nestled against the small of my back. "I'm taking you home," he said. "You get door-to-door service."

I buckled into the passenger seat and yawned. It'd been quite an adventure, and the adrenaline was wearing off. But, finally, Charlie Gong's murderer had been captured.

"Are you sure you're okay? After all that?" Kelvin asked me as he drove.

"I'm fine. A-OK, according to the paramedics."

"I can't believe I left you alone," he said, his hands tightening on the steering wheel. "If only for half an hour." Had it just been thirty minutes? I felt like I'd been trapped in there forever.

"You couldn't have known I'd be left all alone with her," I told him. "There had been a factory full of people when you had to go."

"Still." His jaw tightened. He'd overheard my multiple police statements at this point and knew the entire story.

Kelvin needed a distraction from his perceived guilt or he'd continue beating himself up. He'd really done nothing wrong—it was my own curiosity that had gotten me into that situation. "Hey," I said, plucking a petal off the gearshift box, "what's up with all the flower bits again?"

His nostrils flared. "They're confetti," he said. "Moana came by at the most inopportune time. She wanted—no quote-unquote needed—a special sendoff for the wedding ceremony. Guess her friend Kay texted her about these popular confetti flower cones and got her all excited about it."

"Kay, huh? The friend from court."

"Yeah, I think so. Why?"

I explained that Kay and Cayla were the same person. "No wonder Cayla was tapping away at her phone after her car alarm went off. She probably set the overeager bride on you." The timing worked. If she had seen Kelvin around, she'd figured we would be together and had wanted him out of the way to deal with me alone.

"But I don't think Cayla and Moana are partners or anything like that," he said.

I agreed. "No. All Moana did was ghost Alma and write that angry sweet-and-sour message. But Moana's a talker, and Cayla probably used that fact to keep you busy."

"I did try kicking Moana out of the shop to get back to you quicker," he said.

"A hard task."

"Tell me about it. She had so many ideas about what she wanted. Even the possible types of cones needed to hold the petals. She prefers natural wood fiber ones, in case you're interested."

I glanced at the footwell on the driver's side. Many brightly colored petals littered the floor. "What flower did she end up choosing for the confetti?"

He laughed. "She didn't. Still couldn't make up her mind when I decided I had to go no matter what. I didn't want to leave you alone at the factory for too long."

"You ditched a customer for me?"

"I'm sure she's continuing to swoon at my shop, surveying every flower as a possibility."

By this time, Kelvin had pulled up at my apartment. "I'm walking you inside and waiting until you lock the door before I leave."

"Yes, sir." I got out of the car and stifled another yawn.

"Go and rest," he said with tenderness. "I'll be back with your mom before you know it."

CHAPTER 45

I slept like the dead—or maybe more accurately, like one who'd been close to dying. When I woke up, it was to my mom placing the back of her hand against my forehead.

"You feeling okay?" she asked.

It was like I'd been transported back to my childhood sick bed. I could even smell the herbal broth she cooked whenever I didn't feel well.

"I made your favorite soup," she said.

Actually, it wasn't my favorite, but I was parched, and I didn't want to complain. The soup offered a heavy medicinal tang that announced "I will make you stronger by herbal force" to my taste buds every time.

My mom motioned to someone just outside the curtained entry, and Kelvin walked in, carrying the steaming bowl with both hands. He carefully placed the soup down on the dresser next to me.

Just like when I'd been a child, Mom picked the bowl up and proceeded to sit next to me on my bed. Up close, I spotted the plump red dates floating in the soup, like tiny bobbing apples. A few bright goji berries also added vibrant color to the broth.

She took the porcelain spoon and started scooping

soup up, but I stopped her. Was she really going to feed me?

I sat up in bed. "I'm all right, Mom. I can do it myself." *I'm an adult now*, I wanted to add.

She must have noticed my unease because she backed off. "Of course, of course."

I took a sip to show Mom how strong I felt. We all spent a few prolonged moments together, the silence disturbed only by my slurping. Were they going to stay quiet and watch me drink the entire bowl of soup? I glanced over at Kelvin for help, and he sprang forward.

"Hey, guess what? You're famous, Lissa."

I paused the spoon midway to my mouth. "What are you talking about?"

He held out his phone, and I checked the screen. It was an online article from the *Pixie Courier*. "This posted tonight and will hit the stands tomorrow. It basically says that you're the 'town hero.'"

"For doing what, exactly?" I asked, returning to drinking the soup.

"Helping the police out. Some nosy reporter must have heard about the commotion at Smiley Fortunes and followed up on it."

"Helping the police out" had a nice ring to it. Clearly, I'd been invaluable to them. "Is the case officially closed now?"

Kelvin nodded. "I think so."

"I know so," Mom added, a giant grin on her face. "Detective Sun told me herself. Said I don't need to worry any longer."

The detective really did dote on my mom. Mom continued. "Detective Sun said something else, too."

"What?" Both Kelvin and I pivoted our heads toward my mom.

"She wanted to pass on the message that they'd reevaluate Logan's situation."

I breathed a sigh of relief. Maybe they could reduce his charges or change things in light of his lesser involvement. All he'd really done was move Charlie's body in a moment of panic. I ate better after that bit of good news and soon finished off the whole bowl.

"Good appetite," my mom said with glee.

"Glad you're feeling better," Kelvin added.

"Mark my words," Mom said, "people will be clamoring to see you at the bakery tomorrow."

And even though I was the one with the fortune-telling ability in the family, Mom's prediction did come true.

Despite my extra-long nap, I still managed to sleep in the next day. Mom had to wake me up at the very last minute to get going. I had a touch of a headache, so I popped a few aspirin before going out the door.

We arrived at the bakery to find a mass of people waiting outside. It was the middle of the night (pretty much). What were they doing here so early?

"Sorry," I said. "We won't open for a few hours."

People didn't care. They all agreed, with Sweet Tooth Sally leading the charge: "We'll wait out here. In the meantime, let's take some pictures together."

What? Apparently, everyone wanted to rub shoulders with someone "famous." They asked for selfies with me. Or wanted to shake my hand and congratulate me for keeping the streets of Pixie safe. Guess the residents did really think of me as a town hero.

"You know what?" my mom said as she swung the door to the bakery wide open. "We'll make an exception today. Come on into the shop. Everyone can chat with Felicity inside, where it's warmer."

And that's how I found myself in the front of the shop while Mom bustled around the kitchen in the back, making pastries by herself. As the tantalizing scent of baking bread rose into the air, I shared my harrowing near-death experience with my fellow Pixians.

They wanted all the juicy details of my narrow escape . . .

"Did it feel scary being trapped inside the factory with a hardened criminal?" someone asked. Cayla and her clipboard didn't bear any resemblance to my vision of a tough convict. Then again, she had been trying to attack me with a chunk of concrete.

"It was stressful," I admitted. "Had to think really fast under pressure." Or rather, act fast and throw something *pressurized* into the fire.

I confess, it was kind of fun being the center of everyone's attention. People were cheering on my story and even suggesting that a Felicity Jin Day be instituted in Pixie. That probably wouldn't come to pass, but I liked dreaming about the festivities.

Plus, they were all in such high spirits that they bought loads of pastries. I could envision a gigantic cycle of happiness starting. They'd celebrate now, ingest joy, and spread their cheer forward. More and more residents would pass on the positivity. I beamed. Our family bakery really was the happiness-inducing heartbeat of Pixie, and I was proud of that.

The customers continued to come in waves, and I rode the crest of their encouragement until a little past three in the afternoon when we hit a lull in the business, and I could finally move back into the cozy atmosphere of the kitchen. Hmm. When had I started to feel comfortable in the baking space, surrounded by the steel counters and the warm industrial oven?

I decided to try my hand at another batch of fortune cookies. It felt great to toss together the ingredients and mix up the golden batter. Baking truly was its own sort of magic, creating the edible from a few simple ingredients.

I folded the hot fortune cookies fresh out of the oven. They smelled delicious to me. Perhaps my magic had returned? After all, I no longer felt the remnants of a headache. The throbbing had disappeared with the avalanche of praises and support.

A customer walked into the shop, and I heard her say to my mom, “What is that wonderful smell?”

“It’s my daughter’s homemade fortune cookies. Would you like some?”

“Sure, I’ll take half a dozen.”

I wandered out of the kitchen carrying the tray of fortune cookies and set it down. The customer’s eyes widened with delight at the rows of tasty treats.

“They look fabulous,” she said.

After placing six of the still-warm cookies into a bag, I passed them over, and she thanked me.

“Oh, wait a moment,” I said, placing my hand on her arm in a deliberate gesture. “I forgot the fortunes.”

“No problem. I’m not in a rush.”

I pulled out the paper and pen. Waited for the magic to happen. But nothing came to me. There was a complete blankness in my mind. Sure, I no longer had a headache to contend with, but I still encountered only emptiness.

No rainbow of colors crossed my vision, and everything was silent. I didn’t realize how much I missed my fortune-telling talent until all I was left with was a continuous void.

The customer stared at me. "You okay there?"

"Sorry," I mumbled and scribbled something down on the slips of paper. Hopefully, the words would make coherent fortunes for her.

After the customer left, I sat down heavily on the stool. My mom noticed my moping and asked, "What's wrong? Is the headache back?"

"No, nothing's back. That's the problem."

Mom glanced at the tray of fortune cookies still on the counter and picked one up. She chewed it with deliberate slowness.

"I taste vanilla, sugar, and something more . . ." She wrinkled her nose. "A touch of anxiety."

Clearly. Of course I was worried. Why wouldn't I be? My powers had permanently left me. And who was I without them?

The rest of the afternoon dragged on with just a few stragglers to break the monotony. I didn't dare reenter the kitchen after my most recent failed attempt. I was afraid to bake anymore, and the deep anxiety within me took over like unrestrained yeast.

CHAPTER 46

In the evening, back at home, I mentally retreated inside myself. Charlie's killer might be behind bars, but my magical life had been turned upside down. I forced myself to eat dinner with my mom, in complete silence, and then excused myself to continue my seclusion in my partitioned space.

The doorbell rang, but I didn't bother to get it, although I was the one who usually greeted our visitors. Even when my mom called out to me that Kelvin was on the doorstep, I didn't move from my curled-up spot on the bed.

"Tell him I'm not feeling well," I told her.

She didn't respond. I bet she didn't like my little white lie. But I *didn't* feel good. I felt broken.

I could hear the hushed tones of their conversation, the rise and fall of concerned voices, from beyond my curtained bedroom in the living area. Twenty minutes later, my mom marched in with a vase full of flowers.

"Kelvin left these for you."

They were tiny little blue blooms with sweet yellow centers. "That was nice of him."

"Do you want to give him a call, and say thanks?"

I faked a yawn. "No. Besides, I'll probably see him

tomorrow." Maybe, if I felt up to it. Out of idle curiosity, I wondered what the flowers he'd brought over meant. Kelvin always gave me bouquets full of meaning. Too bad he hadn't provided a cheat sheet with this bunch so I could figure out his intentions.

"You sure you're okay?" my mom asked, breaking into my thoughts.

"I'm peachy," I answered.

"All right then." My mom pulled the curtain shut with obvious reluctance. A rustle of fabric. Whiskers slipped in through the bottom gap.

The bunny and I stared at each other for a moment. Then she twitched her whiskers and waited.

"Fine," I said. "You can stay."

Whiskers took that as an open invitation and hopped right up onto my bed. I scooted over and patted the space next to me, and she jumped even closer.

"My powers are gone," I said. "It's strange, like I'm hollow."

The bunny tilted her head at me, seemingly full of empathy.

"Come here," I said, picking her up and cuddling her.

There was something comforting about having Whiskers in my lap. Up close, her fur looked especially soft and inviting.

I stroked it, feeling the velvety texture brush my fingertips. As I did, I held my breath. Hadn't Whiskers helped me before? When I'd been stumped about my powers, she had saved the day by giving me flashes of insight. Maybe all I needed to do to coax out my powers was to rub her magical fur.

"What's the solution?" I whispered. "How do I get my powers back?"

My fingers tingled where I touched her fur, and a

memory bubbled up in my brain. It was back when I'd stood in the bakery kitchen and traced out my surname in the flour. Jin.

In my mind's eye, though, the character glowed. It gave off an otherworldly golden gleam, like its literal translation.

Chinese characters often combined symbolic pictures to make up a word, and I knew the middle of the character represented an ax. The whole illustrative image of the character had something to do with melting metal, an ax being forged by fire.

The vision before me disappeared in a sudden rush, and my mind was again left blank. And stunned. My fingers continued stroking the bunny as I reflected on what I'd seen.

Was I the ax in that image? Ready to be forged by fire? What could it all mean?

The next morning, I was back in the bakery, but I tried to avoid being in the kitchen. I made some excuse to my mom about feeling drained . . . of power, that is.

Instead of baking, I kept myself busy tidying up the front of the store. The windows and the new glass door were sparkling clear after all my scrubbing. After cleaning, I also made sure to rearrange the pastries in the display case in orderly and appealing rows.

I took the seat behind the register, a position I'd been in so many times over the years that adjusting the stool to the appropriate height had become second nature to me. Everything I needed for serving customers I had within reach: the take-out boxes, bags, and business cards.

Someone banged on the door right then even though we wouldn't open for another hour. Kelvin. I saw him peering through the glass. He'd already spotted me, so I couldn't pretend to be gone. I let him in.

He stood just inside the entrance, wringing his hands. "Did you get the flowers?"

"Yeah, they're beautiful. Little blue ones."

"Forget-me-nots," he said.

"Oh, I've actually heard of those. Hey, sorry I didn't want to talk to you last night." I glanced through the open archway to the kitchen in the back. "Wasn't in the mood to talk to anyone then."

"I know, your mom told me about your, uh, loss. That's why I sent the flowers."

"Yeah? What do they mean?"

He chuckled. "I really should give you a cheat sheet someday like you want. Well, generally, those flowers reflect loyalty. Fidelity."

I stared at Kelvin before me, my best friend.

He shuffled his big feet, shod in his beloved Doc Martens. "Just wanted to let you know that I'm here for you. And always will be."

"I know." We'd been through a lot together, navigating life's ups and downs. The thrill of starting up our businesses, the death of his mom, and now my vanished power. "I appreciate that, Kelvin. I really do."

He smiled at me, and my mom took that moment to enter with a tray of pineapple buns.

"Is there a customer here already? I heard talking," she said before noticing my best friend. "Oh, it's you, Kelvin. Want a pineapple bun? It's fresh from the oven."

"I could never refuse you, Mrs. Jin."

He snatched a pastry, blew on it, and chewed away. I could almost see the bright light fill his eyes as the happiness infused him.

I sighed. I'd always wanted the Jin superpower, that

same cheerful effect on the people around me. And for a moment, I'd had it.

"Felicity, how about you?" Mom asked.

I also took a pineapple bun, ripping it into small pieces, not caring about the many crumbs falling onto the floor. I popped the sugar-crusted morsels into my mouth and relished each bite. My mom stood by my side, smiling at me, while I ate.

It struck me then. I was bringing her joy. Right this moment. Even without handing her a fortune cookie or having a claim to any magical talent. My mom's past words reverberated in my head: that Jin is spelled J-O-Y.

I was Joy manifested. My mom's joy. I was a Jin through and through, with or without special powers. No matter what, I belonged in this family. I took my seat behind the register—and that's when it happened.

CHAPTER 47

With the realization that I was unconditionally a Jin, a whoosh sounded in my head. My toes started tingling, and an electric current seemed to flow up into my fingers. I wiggled them, almost sensing the raw magic in my hands. I felt sure my prognostication skill was back.

I tested the ability a few times throughout the day. On several unsuspecting customers, I slipped in a customized fortune. They were quite happy to receive the positive news I'd predicted—a sudden windfall, an exciting trip, a love connection. I didn't push myself to do more than those few attempts.

At least I didn't feel obligated to do so. The revived superpower didn't make me any more worthy as a person. After all, I thought to myself, hadn't I just solved a case without relying on my magical ability whatsoever?

The inner confidence and subsequent joy that I felt transferred over to my baking. In the kitchen, I even whistled a few musical bars as I worked.

My mom came in and stole a fortune cookie off the cooling tray. When she ate it, she asked, "Do you know what this tastes like?"

I thought about it. "Contentment?"

"Yes," she said, "and acceptance."

By the time the bakery closed, I'd sold out of everything I'd made earlier in the day. Even Mrs. Spreckels had come in asking for an order—after having confiscated (and eaten) a few fortune cookies from misbehaving library patrons. Three people also returned near closing, asking to pre-order more for the next morning. And plenty of customers said they'd spread the word to their friends and neighbors.

Kelvin and Alma joined us that night for a celebratory dinner. It was a simple one-pot meal, and I placed Kelvin's vase of pretty forget-me-nots in the center of the table. I put out the Wishes candle as a special decoration. Its lovely golden hue reminded me of my last name.

I turned down the usual house lights, and Alma lit the candle with a beautiful, long handmade match stick; its head displayed a swirling violet pattern. All at once, the air smelled like promises.

After a delicious meal, we toasted one another with glasses of sparkling apple cider.

"Cheers," I said. "To being a Jin and to belonging."

"To those who seek, they will find," Alma commented.

Mom raised her glass high in the air. "Here's to our bakery thriving again."

Kelvin said, "To all of your triumphs . . . and my own future onscreen credit." He then proceeded to explain how a popular bridal show would be filming Moana's wedding and sharing his floral creations with the television-watching world.

I smiled at him. "About time. You deserve the accolades."

We clinked our glasses together, and I marveled at our tight-knit unit. We were like a little family. But as I sipped, a fleeting thought passed through my mind: if only my dad had stuck around to witness my success.

The candle flickered before me. I blinked. Nope. It was holding strong and steady—must have been my imagination.

We congratulated each other again and began making pleasant small talk. About half an hour into our conversation, the doorbell rang.

"Are you expecting a visitor, Mom?" I asked.

"No." She leaned toward Kelvin. "Could it be your dad?"

"Uh-uh. He's working the night shift."

We all got up, except for Alma who stayed at the table with an indecipherable smile, and walked over together to the front door. Mom opened it . . . to find Detective Sun on the doorstep. Only she seemed so different tonight. She wore a casual outfit, including jeans, and wore her hair down loose and soft.

The detective held up a bag of oranges and offered it to my mom, who accepted the fruit with gratitude.

I, on the other hand, blurted out, "How do you know where we live?"

She raised an eyebrow at me. "It's a small town. I asked around."

My mom darted me a reprimanding look and said, "Why don't you come in, Detective Sun?"

"That's very kind of you, but this will be a quick stop," she said.

Kelvin stepped forward. "Were you in the neighborhood already, Detective?"

"Kelvin. I didn't see you there." The detective tilted her head to look up at him. "By the way, thanks for calling in the incident at the factory. That's actually the reason I'm here."

"To thank Kelvin?" I asked.

"No, to give this to you." She held out a metal object.

What could that be?

"It's from the factory," the detective said. "They shut the building down and liquidated all the stock after the explosion. No longer safe for business. Thought you might want this as a keepsake of your adventure."

I grabbed the item and examined it in the moonlight. It looked like a portable stand with a long metal bar . . . and I'd seen a factory employee using it before. Ah, I understood.

"A fortune cookie shaper," I said. "How helpful." Instead of relying on the rim of a cup for me to fold my cookies over, I could use this specialized instrument. And it'd serve to remind me of my inner source of courage, too.

The detective cleared her throat. "Anyway, I wanted to reiterate that the case is wrapped up. You're all safe now."

Mom breathed a sigh of relief.

Kelvin piped up, a hint of excitement to his voice. "And you got Cayla because of the inhaler, right? That was what cinched the case."

I nudged him. "No, it must've been the texts. From her phone."

Detective Sun looked back and forth between us, probably wondering whether to humor us and how much to say. She hesitated but then decided to respond. "Everything helped. Particularly the supposedly erased to-do lists on her phone app. Captured in her 'Recently Deleted' folder."

Ironic. She must really have organized every minute detail of the murder in advance. Cayla's love of checking off tasks might have actually gotten her time behind bars. A planner's downfall.

Mom rustled the bag of oranges. "These look delicious. And I'm certainly glad we have *professionals*"—she frowned at Kelvin and me—"keeping our streets safe."

She continued. "Detective, know that you always have an open invitation to visit our family bakery. Free pastries for life for you."

"Really?" Detective Sun's face lit up. "I might take you up on that offer. Pixie seems like a charming town to visit, or live in." Though she'd grown on me throughout the investigation, I couldn't help hoping the detective wouldn't be back in town on a case anytime soon.

I traced the smooth contours of the metal bar in my hand. I'd missed out on a lot of baking recently, and I intended to make up for the lost time.

CHAPTER 48

Michael Fu came into the bakery around midday. He walked in with a sheepish grin on his face and swiped at his balding head a few times before approaching me.

"Can I have a word with you, Felicity?"

"Sure." I let my mom take over my spot at the register and picked a quiet corner of the shop to talk.

Michael was a businessman, and I knew he had to have an ulterior motive. I waited him out.

He wrung his hands. "The thing is, there's no more Smiley Fortunes. I considered ordering our cookies from somewhere in the Midwest at first but . . . well, the customers want your fortune cookies."

"What?" I backed up a step. I'd been prepared for a pitch from Michael, not a compliment from his patrons.

"Some of them are repeat diners who clearly told me they liked it better when we ordered from your bakery. That your fortune cookies even enhanced the taste of our food." I bet. A little infusion of joy would help cover the bland flavors found in his typical fare.

He continued. "Others discovered your cookies at the grocery stores around town and were excited to find them in my restaurant."

Business in Fresno must be picking up. I'd have to

check with my contacts there to see if they needed me to come restock their supplies. "I'm not sure why you're here, Michael. Can you get to the point?"

He hemmed and hawed for a bit before speaking. "Okay. I want to apologize for pushing you to make those fortune cookies faster. As you probably know by now, I think in terms of profit and the bottom line."

I'd happily take his apology but . . . "I still don't want to shortcut the quality of my baking."

He held his hands up. "I get it. And I wouldn't want you to. Would you consider working with Foo Fusion again, in a different kind of way?"

"But what about your all-you-can-eat contest? I'd never keep up with the demand of it."

"That's fallen by the wayside. You were right. People do want quality over quantity. And a few eaters complained about stomachaches after stuffing themselves."

"Tell you what, I'll consider it," I said. It wouldn't hurt to keep my options open.

"That's all I want. Look, I didn't even draw up a contract this time," he said, "because I'm going to be flexible. I'll work with you using whatever terms you decide on."

It was nice to be wanted and in demand for a change.

"I could even start calling you the Fortune Cookie Princess"—at my glare, he corrected himself—"I mean, Fortune Cookie Queen."

"It's not that," I said. "I don't need a special title. I'm Felicity Jin. And that's a great name just as it is. No adornment needed."

"Of course." He made a slight bow and backed away. "I hope to hear from you soon."

My fortune cookies were clearly not only a hit in Fresno but in Pixie, because customers kept coming into the bakery. They clamored to buy them by the dozen.

I kept selling more and more. Around the time I realized I needed to whip up another batch, a sudden commotion halted me on the way to the kitchen.

"What's that noise?" I said, echoing the mumblings of several customers in line.

I went out the door and stared at the tall ladder set up in front of our shop. Someone was on top of it, fiddling with the sign of our bakery.

Not only was the guy messing with our signage, but he was actually focused on prying off individual letters. An alphabet thief? "Hey, stop that!" I yelled.

He looked startled but was about to answer when Mom rushed over to stand next to me. She squeezed my hand. "Felicity, he's just doing the job I hired him for."

"I don't get it. You're dismantling our sign?" I said.

"Changing the name to a more appropriate one."

I watched in silence as the man took down G-O-L-D and swapped in J-I-N.

"Jin Bakery." I said the words both in my head and out loud. "I kinda like the ring of that."

"It's more accurate, too," Mom said. "Why are we hiding our heritage? What was I so afraid of? And wait until you see what I special ordered for us."

The final addition to the sign was the Jin character: 金. The man placed it in a prominent spot next to our surname.

My mom cocked her head. "On second thought, do you think it would look better in plural, like 'Jins'?"

"No, Mom. Everyone knows they can find us both here at the bakery."

"But it'd make things more official."

"Make what official?" I asked.

"Us formally running the bakery together"—she

smiled at my confusion—"since I'll be adding you on as a legal co-owner."

"Really?" I whooped with joy. Until that moment I hadn't even known I wanted to run the family business as a true partner. But now, a sudden happiness overtook me. I couldn't help doing a little jig in the street.

Kelvin loped out of his flower shop as I made a fool of myself. "What's with the dancing, Lissa?"

"It's official. I'll be the new co-owner of Jin Bakery," I told him, grinning widely.

"Of what again?"

I pointed to the new sign.

"Why, that's perfect," Kelvin said, slinging an arm around my shoulder.

I took in my surroundings, this little cozy cul-de-sac of shops, and grinned: Love Blooms, Paz Illuminations, Jin Bakery. The lineup was spectacular.

My mom and I thanked the sign installer as he packed up his tools. Then Mom turned to me and added, "Just one more surprise."

She excused herself. A few minutes later, the Jin character on the sign lit up.

It was a beautiful golden hue. When Mom rejoined Kelvin and me, the three of us stared at the glowing neon sign above us in wonder.

I clasped Mom's hand in mine. The gold reminded me of our shiny, strong surname. And I didn't need any predictive superpower to know that a bright future lay ahead for both the bakery and for us.

RECIPE FROM JIN BAKERY

~Fated Fortune Cookies~

Ingredients

3 eggs
¾ cup sugar
½ cup butter, melted
½ teaspoon vanilla extract
¼ teaspoon almond extract
2 tablespoons water
1 cup flour
fortune message (optional—be creative!)

Directions

1. Preheat oven to 375 degrees Fahrenheit. Prepare sheet pan by covering with parchment paper.
2. Combine eggs and sugar in a large bowl. Whip together for a few minutes.
3. Add in melted butter, vanilla extract, almond extract, and water.
4. Mix flour into wet ingredients.
5. Use a tablespoon to spoon batter onto the parchment paper, making really thin crepe-like circles about 3 inches in diameter.
6. Bake for 6 minutes. The edges should turn light brown.
7. Flip the baked circle with a spatula. (If you

are putting in a fortune, slip it in at this point.) Fold it in half and gently touch the golden edges together.

8. Place the middle of the cookie on the edge of a cup. Hold it there for three seconds to create a fortune cookie bend.
9. Put the shaped fortune cookies into separate spaces in a muffin tin to cool down.

Tips

- Bake the cookies two (or three) at a time because you'll have to fold them quickly.
- Use oven gloves if you don't want to singe your fingers.
- The batter should be thin. If it's too thick, add 1 to 2 tablespoons of water to adjust the consistency.

FLORAL TIPS FROM LOVE BLOOMS

Flower of the Day: Forget-me-not

Genus: *Myosotis*
Family: Boraginaceae
Nicknames: Forget-me-nots; scorpion grass
Common presentation: delicate blue flowers with yellow throats; may also come in white, pink, or yellow
Symbolism: true love, respect; remembrance; faithfulness, fidelity
Legend: A drowning knight tossed these flowers to his beloved on the banks, calling out, "Forget me not."
Gardening tips: can be planted in full or partial sun; reseed on their own and may overgrow; considered invasive in several states
Fun facts: The Alaska state flower is the Alpine forget-me-not.

The ancient Greek word for the genus means "mouse ear" and references the shape of the plant's pointed leaves.

~Hand-Tied Bouquets~

Materials

One dozen roses
Foliage (optional)
Floral tape (keep on spool)
Wide ribbon
Pearl floral pins (optional)

Steps

1. Dethorn the roses and pull off the leaves.
2. Hold a single rose directly in front of you, petals up and stem down.
3. Add a second flower to the left of the first one. Turn slightly. Add another rose to the left of that. Continue turning and adding flowers until you make a bouquet. (If you are adding foliage like baby's breath, alternate between the rose and the greenery.)
4. Use floral tape to secure the stems together. Then flip the spool to wind the tape (with its sticky side up) down the length of the gathered stems.
5. Circle the ribbon around the stems. Add pearl pins to decorate and further keep the ribbon in place.

Extra advice:

Use a mirror and hold the bouquet in front of you for a proper frontal perspective.

CANDLE EMBELLISHMENT FROM PAZ ILLUMINATIONS

Special wise saying from an actual fortune cookie message:

"Great prosperity is at your fingertips."

~Golden Glitter Candle~

Supplies

White pillar candle
Mod Podge
Foam brush
Gold glitter*
Tray (for catching glitter)
Wax paper

Directions:

1. Put two coats of Mod Podge on the candle sides using a foam brush.
2. While the Mod Podge is still wet, sprinkle glitter all around the candle. Use a tray to catch the excess sparkles.

*Be aware that some types of glitter may be flammable. Please read the label. You can choose to work with non-toxic cosmetic-grade shimmer dust as a safer option.

3. Brush on a thin layer of Mod Podge to seal in the glitter.
4. Set the candle on wax paper and let it dry overnight.